COLD BETRAYALS

ERIN FARWELL

COLD BETRAYALS

A CABEL EVANS MYSTERY

TATE PUBLISHING
AND ENTERPRISES, LLC

Published by Tate Publishing & Enterprises, LLC
127 E. Trade Center Terrace | Mustang, Oklahoma 73064 USA
1.888.361.9473 | www.tatepublishing.com

Tate Publishing is committed to excellence in the publishing industry. The company reflects the philosophy established by the founders, based on Psalm 68:11,

"The Lord gave the word and great was the company of those who published it."

Cover design by Norlan Balazo
Interior design by Jomar Ouano

Published in the United States of America

ISBN: 978-1-68352-090-0
1. Fiction / Family Life
2. Fiction / Mystery & Detective / General
16.08.15

For my mother,
who shared with me her love of reading and
whose unconditional support makes all things possible

For my father,
who enthusiastically provides whatever is needed
to turn my dreams into reality

ACKNOWLEDGMENTS

While writing is a solitary activity, several people helped me bring this book to life. Thank you, Alex Gurevich, for your comment that impacted Cabel's development.

I also give a big thank-you to my beta readers—Roberta Farwell, Jerry Farwell, Harriet Farwell, and Jodi McKinley—for your insights, suggestions, and overall encouragement.

To my husband, Mike, thank you for your forbearance through my author highs and lows and your bravery in encouraging me to write the next one.

To Willow, the only thing more challenging than surviving middle school is doing so with a mother on a deadline. Thank you for understanding having soup for dinner and my general disinterest in cleaning activities. Though, to be honest, that second one is pretty much a constant.

Finally, I want to say a big thank-you to everyone who shared with me their love of *Shadowlands* and waited, more or less patiently, for Cabel's next mystery.

CHAPTER 1

A slow, lazy smile spread across Jim Evans' face the moment he saw Amanda Channing step from the cab. He knew he looked like a grinning fool, but Amanda had that effect on him. Her legs came into view first, long and shapely, visible through the slit in her blue satin evening gown. Next, her slender arms, shown to their best advantage by the beading at the top of her dress. Now her face, sculpted by angels, framed with sleek blond hair that was bobbed and sophisticated. The fur shawl loosely draped over pale shoulders was her only concession to the chilly late October night. She stood beneath a streetlight illuminated like an actress onstage.

Jim quickened his pace with a silent curse. Rather than waiting for Amanda on the corner as he'd promised, there had been a delay at the office. The meeting with his father and uncle had lasted an eternity. When he realized he would be late for his rendezvous, Jim had rushed through the last few items, scrawling his signature on papers he hadn't bothered to read, before racing the few blocks from his office to the nightclub.

But now, he was here and so was she, and he could breathe again.

She paid the cabbie and turned, frowning as she glanced up and down the crowded sidewalk searching for him. The speakeasy they planned to visit had a new jazz band playing that evening, and everyone had come to hear them. Flappers in short, beaded dresses mingled with women in elegant gowns that swept the tips of their shoes. Men, some in suits and others in formal evening wear, created a dark backdrop for these colorful ladies, each waiting to give the password and enter the Blue Diamond Club. Jim pushed his way through the crowd, apologizing now and then as he trod on toes in his haste to make his way to Amanda's side.

The instant she spotted him her blue eyes widened and a glorious smile replaced the small frown. She glowed as if suddenly lit from within. And she did that because she saw him. The wonder of it still astounded Jim, making him go weak in the knees. Six weeks ago, he hadn't known she existed, but now he couldn't imagine life without her. A cliché, he knew, but true nonetheless. She was his miracle.

The cab pulled away just as he reached her side. A movement on the street behind her momentarily distracted him, but then her eyes caught his and the world faded away.

"Jim," she said in a soft, husky voice that sent his blood racing. She raised a gloved hand to his cheek.

He took that hand and placed a kiss upon it, never breaking eye contact. In those eyes he saw his future—bright, shining, and full of love.

The crack of a gunshot sent the crowd stampeding. Screams filled the air. Jim caught Amanda as she flew into his arms. Grasping her waist, he steered her to the relative safety of the tight space between the bumpers of two parked cars.

Crouching low, holding her close, he murmured reassurances in her ear as others scurried for shelter behind cars, garbage cans, or anything else they could find.

He felt something warm on his hand and raised it to catch the glow of the streetlight. Red drops fell from his fingertips. "No!" His hand began to tremble.

Amanda didn't stir as he pushed away the silky strands of hair that hid her face. Dull eyes stared unseeing into his. "Amanda," he whispered. He gave her a small shake, as if to wake her. "No, please," he cried.

A shadow fell over him. Jim looked up. A man stood in front of the streetlight.

Scooting back, dragging Amanda with him, he tried to move her to safety. Amanda lay heavy in his arms, hindering his efforts. The space between the parked cars was too narrow to allow him to shift her body behind his. He couldn't shield her from the large gun pointed at them.

The brim of the shooter's fedora shadowed his face as he raised his weapon. He fired.

Amanda's body jerked. Jim felt a terrible, hot pain pierce his chest. He gripped her to him as the darkness closed in. "Amanda," he sighed and fell into oblivion.

CHAPTER 2

Lake Michigan churned cold and gray. Strong winds capped the waves in white froth. Dark clouds blocked the sun as they scudded low across the sky, heavy with the promise of icy rain. From the vantage point of his bedroom window, Cabel Evans couldn't see the beach that lay at the base of the bluff but was certain that no one walked along the sandy shoreline on this bitter October day. The Silver Beach Amusement Park was closed for the season so there were no rides or games to tempt anyone to visit its grounds in this inhospitable weather.

He turned away from the dreary view and surveyed the inviting room in which he stood. The new bed, wardrobe, and nightstands were of light oak and carved with simple, classic designs that fit well with the pale blue walls. A brightly patterned quilt made by his nimble-fingered housekeeper lay across the bed. A warm fire blazed in the brick hearth on the adjacent wall. In front of it stood a comfortable reading chair and a small table, offering warmth and relaxation.

Yet it was the bleak landscape outside his window that called to the darkness in Cabel's soul, for there lived a black beast which had taken residence during the first months of the war. His dearest friend, Jon Warner, had died, Cabel had lived, and nothing had been right again.

The fact that he stood here, in this cheerful bedroom that kept the darkness at bay, was less a testament to his own healing than evidence of the tenacity and deviousness of his meddling housekeeper, Marta Voss. She had created this haven of a bedroom, had pushed to change his house into a home, complete with a family of sorts, cobbled together from bits and pieces of his life over the last few months. From the ashes of his past arose a glimpse of a future, still unformed, yet within reach. Was he brave enough to grasp it?

Cabel settled into the chair in front of the fireplace, picked up the *Chicago Tribune* and turned to the business section. Among the usual stories of stockholdings and new partnerships was an extensive article about Charles Banton who had been installed as the president of Banton Construction, a large Boston-based firm. The only reason Cabel took notice of the article was that young Jefferson Banton was to have taken over his father's business but had hanged himself a few months ago. The papers had handled the matter delicately, of course, but their meaning was clear. At first Cabel assumed that the young man had been in the war, for many found death preferable to living with the memories of what they had seen and what they had done. Instead, a woman had broken Jefferson Banton's heart and he hanged himself in a fit of despair. With all the needless death Cabel had witnessed on the battlefields of France, he had been angry with this man he had never met for wasting the gift of life. But he was a bit envious as well. Jefferson Banton had done something that Cabel had considered not so long ago, though he never had the courage to act. Only recently had he come to understand that it took more courage to live than to die. Without this reaction to the man's death, he never would have remembered the name or made the connection to the current article.

Still the tragedy had not been his, so he set it aside and finished the rest of the articles. Folding the newspaper, he picked up a pen and started to doodle in the margins as he debated the question that had begun to plague him over the past few weeks: should he start his own company? The idea was foolish, he knew, but the question persisted. From his success in running his family's large manufacturing company in Chicago, he knew he was capable, but he had left that business almost five years ago and it continued to thrive without him. Although he had money, he had no experience in starting a business from nothing. To succeed he would need to make connections with other businessmen. Those men would check into his background and learn of the violence that had driven him from Chicago to New Orleans. Once this shame was known, none of these men would work with him.

This was a fool's dream.

Failure was a near certainty.

Maybe he would start with a small tool and die shop.

Through his open bedroom door, Cabel heard the telephone ring in the hallway below, followed by the scurry of Marta's footsteps as she rushed to answer it. He listened to the muffled sound of half of the conversation and decided that the call had nothing to do with him. Picking up a pen and using a corner of the newspaper as a notepad, he began listing the things he might need to start his hypothetical company.

"Cabel."

The despair in Marta's voice had him hurry to the top of the stairs. Below, Marta clutched the newel post and stared up at him with red-rimmed eyes.

"It's Jim, Cabe," she said, a small sob escaping with her words. "Something's happened to your cousin."

Bounding down the stairs and past his housekeeper who had slumped on the lowest step, Cabel rounded the corner and saw the earpiece of the phone dangling from its cord. Picking it up, he stepped to the mouthpiece and spoke.

"This is Cabel Evans."

"Oh, Mr. Evans, I'm so glad that I was able to reach you." The woman on the other end of the line sounded young and close to tears. "I'm Katherine, Katherine Anderson. I'm Mr. Jim's secretary." She began to cry and Cabel felt his heart drop to the floor.

"What is it? What's happened?"

The woman gave a loud sniffle then tried once again to speak. "Mr. Jim was shot on Saturday night, downtown, near a club." The woman cried more tears, holding Cabel in agonizing suspense.

As the sobs began to subside he gathered his courage and asked, "How is he?"

She gave a small hiccup as her tears ended. "He's in the hospital. He's had surgery on his shoulder and chest."

So Jim was alive, injured but alive. Tightness eased in Cabel's chest and he drew a deep breath.

"He's unconscious," the girl continued. "And the doctor's aren't sure..." Her voice caught. She cleared her throat and said, "A few weeks ago, Mr. Jim told me that if anything happened to him or someone else in the family, I was to call you. He was concerned that your mother or aunt would be too upset to do so."

Jim had been shot on Saturday night and now, Monday morning, a secretary was calling with the news. His position within the family was once again confirmed.

"He hasn't awakened since the surgery. The doctors are worried that if he doesn't wake up soon..." She left her sentence unfinished, as if by not speaking the words she somehow kept Jim alive. "Even though he's not awake, I know he'd like you to come." She paused as if she had a vague notion of how awkward that might be. "He's spoken of you often these last few months. I think you should come."

Cabel thanked the young woman before ending the call and replacing the earpiece. The world was suddenly out of balance and he moved with great deliberation to sit next to Marta. Putting an arm around her shoulders, he held her close as she cried.

When her tears abated, she dabbed at her cheeks with a lace-edged handkerchief. Her careworn face seemed to have more sags and wrinkles than it had just an hour before when she had served him breakfast. Sitting up straighter, she squared her shoulders, blew her nose, and patted her gray hair back into place. "I'll pack your bag while you call down to the station and find out when the next train leaves for Chicago." She marched past him up the stairs.

Chicago. The city lay only sixty-two miles across the lake from St. Joseph, Michigan. The train ride would take less than three hours. Yet the journey itself would span years as well as distance. Visiting Jim at the hospital would also mean seeing the rest of his family. There were few people for whom Cabel would make such a sacrifice. Unfortunately, his cousin was one of them.

He went to the phone and rang the operator.

CHAPTER 3

The crowded hospital corridors hummed with the activities necessary to care for the ill and injured. Nurses walked briskly down the hall, their starched white uniforms bright against the dull beige walls. Doctors conferred with family members huddled outside of patient rooms, speaking in hushed tones as orderlies maneuvered wheeled chairs through the maze of humanity with professional detachment.

The sounds, the smells, the sights were different from the medical stations near the battlefields of France but they were similar enough, too much so. Cabel moved through the hallway ruthlessly shoving aside memories of dank trenches, gunfire, and death.

A nurse came out of a patient room, bringing with her the sharp smells of antiseptic and bleach.

Mud, thick and deep, threatened to suck the boots off his feet. A wounded soldier leaned heavily against Cabel's shoulder as they struggled through the muck to reach the medical station. A bitter wind howled through the bare limbs of the trees and blew open the canvas flap of the hospital tent, releasing the screams of the wounded and dying.

Stumbling to the wall, Cabel leaned against it, shaking so hard he feared he would break into pieces. No one paid him any attention as they hurried about their business. He closed his eyes and willed his nerves to steady as the memory sank back into the depths of his mind.

One deep breath followed another and slowly, slowly, breath by breath, Cabel calmed. He was sure his face was pale, but under the harsh lights, he doubted anyone would notice. His hands still shook, but less so than they had a moment before. With a last, deep breath he shoved his hands in his pants pockets and pushed away from the wall.

As he moved toward the end of the corridor, Cabel silently damned the war that had taken so much from so many. He needed every ounce of courage and strength that he could muster to face what lay ahead, and this brief foray into the past had stolen some of those precious commodities.

When he first reached the third floor, the hallway had seemed impossibly long, a gauntlet to be run. Now the room numbers sped by. His heart beat faster as he neared his goal, room 328. The door was closed. His stomach churned as he reached for the knob, afraid for Jim, afraid for himself.

The small room was empty except for the prone figure on the white metal-framed bed. Flowers wilted in a small vase perched on the chipped metal table that stood nearby. Hard wooden visitors chairs had been shoved haphazardly against the wall, as if their occupants had fled the room in despair. Cabel's brief surge of relief at the absence of the rest of his family was doused by the sight of his cousin, unresponsive and unmoving, with various tubes and bandages taped to his arms and chest.

Pale but relaxed, Jim appeared to be sleeping rather than unconscious. Cabel stepped to the bed and picked up Jim's hand. Its warmth offered proof that, whatever was to come, in this moment his cousin was alive.

"Are you a member of his family?" asked a quiet but commanding voice.

Cabel turned. He wouldn't have needed to see the woman's uniform or the nurse's cap pinned into her dark curls to know her occupation. She had the bearing of a leader and the chapped hands that seemed to be a hazard of her vocation. Her eyes were weary, yet held a calm intelligence, and she spoke as someone who was used to having people obey her without question. Cabel had met many such women at the medic stations and makeshift hospitals near the front lines of the battlefields. He guessed that her age was near to his own and wondered if she had been there, in the midst of the horrors, though he would never dare to ask. If she were like him, she would find such a question an unwelcomed intrusion that risked awakening the ghosts of a bloody past.

"Sir?"

"Yes," he said, realizing that she now studied him as if he were a patient escaped from the mental ward. "Jim's my cousin."

She looked from his face to Jim's then nodded. "I should have noticed the resemblance. The rest of your family has stepped out for a few minutes, but I expect they will return soon." With a formal smile and brisk manner she turned, leaving Cabel alone to wonder if he should follow her out the door or wait and let the inevitable disaster occur.

Jim's hand squeezed his own. Though he doubted the action had been intentional, Cabel took it as a sign that he should stay. Moving one of the chairs closer to the bed, he settled himself in as best he could and found himself at a loss. This was not the time to tell his cousin the outcome of his amateur investigation and unexpected encounter with the mobster, Capone, nor did he wish to recall memories of their shared childhood. Although most were pleasant, humorous even, many included Jon, lost to battle in France, or Elizabeth, Cabel's former fiancé. Such memories brought with them the devastating reminder of all that was lost. With his nerves already stretched near the breaking point, Cabel searched for more neutral topics of conversation. He pulled that morning's edition of the paper from his valise, skipping over the front page with its lurid description of a sensational gangland killing at a speakeasy on the near north side, and turned instead to the business section. Self-conscious but determined, he began to read to Jim articles that his cousin might have found interesting if he were awake.

They were in the midst of an article about the new municipal airport that was to be dedicated and opened in mid-December when a gasp from the open doorway caught Cabel's attention. In an odd tableau stood their shared parentage, mouths agape in identical looks of horror and loathing. Jim's mother, Eunice, was as thin as Cabel remembered though there were more gray strands than brown in her straight, thin hair. Jim's father, Frank, stood next to his wife. He appeared to have put on a few pounds since Cabel had seen him in August and his vest buttons now strained to contain his belly.

Edward Evans stood next to his brother, Frank, and stared at his son with cool disdain. His once dark hair had lightened with age and there was a small scar above his eyebrow, but otherwise he seemed fit, slender and dapper as ever. Cabel's stomach lurched as he realized that he had caused the scar. Bile rose in his throat when he saw the cane clenched in his father's hand. His fault, he knew, all of it. The hatred he saw in his father's eyes confirmed that there would be no forgiveness for his transgressions. Though he expected no less, he felt the pain of having hoped for so much more.

Someone behind him must have spoken because Edward turned and shifted from the doorway to allow the fourth member of their party to enter. Cabel's breath caught as he saw his mother for the first time in almost five years. Margaret was as she had always been, aloof and beautiful, yet overshadowed by the more aggressive personalities of the others.

"Get away from him. Get away from my boy." Aunt Eunice stepped forward, breaking the spell that had held them all. Her fists clenched at her side, prepared to do battle to protect her son. As if Cabel were a threat.

As they faced each other across Jim's battered body, Cabel couldn't help but notice that despite her son's grave condition, his aunt's hair looked freshly set and her makeup pristine. The purplish woolen dress she wore must be the height of fashion for it had nothing else to offer her. The color enhanced the sallow tones of her skin and the drape emphasized her too-thin frame, giving it an unpleasantly skeletal appearance. She had always dressed to the standards of society and the tragedy of her son's condition had not altered her devotion to those critical expectations.

"You need to leave now, before anyone sees you." Pure hatred burned in her dark brown eyes. "We can't have anyone believe that we've accepted you back into the family."

"I think I need to sit down," Edward said. He swayed before reaching out with his free hand to steady himself against the wall. Margaret rushed to his side to help him into a chair. She knelt in front of him, speaking in low, soothing tones.

Cabel and his aunt continued to face each other across the bed. He saw the judgment in her eyes and felt anger surge from her in dark waves. She despised him. Here, at least, was common ground.

He lived for years with the guilt of having harmed his father and failed his family. Until recently all he could see were his own faults, his own mistakes. Then he and Jim had met for the first time in years and his cousin had helped Cabel to understand what he couldn't see for himself—his father's jealousy. Cabel had grown up knowing that his uncle and father had competed for positions in the family company. What he hadn't understood was that they were also competing for their father's respect. Instead it was Cabel, the eldest grandson, who had impressed James Cabel Evans. The patriarch bestowed upon Cabel the majority share of stock in the company, and with that the implied expectation that Cabel would someday succeed him. Perhaps this was why Edward had volunteered his only son to go off to war, why he had pushed Cabel to the breaking point upon his return. But did it matter? It was Cabel who had raised his fists in anger and they had both paid an awful price.

Now, standing in the cool, sterile hospital room with its white walls and tiled floor, Cabel knew there would be no redemption, no forgiveness, not that he deserved either. But he would not let that keep him from Jim's side. Cabel could do nothing for the dead, but he would stand for his cousin and help him in every way possible.

"Nurse," Eunice's shrill voice cut through the air like broken glass. "Nurse," she shouted again.

The same composed nurse appeared in the doorway. "Please keep your voices down, not only for your son's well-being but also for the other patients on the ward."

"How dare you speak to me this way? I will report you to the head nurse."

"Please do so if you feel it is necessary, but if you do not keep your voice down, I shall have to ask you to leave."

Eunice stood dumbfounded as the younger woman stepped around her to adjust Jim's blanket and assure herself that all was well. "His color is a bit improved since I checked on him an hour ago. Your company seems to be helping." She addressed this comment to Cabel.

Over her shoulder, Cabel saw his aunt turn an unfortunate shade of puce. "Young woman, I demand that you escort this, this, person from the room." It was clear that she didn't wish to claim Cabel as family, but was at a loss as to how to refer to him.

He would have found the situation humorous if it wasn't so ghastly painful.

The nurse turned back to Eunice with a professional smile and shuttered eyes. "My name is Maude Adams. You may address me as Nurse Adams."

Eunice opened her mouth to protest but Nurse Adams soldiered on. "As this man is clearly a member of the patient's family, I cannot ask him to leave during visiting hours unless his presence is disruptive to the patient or the other patients on the ward."

"But I'm Jim's mother and I find this man's presence to be disruptive. I wish him to leave."

Nurse Adams nodded. "I understand and if voices continue to be raised, I will be asking *someone* to leave."

The two strong-willed women were nearly toe to toe. Although Eunice towered nearly six inches over the nurse, the smaller woman refused to give quarter.

"Cabel, you need to leave." Although Frank Evans spoke the words with authority, there was an underlying note of a plea within them. No one enjoyed seeing Eunice Evans in one of her rages.

"You're right, of course," Cabel said, both for his family's sake as well as his own. "I'll come back another time."

"No. I don't want you anywhere near my son." Eunice turned to glare at him. Nurse Adams took the opportunity to move toward the door. "Jim wouldn't be lying in that bed if it wasn't for you."

Cabel shook his head, too stunned by the accusation to form a response.

"I'm sure that your gangster friend had something to do with this. Did you ask Al Capone to get your cousin out of the way so you could take over the company?"

Although she was a consummate professional, this statement was too much for Nurse Adams who turned to gape.

Cabel shook as he struggled to hold his anger in check. "I am not friends with any gangster, especially Capone." He looked down at his cousin, giving his hand a brief squeeze then gently returning it to the bed. Calmer, he faced his aunt again. "I don't know what happened to Jim, but I do know it had nothing to do with me. He and I have spoken about the company and that I no longer have a place in it. We both agreed."

The conversation with Jim had occurred in a hotel room a few months ago. During that meeting, Jim realized that he could stand up to his father and uncle and lead the company. Cabel accepted what he had known for some time, he would never again assume a leadership role in Evans Manufacturing. Jim knew he had Cabel's full support. In turn, Cabel learned that, despite everything, Jim still loved him.

"I don't care what you told him, you're still the majority shareholder and you forced Jim to side against his father. This is your fault."

Cabel looked over at his uncle who was staring down at the floor with a decidedly guilty look on his face. Risking a glance at his father, he found Edward looking similarly disconcerted. He wondered what lies these men had told Eunice to have her believe so strongly that it was Cabel who had changed Jim's behavior toward the older men, rather than Jim's own common sense and business experience. *It didn't matter*, he told himself, though in his heart it did.

Jim stirred in the bed, turning his head and sighing.

"You see, you're upsetting him. Leave."

Nodding, Cabel stepped around the bed, taking care not to look at anyone, even Nurse Adams, as he made his way to the door. He had just reached the threshold when a weak voice called out, "No, Cabe, stay."

For a moment no one moved. Eunice cried with joy, threw herself over her son's body and wept with relief.

IIIII

The walls of the narrow hallway closed in on him. Deep breaths did little to ease his claustrophobia. Cabel had positioned himself down the corridor from Jim's room but close enough to keep it in sight. His parents, aunt, and uncle huddled near the closed door, waiting for the doctor to step out and declare his prognosis. Although they did not acknowledge him, their turned backs and surreptitious glances made it clear that his presence was noted and not desired.

How foolish he had been to believe that he had needed Lake Michigan between himself and his family to keep them at a distance.

The door opened and all attention turned to the middle-aged, bespectacled man in a white coat who emerged to confer with Jim's parents. Aunt Eunice's hand flew to her mouth and she swooned into her husband's arms. Cabel's heart leapt into his throat until his mother turned and gave him a radiant smile. Jim would live.

Uncle Frank gave the doctor's hand a vigorous shake, until the other man pulled his hand away and with a professional smile turned on his heel and walked away. Cabel waited until the doctor was nearly abreast of him before calling out to him.

"Excuse me."

The man turned. His harried expression transformed into wonder as he looked at Cabel, then down the hall, then back to Cabel again. "You must be a relative," he finally said.

Cabel nodded. "Jim is my cousin and I'd like to know his condition."

The doctor hesitated a moment. "The young man's parents made their wishes clear. They don't want me to discuss their son's diagnosis with anyone but them."

"Please. I'm Cabel Evans and Jim asked me to stay. I don't want to leave until I can see him, or at least know how he is doing."

Down the hall Nurse Adams ushered a reluctant Eunice and the rest of the Evans clan through a set of double doors. The doctor watched the proceedings, nodding his approval.

"What the patient needs now is rest so I sent his family away, telling them to come back tomorrow morning." He waited until the doors closed firmly behind them before turning back to Cabel. "Mr. Jim Evans was a very lucky man, under the circumstances. Had the bullet gone directly into his chest, he would have died, but its velocity was slowed when it passed through the other..."

When the doctor's words faltered, Cabel realized that he knew that Jim had been shot, but not the circumstances in which it occurred. His confusion must have shown on his face because the doctor proceeded to explain.

"Your cousin was with a young woman who was also shot. From what I understand, your cousin had tried to pull her to safety once he realized that someone was firing into the crowd. When she was hit a second time, the bullet passed through her body and into his." The doctor fiddled with his tie as he seemed to struggle with an internal debate. Finally, he continued his story. "I read her autopsy report. Your cousin couldn't have saved her. The first bullet went directly into her heart. She died instantly."

A woman had died in Jim's arms. Cabel wondered if his cousin had known her, if he knew she was dead. "I appreciate this information, Doctor, but please, how is he?"

The doctor smiled. "He has awakened, as you know. Although we will continue to monitor his condition, there is no apparent impairment of his faculties as can sometimes happen with severe blood loss."

Cabel nodded as one more weight was lifted from his heart.

"He's weak," the doctor continued, "but young and otherwise in good health. With rest and care I expect him to make a full recovery."

"Thank you." The words were inadequate but all Cabel had to offer.

The man nodded but a slight frown had settled upon his face. "I'm only telling you this because your cousin asked for you several times while I was examining him." He sighed and his shoulders sagged, pressed down by exhaustion and responsibility. "It's clear that his parents do not want you meeting with their son and to tell you the truth, I'm of two minds. Because he has asked for you repeatedly, I believe it is in his best interests that you see him, but his parents, especially his mother, are adamant that this not happen." He took off his glasses and began to polish them on his coattail, giving the activity his entire focus. "In my profession, I often find myself in the center of ongoing family disputes. The need of the patient has to come first." He put his glasses on, smudging one of the lenses in the process. "Speak with Nurse Adams. I suspect she knows the family's schedule by now and could recommend a time for you to visit that will not be disruptive."

The doctor turned to find a nurse hovering nearby with a clipboard and pen. With a sigh, the doctor took the clipboard and walked down the hall, signing papers as he went.

CHAPTER 4

Bright and cool, the day held the hint of Indian summer and Cabel enjoyed his walk from his hotel to the hospital. Despite the possibility of meeting his parents, the knowledge that Jim was awake and asking for him overrode all other concerns.

The sun had little opportunity to make its presence known in the hospital corridors and Cabel found the curtains drawn closed in Jim's room. His cousin lay on the bed, eyes closed and breathing deeply. Disappointed to find Jim asleep but not wanting to disturb him, Cabel turned to leave.

The bedclothes rustled as Jim turned toward the door. A smile lit his gaunt face, drawing Cabel back into the room.

"Jim."

As Cabel stepped closer, he could see the sharp edge of pain whiten the corners of Jim's mouth. "Do you need anything? Should I call the nurse?"

"No. Please just get me some water."

Cabel poured a glass from the pitcher on the bedside table and helped Jim to drink. The small exertion seemed to take all of his cousin's strength. He would live, Cabel reminded himself. He would heal.

Jim settled back on the pillows and waved Cabel into a nearby chair. For a moment neither spoke, just looked at each other as a thousand unspoken conversations flowed between them.

Finally, Jim nodded. "I'm glad you're here. I know it can't be easy for you." He coughed then winced in pain. Rubbing the bandage that covered his chest he said, "It was a near thing."

Cabel nodded. "Too close."

"The woman I was with, Amanda, she…" Jim's eyes filled with tears as he turned his face away.

So Jim had known the young woman who had been killed. Cabel wanted to offer words of comfort but knew from his own experience that none existed. Instead he took his cousin's hand, letting his presence provide what comfort it could.

Using a corner of the sheet, Jim dried his eyes and gave another painful-sounding cough. Staring at the ceiling he said, "Mother told me that it was a random shooting. We were just unlucky to be there when it happened." Tears again filled his eyes but he blinked them away. "It's not true, you know. The man who did this was looking for her. She was the target and I couldn't protect her." His hands balled into fists as he turned to look Cabel in the eye. "I couldn't save her."

Guilt. Guilt for not being able to protect those around you. Guilt for surviving when others didn't. Guilt at your helplessness in the face of the unthinkable. Cabel understood all too well what his cousin felt. He had lived with it himself since the first night he had ordered his men over the side of the trench and into the arms of death. He hadn't found his own way out of his private hell and had nothing to offer his cousin as he navigated his own dark path.

"The man was gunning for her, for Amanda," Jim said. "Mother won't listen and father just stands with his hands behind his back, looking at his shoes. No one believes me."

"I do," Cabel said, not knowing enough to have an opinion but sure of what Jim needed to hear. "Tell me about Amanda."

A sad smile lit Jim's face. "She was amazing. We met at the theater during intermission. I was there with friends and she had lost her escort in the crowd. He had her ticket and she couldn't remember where she was seated so we offered to let her join us in our box." Jim's smile widened. "She sat next to me for the rest of the play. It was something truly awful and we had a lovely time adding our own views to the production." His smile slipped. "I never knew what became of her escort that night. After she joined us, she never mentioned him again."

"Well why would she?" Cabel offered. "She now had you."

Jim gave him a weak grin. "Exactly. Anyway, I asked her out on a date and she said yes. That was six weeks ago." He looked at Cabel again, his eyes filled with pain and resolve. "I loved her, Cabe. We hadn't known each other long but I loved her. She was perfect, as if she were made just for me. I hadn't asked her yet, but I wouldn't have waited much longer. Now..."

Jim had been in love. Cabel remembered the exhilaration of romance, but as if from a great distance. Now only an echo remained. "I'm so sorry."

With a feeble gesture, Jim waved the words away. "I appreciate that, Cabe, I do, but what I really want is your help."

"Of course. What do you need me to do?"

"Find out who did this, who killed Amanda."

Cabel stared at his cousin in shocked silence. After a moment, he realized that he was shaking his head, an involuntary but decisive motion.

"I know it's a lot to ask, Cabe, I do, but I don't know who else to turn to except you." Jim leaned back and closed his eyes a moment then looked up at his cousin.

Cabel could barely stand to witness the pain in their depths.

"Mother and Father had met her, liked her, but now they act as if she never existed, as if she were some stranger who happened to die in my arms." His voice broke but his anger carried his story forward. "I asked Father and Uncle Edward to authorize the company to hire the Pinkerton Agency and find out what happened, but they refused, told me to forget about her." He shook his head. "As if that were possible."

Cabel placed his hand on his cousin's shoulder.

Jim shrugged it off as his eyes turned hard. "I don't want your pity. I need your help. I must know why she died and I have no one else to turn to."

The words were almost a perfect recital of what Walter Arledge had said to him four months earlier. The only reason he had investigated the death of Walter's daughter was that he had owed the man a soldier's debt of honor. His success in the investigation had more to do with luck than ability. In the end, he had learned the truth but true justice was beyond his reach. Still, the answers Cabel had found gave Walter and his family some peace and, despite himself, he had gained a small measure of redemption for his many sins.

Cabel knew Jim was in pain and understood his need for answers, but he couldn't help him, not in the way his cousin wanted. Jim needed to understand that Cabel's success over the summer had been accidental at best. "Jim, I'll help you of course. I'll hire the Pinkerton Agency myself."

"No," Jim said. "Father and Uncle Edward both know the head of the agency here in Chicago. Given how adamant our parents were about not pursuing the matter, I doubt the Pinkertons would accept the case."

"Okay," Cabel said. His chest tightened as he felt his panic begin to rise. "I'm sure the police are investigating and there are other agencies in Chicago. I will find someone..."

Jim shook his head. "I don't know who killed her or why she died. Capone owns half the police department, so I know it's corrupt. I would trust the Pinkerton Agency, but anyone else, I'm just not sure."

"But, Jim, I'm not a detective. Before, with Walter, I was lucky. I discovered who had killed his daughter more in spite of myself than because I knew what I was doing."

This statement brought a brief smile to his cousin's face. "I know, but you made a promise and you kept it. I'm asking you to do the same for me."

Cabel looked at Jim, injured and in pain, both physical and mental. There was only one answer he could give though he dreaded saying it. He didn't want to accept the responsibility that came with that promise.

"At least speak with the detective who is looking into the shooting," Jim pleaded. "I think he came by to see me today but my parents wouldn't let him in." He lay back on the pillows, pale and exhausted. Although Cabel deplored agreeing with his aunt and uncle on anything, they had been wise to keep the policeman away, at least for now.

"Please," Jim said again, his voice fading with his strength.

"Of course," Cabel said, as Jim closed his eyes. "I'll find out who killed Amanda." And who shot you, he added silently. Although the answer would be the same, the second question was the one that mattered to him.

The lines of pain eased from Jim's face as he succumbed to sleep. Cabel crossed the room and quietly closed the door as he stepped into the hall. The weight of the commitment disappeared as a new thought occurred to Cabel. Had the girl been the target, or was someone after Jim? Could his cousin still be in danger?

CHAPTER 5

Cabel had no information on where the actual shooting took place. He had to start somewhere so he asked for directions to the police station closest to the hospital. Located on LaSalle Street, near the heart of the city, the gray concrete building encompassed an entire city block. Uniformed officers hurried in and out of the glass doors, past members of the general public who took a more timid approach to the imposing edifice.

Inside the large marble and plaster foyer, Cabel waited in line to speak with the duty officer posted at a raised desk. The line inched forward as, one by one, people were directed to their various destinations. After a few minutes, the burly sergeant with a luxuriant mustache and strong Irish accent directed Cabel to the third floor. There he found a large open room with several offices around its perimeter. The center of the room held a maze of desks and file cabinets. Police officers, some in uniform and others in suits, moved about in a purposeful manner. Taken as a whole, the scene was one of choreographed chaos.

An older woman sat at a desk near the entranceway, efficiently typing from a stack of handwritten notes. Cabel waited until she acknowledged his presence before explaining that he wished to speak with the detective in charge of Jim's shooting. The woman reached for a red leather-bound ledger and flipped it open. She ran her finger down a column of names and dates then stopped when she found Jim's name. At this point, the finger changed direction, moving to the right until it came to rest on the name of the investigating detective.

"You'll need to speak with Detective Finch. His desk is near the windows, over there." She stood and pointed. "Oh, good, he's there. Just head over. I'm not sure if he'll have time to meet with you now, but you could at least set up an appointment." Offering a distracted smile of dismissal, she resumed her seat and continued typing.

Several desks stood beneath the bank of windows that allowed some natural light into the room. Unfortunately, the receptionist hadn't been specific as to which one belonged to Detective Finch and Cabel spent a few minutes wandering through the maze until he located one with a nameplate for the detective he sought.

The man who looked up from a file was younger than Cabel expected and for a moment he wondered if he had the right person. His sandy brown hair was neatly trimmed and his deep brown eyes assessed him with a level gaze. "May I help you with something?" he asked, smoothing his tie as he stood. The detective didn't offer a hand, just stood, waiting for Cabel to state his business.

"My name is Cabel Evans. My cousin Jim, James Evans, was shot Saturday night and I was told you are the detective in charge of the case. I came by to see if you'd made any progress and to learn more about what happened."

Detective Finch's mouth tightened but otherwise gave no indication of having heard what Cabel had said. After a moment, the detective pulled a chair over from another desk and gestured for Cabel to sit before resuming his own seat.

He opened a drawer, pulled out a file, and placed it on the center of his desk. Neither thick nor thin, the dark brown folder sat unopened and Cabel found himself once again under the detective's scrutiny.

"What did you want to know?" The clipped tone did not invite a lingering conversation.

"I just arrived in town and would like to start at the beginning. Where did the shooting take place?"

The man nodded. Flipping the file open, he looked down at the document at the top of the stack and read for a moment in silence. Cabel suspected the man already knew every word in the report and wondered at the reason for the charade.

"Your cousin was just off of State Street, near Monroe. There are a few theaters and restaurants nearby. I'm sure your cousin was planning to patronize one of those establishments with his young lady when the shooting took place."

Only a deaf man would have missed the sarcasm in the detective's voice. Deciding to be honest with the detective in an effort to encourage cooperation, Cabel said, "Odd, I thought he was going to a speakeasy."

A small quirk of the lips changed the young man's face from stern to approachable. He studied Cabel again, but with a different air. His shoulders relaxed as he leaned back into his chair. "Many relatives couldn't imagine their loved ones frequenting such establishments."

"I understand, but we both know the truth. In fact, Jim and I hadn't seen each other for several years and became reacquainted at the Charades Club a few months ago."

"I wouldn't recommend you mentioning that fact too loudly in here." He leaned forward, resting his hands on the file. "The mayor and the chief of police might enjoy a few indulgences, but us working stiffs still have to enforce the law." The words were spoken with humor but there was an underlying note of frustration.

"Thank you, I'll keep that in mind." Deciding it was best to move off of the subject of speakeasies, he returned to the purpose of his visit. "Do you know which, ah, establishment Jim and his date were headed to?"

"The shooting took place in front of a place called The Blue Diamond and I suspect that was their destination. According to witnesses, the woman, Amanda Channing, arrived by taxi and your cousin met her on the sidewalk."

Cabel nodded. "Jim's offices are just a few blocks away. If he was working late, he probably walked over."

The detective nodded. "That's what I thought, though when I questioned the victim's father and uncle, they were rather vague about the events of the evening prior to the shooting."

Hearing Jim described as a victim unsettled Cabel and for a moment he was distracted from the rest of Detective Finch's statement. "I don't understand. How could my uncle and father not remember what happened that night?"

"That's an interesting question, isn't it?"

"You can't suspect that they had anything to do with the shooting. My relatives and I have a strained relationship, but I can promise you that neither of them would do anything to hurt Jim."

"Hmmm." Opening the file again the detective flipped through a few pages until he found what he was looking for. "The staff at Evans Manufacturing is very loyal to the business and your cousin. Still it seems that there was a disagreement about the direction the company should take. Your cousin was of one mind and your uncle and father of another." He looked up. "Which side did you take in all of this?"

"Jim's." Cabel wondered what the detective might read into his brief answer.

Nodding, the man looked down, sorting through more of the papers. "It seems that the two elder Evans were concerned that an estranged relative might have had a hand in this, wanting to regain control of the company." When Detective Finch raised his eyes again it was clear that he had known from the beginning who sat across from him.

Cabel's stomach tightened. His concern for Jim blinded him to the obvious. Any investigation would unearth his past. He felt his face redden and wondered if the detective would read that as a sign of guilt. "I didn't. I would never hurt Jim. I…"

The detective's raised hand halted Cabel's words. "I've looked into your background, which I have to say is a bit unusual." He picked a report out of the stack and laid it on top of the others. "You were a decorated army officer in the war, yet you have a history of violence against your father. There was only one public incident and witnesses claim that your father provoked the attack, though they felt your response was extreme." Detective Finch paused and met Cabel's eyes. "You might not realize this but there are many on the board who think well of you. Several of them believe that your behavior might have been affected by the war as much as your father's callousness." He studied Cabel a moment before returning to the report in his hand and continued his recitation. "Although you were next in line as head of Evans Manufacturing, you disappeared for several years after the incident with your father and have had no contact with any family member until recently. According to Mr. James Evans' secretary, you had reconciled with your cousin and he did not view you as a threat to his person or position in the company." He set the report on top of the others and waited for Cabel to respond.

"It's true, at least what happened, what I did." Painfully, humiliatingly true. "As to the opinions of the board members, I'm at a loss..." He swallowed hard against the lump that made a sudden appearance in his throat. There was no explanation as to why these men would stand by him, not after what he had done. He looked at Detective Finch and spoke the only truth he knew, "The incident between my father and myself was my fault alone and I take full responsibility." Rather than condemnation, Cabel saw respect in the detective's eyes, though he didn't understand why. He had just admitted to nearly beating his father to death, and there was no justification for such a horrendous act.

"Despite all of this information, I have to tell you that you are a suspect in the shooting." He held up a hand to forestall Cabel's objections. "According to your father and uncle, you are the only one that benefits from James Evans' death. They also claim you have ties to Capone, that you work for him and could have arranged for him to help kill your cousin."

Cabel sat a moment to consider what he had heard, shaking his head both in bafflement and denial. He cleared his throat and met the detective's eyes. "First, I have nothing to gain from Jim's death. To be honest, I wouldn't want to see my father and uncle back at the helm of Evans Manufacturing, but I promise you I know my place and it isn't there." He paused, trying to decide how best to explain his bizarre connection with Al Capone and decided that there was nothing to do but to tell the man the truth, or at least a reasonable version. "In August, I came back to Chicago only as part of an effort to help a friend. My search led me to the Charades Club which happened to be run by someone I was acquainted with long ago. Purely by accident, I found myself caught in a shoot-out between Capone and men who worked for a gangster named Malone."

The detective blinked then leaned forward, his hands now flat on the blotter. "Bugs Moran. You *accidentally* found yourself in the middle of a shoot-out between the most powerful gang leaders in Chicago?"

"Moran wasn't actually present at the time," Cabel said, realizing how bad this probably sounded.

The detective blinked again, shook his head in disbelief. "Okay, then what happened?"

"My arm was in a cast," he said, hoping for some sympathy. From the look on Det. Finch's face, it wasn't forthcoming. "I found myself more or less taken hostage by Moran's men. When they attacked Capone in the office of the Charades Club, they threw me on the floor and ..." How could he explain to this man the effect of being in the middle of a gunfight had had on him? The past and present had mingled until he found himself back in France, fighting a war that was long over. When he had come back to himself, he was holding a gun on two of Moran's men, effectively ending the shoot-out and unintentionally saving Capone's life.

He looked up to find Detective Finch patiently waiting for him to continue. Finally he said, "Moran's men had forgotten about me. Capone's men were more concerned with shooting people who were shooting at them, so no one noticed me." He paused, for here was the point at which he had lost himself, something he could never admit to anyone. "A man was shot and his gun fell, sliding toward me. I picked it up, pointing it at two of Moran's men who were in front of me. They surrendered and Capone decided that I saved his life. I felt it was best for my health if I agreed with that assessment."

The two men looked at each other across the desk. Cabel did his best not to flinch under the detective's scrutiny. After several uncomfortable moments, Detective Finch leaned back in his chair. "Is that the last time you had contact with Capone? That night at the club?"

Cabel nodded, deciding that this was not the time to mention that Capone felt that he owed Cabel a debt and had given him a ring to hold as a token of that debt. Cabel didn't want it, but found it prudent to accept as he had been sitting in the middle of a group of armed men at the time. After another long moment, he said, "I don't work for Capone, I never have. Jim's attack had nothing to do with me."

The detective shrugged as if not accepting Cabel's statement as truth. "What about Capone? Could it have something to do with him?"

"No, at least I can't imagine that Jim would have any reason to be connected with the mob leader."

"But didn't Jim also go to the Charades Club? Didn't he also have a connection to this acquaintance of yours?"

Cabel closed his eyes, trying to find the words that would help Detective Finch see the truth. "Yes, Jim went to the Charades Club, as did many wealthy Chicagoans. I presume they still do.

But Jim is a businessman. Evans Manufacturing makes machine parts for other companies. I can't imagine any reason for Capone to be interested in the company or Jim."

"Except through you." The detective let that statement hang in the air between them a moment, waiting.

Cabel met the other man's gaze. There were things he would not reveal to the police officer, but he knew that his odd connection to Capone had nothing to do with the shooting.

The detective nodded a moment, then rummaged through a drawer and produced a battered package of cigarettes. He offered one to Cabel before taking one himself. Cabel rarely smoked but decided to accept this unexpected gesture of courtesy. Using the detective's lighter, Cabel lit his cigarette, inhaled deeply, and felt his tension dissipate as he exhaled. The detective was a clever young man, he decided.

Detective Finch searched his desk a moment, lifting a stack of reports and shifting through papers, until he uncovered a saucer smeared with ash and set it between them. "You have to know how unbelievable your story is," he said.

Cabel smiled ruefully before blowing a wisp of smoke into the air. "I have a hard time believing it myself, and I was there."

The corners of the detective's mouth twitched. "I have to say that with your connection to Capone and your family's insistence that you are involved, I should arrest you right now."

Cabel's chest tightened. He stabbed out his cigarette before saying. "Why don't you?"

Detective Finch blew a perfect smoke ring in the air. It floated between them a moment before drifting away to join the cloud of smoke that hung over the room. "Several things trouble me about this shooting. According to the witness accounts, Amanda Channing was the intended victim, not James Evans."

"I don't understand," Cabel said. "How could anyone be sure?"

"First, it seems that her cab was followed to the nightclub. A car stopped down the block from the entrance as her taxi pulled up. The shooter stepped out and headed straight for the girl." The detective rubbed his hands over his face as if to wash away what had happened next. "Second, the shooter didn't hesitate. He aimed at Amanda Channing and fired. This wasn't a drive-by shooting or people caught between two warring gangs. It has all of the elements of a professional hit." He crushed out his cigarette and studied the saucer a moment as if he were trying to organize his thoughts. "It is possible that someone knew Miss Channing was meeting your cousin that night and followed her to get to him, but that seems unlikely. If someone wanted to kill your cousin, they wouldn't need to follow her to locate him."

Cabel nodded, relieved but confused. "What you say makes sense, as far as Jim is concerned, but what of Miss Channing? I don't know anything about her, but if she moved in the same level of society as Jim what could she have done that would have put her in the sights of a killer?"

"That is a very good question. I'm hoping your cousin might have a few answers for me when I have a chance to speak to him."

"I doubt he knows anything important," Cabel said, reviewing the bedside conversation in his head. "He's weak from his injuries, but he wants to understand what happened. When he's able, I know he will help you in any way he can."

"That would be appreciated." Detective Finch closed the file with an air of finality, but added, "What I find odd is that when there is a shooting which involves someone from a family as prominent as yours, I receive a lot of pressure from that family and from my superiors to solve the case. Aside from you, no one has even asked about it. Why do you think that is?"

"I don't know." Though maybe he did. Perhaps his family had already judged him, found him guilty, and were waiting for the police to make an arrest. Pushing aside these bitter thoughts, he realized he had a few more questions. "What about Amanda's family? Haven't they been here, seeking answers?"

"That's another thing I'm hoping your cousin will be able help me with. We can't locate any family, any next of kin. Amanda Channing rented an apartment approximately two months ago. It's near Clark and Addison. The landlady's husband had purchased two homes side by side, converted one into apartments and they lived in the other until he died. Mrs. Marshall still lives there and keeps a close eye on her tenants. She is sure that Miss Channing's only visitor was Jim Evans."

"But the lease agreement…"

"Mrs. Marshall doesn't bother with them, just first and last months' rent and two references, which Miss Channing supplied without hesitation. One was supposedly from a former employer and the other from her previous landlord. Both are located in the Boston area. Mrs. Marshall was so taken with Miss Channing and, not wanting to incur the expense of long-distance telephone calls, she didn't check them. I'm trying to follow up myself, but the company she listed as a reference is large and though no one I spoke to knew her, no one can say for certain that she didn't work there. I'm waiting for someone from the accounting department to get back to me. As for her former landlord, the number she gave is for a deli. It's possible she could have written the number wrong, but it seems odd that both of her references are so difficult to confirm." He shook his head. "In fact, I'm beginning to wonder if Amanda Channing is her real name."

"That doesn't make any sense." Cabel had never met the woman, but he trusted Jim's instincts. Granted his cousin was in love with Miss Channing, but he couldn't imagine him being duped.

"Maybe the woman was after your cousin's money or running away from an abusive spouse. There are many reasons why someone might want to hide their past. The question I have is: was it her past, her present, or her relationship with your cousin that led to her death?"

CHAPTER 6

Icy rain pelted against the panes, sounding like distant rifle fire of a forgotten war. Cabel lay against damp sheets as the last remnants of his nightmare faded. Exhausted by the battles he had fought in his sleep, only thoughts of seeing Jim had him draw back the covers and stumble toward the bathroom.

A short time later he arrived at the hospital and made the trek down the now-familiar corridor, more relaxed than he had been the two previous days. Jim was improving and, if Nurse Adam's was correct, he would avoid meeting his family. His steps faltered as he neared the nurses' station and he saw Detective Finch with Frank and Eunice. The detective wore an expression of unraveling patience as he spoke in low tones to Jim's parents. Eunice's arms were crossed over her sparse bosom as she glared at the young detective while Frank gestured with sharp hand motions, making it clear that he wanted the detective to leave.

Knowing his presence would make matters worse, Cabel decided to return later in the day. He turned to leave when he heard his aunt exclaim, "He's the one you should be talking to, not Jim." Cabel looked back. Aunt Eunice stood, eyes wild with anger and one long, bony finger pointed at him in accusation.

Her hatred was palpable and he felt his anger rise in response, not the mindless anger that would not be contained, but the reasonable one that said enough is enough. Many sins could be laid at his feet but not Jim's shooting, and he grew tired of the assignment of blame.

Cabel approached the group with measured steps. His aunt and uncle squirmed with discomfort and drew back a step as he reached the nurses' station. Detective Finch shot him a look of sympathy.

"Tell the detective what you know about that girl," Aunt Eunice demanded.

"Do you mean the one that Jim was in love with and who died in his arms?"

Several emotions chased each other across his aunt's face. There was anger certainly, and concern and defiance. He could have sworn that guilt passed by as well, only to be replaced with arrogance.

"How dare you tell me how my son felt about that, that female? I doubt he had known her for more than a few weeks."

Cabel nodded. "That's what he said, just before he told me he loved her."

The hatred in Aunt Eunice's eyes held a moment longer before it slipped away and only sadness remained. Her chin trembled slightly as tears sprang to her eyes. Shaking her head as if to dismiss Cabel's words, Eunice turned and sagged against her husband's shoulder. Her voice trembled as she said, "Take me home, Frank."

Uncle Frank placed his arm protectively around his wife's waist before turning back to the detective. "If you do anything to upset my son or cause him any relapse or delay in recovery, I will have you fired."

Detective Finch bore the news stoically, nodding to Jim's parents as they retreated down the hall. Turning to Cabel, he said, "Interesting family you have."

Cabel gave him a rueful smile. "I'm just thankful I don't have more of them."

Nurse Adams had monitored the situation from the safety of the nurses' station but now stepped forward to address them. "Mr. Evans requires rest to complete his recovery. I understand your need to interview him," she said to the detective. "And that you wish to see him again," she nodded to Cabel. "However, he often finds his parents visits taxing. If you wish to see him now, please keep the visit short." She turned and walked away, confident that her requirements would be met.

Detective Finch said to Cabel, "Given that you and your cousin are so close, why don't you go in with me. Your presence might reassure him as we discuss Miss Channing."

Cabel nodded, pleased both to be asked and relieved that he would not be the one to tell his cousin about the odd aspects of Amanda Channing's life.

Detective Finch opened the door, motioning Cabel to walk in first. His heart warmed as Jim smiled at him, genuinely pleased that he had come. The smile stiffened as he saw Detective Finch.

"You can't be another specialist, you don't have the white coat."

Detective Finch smiled as he approached the bed. "My mother would have loved it if I had become a doctor, but she had to settle for a police officer instead."

Jim looked at Cabel. "Thank you," he said. "I knew you would be able to help me learn the truth."

Cabel and the detective exchanged glances before the police officer took a chair on the side of the bed nearest the door and gestured for Cabel to sit in the one near the wall. They flanked the injured man on the bed who looked at both of them hopefully, then with growing concern.

"What is it? What's wrong?"

Detective Finch took charge and gave Jim a straightforward account of what he had learned about the shooting and, more important, what he hadn't been able to learn about Amanda Channing. When the detective completed his statements, Jim looked at him stricken and confused.

"This makes no sense. I knew Amanda. She had family in Boston. Her parents live there, her brother, aunts, uncles, cousins. They can't all have fallen off the face of the earth."

"I agree," Detective Finch said, not without compassion. "We just don't know how to locate them. I haven't heard back from the company she said she worked for and no one I've spoken with has any further information." He paused for a moment, weighing his words carefully. "I've begun to wonder if Miss Channing has been using a false name."

"No." Jim was emphatic. "No. She wouldn't lie, not to me." His eyes pleaded with Cabel and Detective Finch to believe him. "I knew her," he said. He looked up at Cabel in confusion. "I thought I knew her."

CHAPTER 7

After a few false starts and with the aid of a helpful newsagent's boy, Cabel found Amanda Channing's apartment building tucked away on a residential side street off of Addison Avenue. The two-story home had white siding, a minuscule front lawn and a well-swept walkway leading to the front stoop. An identical house stood at an angle on the adjacent lot and together they were part of the ten or so homes that lined the little dead-end street. The second house lacked the Apartment for Rent sign in the front window and thus marked it as the landlady's residence. A twitch of a lace curtain let him know that he was being observed by someone in that house. Flowers flanked the walkway in a riot of color, a last hurrah before winter set in. Yet for all of their brightness and profusion, they had the fragile look of blooms awaiting that first, killing frost. The walkway ended at a wood door where a cheerful mat lay at his feet and bid him Welcome. He paused, wondering again just how to approach this woman. She had no reason to help him as he wasn't a detective, merely the cousin of her murdered lodger's suitor. Still this dubious distinction was all he had to offer by way of an explanation for his presence on her doorstep. He prayed it would be enough.

Rather than knock, he turned the key in the center of the door and listened to the harsh ring of the bell. The brassy clamor still echoed in the late autumn air when the door flew open and before him stood a small woman, pudgy, but with a pleasant face and sparkling eyes. Her tight curly hair was an improbable shade of silver, reminding him a bit of a poodle he had once seen. The woman's smile was welcoming though her bright eyes were shrewd as she considered him.

"I'm Mrs. Marshall and you must be a relative of Mr. Evans, you have much the same look about you. You'd better come in." She turned and disappeared down a cluttered hallway.

Cabel stood in the doorway a moment, surprised at Mrs. Marshall's trusting nature. Deciding to accept his good fortune, he stepped over the threshold, closed the door, and followed the sounds of the woman's voice.

The parlor nearly defeated him. Flowers festooned the walls, draperies, and furniture. Vases and bowls of fresh-picked blooms covered every flat surface from the tabletops to the mantelpiece. Even the carpet had interwoven roses and ivy vines around its border. Underlying the competing scents of the various bouquets of flowers was the cloying aroma of Mrs. Marshall's toilette water.

Devastated by the olfactory and visual assault, Cabel tried to blink back his tears, but in the end had to pull out his handkerchief to wipe his eyes. On the far side of the room Mrs. Marshall sat on a chaise lounge covered in a fabric awash in purple peonies. A young girl in the dark dress, white apron, and cap of a maid stood near her mistress, listening to the older woman's instructions while looking longingly toward the hallway. Cabel had the distinct impression that the girl was attempting to hold her breath and was nearing the end of her reserves. Silently cursing his upbringing that required him to be gallant when faced with a female in distress, he took his own last breath of unadulterated air and crossed the room to where Mrs. Marshall sat.

"That will be all, Lucy," she said, shooing the girl away with a quick motion of her hand, though the girl was nearly out of the door before Mrs. Marshall's words had left her lips. The maid looked back over her shoulder and offered Cabel a smile of thanks mingled with pity.

"Sit down, young man, sit down," the landlady said, making the same shooing motion at Cabel as she had to the maid.

The same sense of self-preservation Cabel had trusted as a soldier came to his aid yet again. A side window near the settee was raised a few inches and a comfortable chair stood nearby. Forcing himself to take measured steps, he claimed the chair and took a shallow, tentative breath. While the smell of perfume and flowers still pervaded, the gentle breeze from the window diluted it to a manageable level.

Mrs. Marshall looked at him in disappointment. "You too? I have all of these lovely chairs that give a better view of the room, but all of my guests choose the one you're in." She sighed. "I don't understand it. Just last week, the reverend and his wife called and they practically raced across the room trying to reach the chair first. The poor reverend's frock coat caught on the corner of the desk, so his wife claimed the prize. She seemed quite pleased. It was rather unseemly. They didn't stay long." Her voice trailed off as she pondered these mysteries for a moment. She turned back to Cabel. "My husband hated this room, wouldn't step foot inside it. Said there were too many flowers, but how can you have too many flowers?"

She looked at Cabel expectantly.

"I would have thought that would be impossible," he managed with what he hoped was a sincere tone of voice.

"Exactly," she said in triumph. "Most men just don't understand, but I knew you would." Her gaze wandered over the room, pausing to caress a floral arrangement here or a botanical print there. "I had an infection of the sinuses as a young girl and lost my sense of smell. I had always loved flowers, but I can no longer enjoy them fully, the way that I had as a child, so I made this room to enjoy them in the only way I can. It's lovely, isn't it?"

Cabel nodded in polite agreement. He silently blessed the young maid who undoubtedly kept the window cracked for the benefit of visitors.

"Now," Mrs. Marshall continued, "I know you must be a relative of that nice young Mr. Evans. Are you brothers?"

"No, ma'am. I'm his cousin, Cabel Evans."

"How is he, your cousin? When the nice young policeman came by to tell me what happened to poor Miss Channing, he said that Mr. Evans was in the hospital, his outcome uncertain."

"He's doing much better, thank you for asking. We're hoping for a full recovery."

"Oh, how wonderful. I was quite worried for him and of course so upset about Miss Channing. Have they located her family yet?"

The arrival of the maid pushing a tea cart laden with trays of pastries and sandwiches interrupted the conversation. Tea was poured, delicacies selected, and Cabel found himself perching a plate of watercress sandwiches on his knee while sipping a cup of floral tea. He had imagined hell as the battlefields of France, but he now had a new version to consider.

"I hope you don't think me a poor hostess, we really should be talking of more polite topics as we have tea,"

"I don't mind at all, ma'am," Cabel said. "To be honest, I'm not even sure why I'm here except that I wanted to know more about the woman whom Jim was seeing."

"You mean in love with, don't you?" Mrs. Marshall smiled as she raised her rose-patterned tea cup to her lips. "I saw him several times, coming to collect her for an evening out. His feelings grew quickly and he wasn't able to hide them as well as he probably would have liked."

The words cut through Cabel's heart and he took a bigger sip of tea than he intended. He coughed briefly but managed to control his face enough to hide his grimace. "He is usually quite level headed but seemed quite the opposite where it came to Miss Channing. He was quite taken with her."

"Yes, he was," she said, looking out of the window.

Something in her tone, more serious now than it had been a moment ago, had him ask, "Did you not approve of my cousin, or was there something else that concerned you?"

She gave her head a small shake. "Oh, there was nothing wrong with Mr. Evans. He was quite gallant and it was nice to see a young man come calling on a pretty girl. It took me back to my own, younger days."

Cabel waited, forgetting about the tea and the overwhelming fragrances that choked the room like mustard gas.

"I tried to tell the nice policeman, Detective Finch, but all he wanted was to ask a few questions and collect the key to Mrs. Channing's apartment. If he had stayed longer I would have told him, but he was in such a hurry."

"I'm sure he had much on his mind," Cabel said. Next time he saw the detective he would have to chide him for being a coward in the face of an overabundance of flowers. "I have spoken with him twice and would be happy to pass along any information you could tell me."

She nodded, then set her tea cup on the trolley, signaling the completion of the social ritual. Cabel did the same. "This road is just a little afterthought, coming between two angled streets, near enough to sometimes hear the traffic, but isolated enough that it doesn't have such a city feel to it. Do you know what I mean?"

He considered her words, and then nodded. She had described her little neighborhood quite well.

"There is a cut through in the back yard, just over there by the corner." She pointed to a place where two tall wooden fences joined behind the house she leased out. "It's a bit of an optical illusion, those fences. From here it looks quite solid, but actually there is a small alleyway that leads past the buildings behind us and over to Addison Avenue. Few people notice it and even fewer use it."

"Did Miss Channing use it?"

Mrs. Marshall nodded her head in a slow, thoughtful manner as her gaze drifted back to the view from the window. "Yes, she did, rather frequently as a matter of fact." She turned her head to look at Cabel again. "She had the upstairs apartment. When my husband added the porches above and below, you can see, he also added a stairway from the second floor apartment to the yard."

Cabel could see both from where he was sitting, grateful that he was able to lean closer to the open window in the process. "So Miss Channing came down the backstairs and cut through the little alleyway."

"Yes," Mrs. Marshall's hesitation had him turn back to her. She had taken out a tat-edged handkerchief and now sat twisting it in her hands. "I had promised my husband that I would only accept quality tenants, that I would check all references before I leased an apartment to anyone, but Miss Channing seemed so nice, that I…"

"Mrs. Marshall, I never met Miss Channing but my cousin cared for her very much. I can't tell you yet if she had deceived you, but if she did, she deceived Jim as well."

"I feel responsible for his injury," she said. The anguish in her voice matched what he saw in her eyes. "If I had asked Miss Channing for references or told Mr. Evans what I had seen, it all might have turned out differently."

With those words Cabel felt the weight of someone else's needs settling on his shoulder, joining the burden Jim had already placed there. "I doubt you could have changed what happened to either of them, but you can help us understand why. We still don't know if the shooter was trying to harm the girl or Jim."

"I can't say, of course, but, well, Miss Channing's behavior was a bit odd." She sighed. "You must think me an old busybody with nothing to do but sit at this window day and night, spying on my tenants, but it really isn't true. From here I can't see the front of the house and I've never wondered about people coming and going. As long as my tenants paid their rent on time and kept the property up, I let them live their lives."

Cabel nodded. "If Miss Channing hadn't gone out the back way, you never would have seen her."

Mrs. Marshall gave a small smile. "Exactly. At least at first, then I must admit I was curious. It wasn't just that she used the alleyway to get to the other street, it was how she dressed as well."

"I don't understand."

The landlady considered her words carefully. "Most of the time she dressed in lovely clothes, expensive and tasteful. But when she left from the balcony, her clothes were gaudier somehow, and her hair was different as well. Even the way she walked seemed changed, turning her into someone very different from the young woman to whom I leased the apartment. It reminded me of an actress putting on a costume, getting into character. Do you know what I mean?"

Again Cabel nodded, trying to understand a woman he had never met.

"She paid her rent for four months. The apartment came fully furnished, and Miss Channing told me she wasn't sure what her plans would be after that. Normally, I don't like to take short-term leases, but she paid in cash and it kept the apartment occupied."

"So she wasn't planning on staying in town long?"

"She didn't say, but that seemed to be likely. I was hoping that your cousin would change her mind, but then she started her odd behavior and I didn't know what to think."

Cabel nodded. "I realize that my next request may seem unusual but..."

"You'd like to see Miss Channing's apartment," Mrs. Marshall said. "Yes, I think that might be a good idea, but only if you promise to tell me what you learn."

"I promise, though I don't know when that will be."

Mrs. Marshall's smile was bright but tinged with loneliness. "Just come back when you can. If nothing else, I need to know what to do with Miss Channing's belongings." She raised a small silver bell from the table beside her and rang it vigorously. "My maid should be here in a moment to see you out."

Cabel stood, debating with himself a moment. He offered his hand as he reviewed the social training that was drilled into him during his youth. There were some things that were not discussed, but if a delicate matter must be broached, it should be surrounded by flattery. Mrs. Marshall took his hand, giving it a brief squeeze. Her eyes widened when her fingers were not released. Cabel knelt next to her, nearly suffocating, but knowing that she had given him aid for no reason other than that he had asked, and he would offer her some in return. "Mrs. Marshall," the words came out choked, though not from emotion. "You have done me a great service and I want to thank you for it."

She gently tugged her hand free and laid it on his arm. "It is of no consequence."

"You have a lovely home," he said, soldiering on. "This room in particular is exceptionally beautiful, like a garden in spring."

Her hands fluttered to her throat as she beamed with pleasure. "I am so glad you enjoy it."

"It is so sad that you can't enjoy the lovely fragrances of the flowers." He paused, unsure of what to say or whether he should continue at all. The fact that his eyes had begun to water gave him his answer. "I just thought I would mention that for those of us who can smell them, the number and variety of blooms in this room is a bit overwhelming to the senses."

Her smile faltered as she took in his words. Her eyes widened as his meaning became clear. She looked around the room, from vase to vase, tabletop to the mantelpiece, then settled on the window, opened just enough to provide a breath of fresh air.

"Oh my," she said. Her hands flew to her reddened cheeks. "I am so embarrassed. No wonder no one stays long when they visit me. And that chair." She pointed to it, her hand shaking. "It's the only safe one in the room, isn't it?"

"Your pastor and his wife seemed to think so."

She looked at him a moment, then she started to laugh.

"Oh, dear. What everyone must think of me?"

"They must think you are a wonderful person, if they are willing to visit you at all, knowing what awaits them."

Mrs. Marshall smiled at him, warmth and embarrassment clear upon her face. "I shall banish the flowers immediately and hope my friends might give me another chance."

"You don't need to remove all of them," Cabel said.

"True, but most of them I think." She looked around the room again with a more critical eye, nodding to herself as decisions were made.

The maid appeared in the doorway and Mrs. Marshall smiled. In short order, she gave the girl instructions regarding the key and Cabel's desire to see Miss Channing's apartment. "After that, Lucy, please come back. I have a task for you that I believe you might enjoy." She then turned to Cabel. "I will hold you to your promise of letting me know what you discover about Miss Channing. In the meantime, thank you for telling me what my friends should have mentioned years ago."

Cabel nodded, thanked his hostess for the tea and the assistance before following a very curious maid to the hallway.

There were two keys on the ring that the maid handed him, one for the front door of the building next door and one for the apartment.

The door of the apartment house opened into the same general hallway as with its sister next door. Instead of the inviting foyer of Mrs. Marshall's house, all of the doors were closed and a wall had been added near the back of the stairwell, enclosing the first floor into an apartment. A stack of letters sat on a polished table near the front door. Cabel sorted through them, uncomfortable at invading the other tenant's privacy, but it had to be done. None of the envelopes were addressed to Amanda Channing or any other occupant of the second-floor apartment. He put the letters back on the table and climbed the stairs. He paused at the small landing and used the second key to open the door, anticipating his first glimpse of the elusive Miss Channing.

CHAPTER 8

He pushed the door open and found chaos. Cushions had been pulled from the sofa and slashed, disgorging fluff and stuffing over the worn carpet. An armchair lay on its side, the underside cut to reveal springs and bits of fabric. Lamps and small tables lay smashed on the floor, as if whoever had done this had been frustrated in his search.

For the first time, it occurred to Cabel that he might not be alone. He stepped inside the apartment, careful to avoid crunching the broken glass underfoot and listened, not with his ears but with all of his senses, a survival instinct honed in the war. A few minutes later he was certain he was alone and stepped further into the room.

The doorway opened directly into a large sitting room that stretched the width of the house. With its many windows and bright yellow walls, the room would have been cheerful but for the wreckage that laid waste to Miss Channing's possessions. Directly across from Cabel, the door to the back porch hung drunkenly from broken hinges. This was how the thief entered and left the apartment, the same clandestine manner as Miss Channing.

Cabel knew he should contact the police, or at least return to Mrs. Marshall and inform her about the damage. Still he hesitated. This might be his only chance to learn something about Miss Channing. Besides, he couldn't make the room look worse than it already did. With the decision made, he closed the apartment door and began a search of his own.

Whoever had come before him had been thorough if not tidy. In the bedroom, clothes had been flung from the wardrobe and yanked from the dresser drawers. As with the furniture in the other room, the mattress and small chair had been slashed, their stuffing added to the overall mess. Until they had been torn and stepped on, Miss Channing's clothes had been of excellent quality, though something felt wrong. After a moment he realized that the way the dresses lay strewed about the room gave the impression that there were more of them than was actually true. He could only see three evening gowns, two or three walking skirts, and four fashionable day dresses. He would have expected that a woman of Miss Channing's station in life to own several more than she in fact did. Perhaps Detective Finch had guessed correctly when he suggested that she was running away from something.

In addition to the clothes, something else seemed odd. There were only token amounts of perfume and a bit of cosmetics scattered across the floor. There were no photographs tucked into the mirror frame, no knickknacks brightened the windowsills or lay broken beneath them. Even the shattered picture frames that had been torn from the walls held only mundane scenes of children and flowers. Most likely they were part of the furnishings that had come with the apartment. Unless the intruder had taken all of Miss Channing's personal items, there had been none to begin with. On the surface there was no evidence of the bright, vibrant woman whom Jim had loved.

Cabel turned to leave the room when he saw a battered straw hat, half hidden under the dresser. This item was so out of place amongst the silks and satins that he picked it up and examined it closely. The wear on the brim and tie ribbon were from long use, but was further damaged from being trampled by uncaring feet. It was of poor quality and not of the current fashion. Turning it in his hands, he wondered if it had been left by a prior tenant or if Miss Channing had kept it for some reason. Part of the pink band that decorated the top of the brim felt thicker than the rest. With a quick tug the fabric came off in his hand and a folded piece of paper fluttered to the floor. Retrieving it, he opened the heavy paper with care to reveal a photograph, faded and creased but sharp enough to see the details.

Two girls, about twelve and fourteen he guessed, stood close together, arms around each other's waists, the older one smiling toward the camera with the younger one looking up adoringly at her. Sisters, he was sure, based on their facial features and ages. They wore simple dresses and straw hats similar to the one in which the photo had been hidden. Behind them stood a brick archway, ivy growing up the sides, obscuring some of the letters carved into the brick. Something about the location was familiar to Cabel, though he couldn't place it. The harder he tried, the more elusive the memory became.

Perhaps one of the girls was Amanda. He had never met her but Jim might recognize her. Rather than leave the photograph for the police to find, he tucked it into his jacket to give to Detective Finch the next time they met.

Leaving the bedroom, Cabel went to the dining room and kitchen that were on the opposite side of the apartment. Dining room was too grand a word for the small alcove that held a simple, square table and four matching chairs. A small vase of flowers lay smashed on the floor, the only attempt to decorate the room that Cabel could see. Other than the vase, there were no other casualties here, as there were no places to hide anything.

The kitchen made up for the restraint shown in the last room. Cupboards and drawers were open, their contents thrown against the walls or the floor. The small icebox had been tipped over and the melted ice had made a puddle beneath the counter. There had been little food in the icebox and pantry. The dishes and utensils were mismatched, probably remnants of sets once owned by Mrs. Marshall.

The only thing that the intruder had left alone was a small, wood-burning oven in the corner of the room. Dusty and clearly unused, the cast-iron oven was too heavy to tip over and the door latch was stuck. The thief hadn't bothered with it either out of frustration or the belief that it made a poor hiding place. For that reason alone, Cabel thought it made a perfect place to store things that someone wanted hidden from prying eyes. He tugged on the door latch but it wouldn't give. Kneeling down, Cabel saw a small stick, maybe a match, had been wedged into the latch to keep it closed, a clever way to lock something away in an apartment with no safe. He pried the stick out and the door opened with ease. A lumpy package wrapped in brown paper and tied with a string sat in the center of the rack like a Sunday roast. Cabel lifted it out, placed it on the kitchen counter, and cut the string. Pulling the paper back, he found a woman's overcoat, two dresses, and a pair of shoes, all very different from the ones Miss Channing had kept in the bedroom.

The dresses were brightly colored and low cut, one with beading and one with small disks sewn into it that caught the light. Tawdry was the word that came to mind and he doubted that Jim had ever seen her in them. The material and quality were cheap, especially in comparison to what lay destroyed in the other room. The shoes were high-heeled and heavy, a basic black that could coordinate with either dress. Wedged into the toe of one of the shoes, wrapped in a handkerchief was a key, probably to a door from the look of it, but it didn't match the ones to the apartment. The coat itself was made of dark-patterned wool with large cloth-covered buttons down the front. As with everything else, the material was cheap and it was poorly made. The seams were frayed and even the fabric over the buttons was misaligned with the rest of the coat, making it impossible to ignore.

Here were the dresses that the landlady had seen Miss Channing wear as she disappeared through the backyard. Once again he debated leaving the items for the police to find but decided it was best to take them away with him. He wrapped the items back in the brown paper and did his best to retie the string.

He stood another moment and surveyed the ruined kitchen. There was no way to know if anything had been taken by the thief. The break-in raised more questions about Miss Channing but offered no solutions. He needed to inform Mrs. Marshall of the situation and leave the rest to the police.

IIIII

Mrs. Marshall was still ensconced in her garden room, though the air was noticeably fresher than before. She seemed more excited than upset about the intruder, though she was annoyed at Cabel's description of the damages incurred. She sent her maid to telephone the police and told Cabel he could leave unless he wished to speak with them himself. Since he knew little that would aid in their investigation, he simply reminded Mrs. Marshall to direct the officers to Detective Finch for further information and took his leave.

There was one more thing he wanted to see before he left Miss Channing's lodgings behind. The grass in the backyard was more brown than green, patchy in places due to the colder autumn days. From below it was impossible to see the damage to the second-floor door. The railings were unmarked and offered no witness to the fact that an intruder had used the stairs to gain access to the upper level. A path of sorts had been worn into the grass, leading from the steps to the far corner of the yard.

Mrs. Marshall had been correct about the optical illusion created by the fencing. He couldn't see the opening to the narrow walkway until he was nearly upon it. Weeds grew along the edge of the narrow path that slipped between two brick buildings and ended at Addison Avenue. A telephone booth stood near the corner and taxis idled near the entrance to a small hotel across the street. Amanda could have disappeared in any direction from this point. Without more information, Cabel had no way to track her movements. How would he explain this to Jim?

Admitting defeat, he hailed a taxi and asked to be driven to the police station on LaSalle Street. Perhaps Detective Finch would have some thoughts on the matter.

CHAPTER 9

The cab pulled up in front of the police station as Detective Finch exited the building. Cabel thrust an assortment of bills and change at the driver, then hurried down the sidewalk to catch the detective before he left for the day.

"Detective Finch."

The detective turned as did the man walking next to him. In his rush to catch up with Finch, Cabel hadn't realized that he wasn't alone. Detective Finch looked steadily into Cabel's eyes and gave a small shake of his head. The other man, older, gray-haired and unsmiling missed the gesture as he studied Cabel with cold dark eyes.

"John, you're early. We weren't to meet at O'Malley's until six." The detective stared at Cabel as if willing him to understand.

"Of course, I must have confused our plans," Cabel responded, understanding what Detective Finch wanted but not why.

"Good. I'll see you then." With a brisk nod, both men turned and continued on their way.

Cabel glanced at this watch. He had two hours until his meeting with the detective and it was too late to visit Jim at the hospital. His stomach chose this moment to remind him that, except for the light snack at Mrs. Marshall's, he hadn't eaten since breakfast. The decision made, he raised his hand, flagging a taxi. An early dinner, brief rest, and he'd be ready to face whatever Detective Finch had to tell him.

IIIII

The green-trimmed sign in the window of O'Malley's identified it as a soda fountain, but that small piece of paper couldn't disguise the true character of the building. Cabel opened the door to find what the exterior promised, an Irish pub. The air was thick with smoke and redolent with the scent of house-brewed beer. Instead of beer mugs, drinks were served in soda glasses and Cabel wondered if this was a nod to the law or a bit of ironic humor. Either way the sight made him smile.

A long, polished wood bar with gleaming brass rails stretched across the back of the room. Booths lined the walls and tables filled the rest of the space. Unlike some sophisticated speakeasies which offered music and dancing in addition to the illicit drinks, this was a working-man's bar. A place to drink and gossip, letting the day slip away and tomorrow seem more distant. He had spent much time in places such as this during his exile in New Orleans and felt at home.

Cabel searched the room twice before he spotted Detective Finch slouched in a booth near the window. The corner was dark as the window had been painted over, hiding the activities of those within. Wending his way through the tangle of tables and boisterous men, Cabel slid into the booth, sitting across from the detective.

The young man had removed his tie but there was no mistaking he was a policeman, yet no one seemed concerned at his presence. Cabel glanced around the room again then back to the detective. "They know you here."

Det. Finch nodded. "I grew up around the corner. My mother's maiden name was Callaghan and her people live in this neighborhood, so yeah, they know me." He took a sip of his beer then looked out across the bar patrons. "I like this place. It's far enough from my precinct that I don't have to worry about being seen by the wrong people. Still enough of the beat cops know my habits that the right ones can find me here if I'm needed."

Cabel nodded as he considered this. "And you're not worried about it being raided?"

Finch laughed. "This place? No. It isn't big enough, and it's run by the owners not gangsters, thank the Lord." He took another sip of beer. "There's always violence when a place is run by thugs, but it's worse right now. There seems to be some kind of power struggle in Capone's ranks. No one's talking, but we've had a few more dead bodies than normal." He looked around the pub with a smile. "Everyone's focus is on Capone or Malone. No one cares about this place except people from the neighborhood."

A young barmaid stepped up to the booth. Her serviceable dress was covered with a simple white smock. "Would you like a soda or a root beer?"

Expecting her to say something else, Cabel hesitated.

"My friend will have a root beer," Detective Finch supplied. The young woman nodded, giving Cabel a curious glance before turning toward the bar.

The detective gave a wry smile over his soda glass as he studied Cabel again. "Where do you live, when you're not causing trouble in Chicago, the middle of a cornfield?"

"What?"

"Once prohibition started, most of the smaller bars in Chicago became soda fountains, at least on their licenses. Some are speakeasies and you need a password to get in, but many of them keep doing business as usual."

The barmaid returned with a soda glass that held a deep, amber-colored beer with a nice head of foam. She placed it on the table, adding a drinking straw and a saucy wink before turning to the other man. "Would you like another?" The detective nodded and the girl left to fetch a second glass.

"A drinking straw?" Cabel asked.

"Keeping up appearances," the detective said with a smile. "Again, I ask, where do you live that you don't know how to order a drink in a soda fountain?"

Cabel shrugged. "I don't drink much since, well since." He left the words hanging, finding any mention of the war difficult as it was always accompanied by memories of horror and death. Even this brief, passing thought brought the darkness close. He took a deep breath and willed the past away. "The bars near the docks in New Orleans didn't bother with pretense, or drinking straws."

"Ah." The detective nodded to the girl as she placed another drink on the table and left them to their business.

"Other than the Charades Club, I haven't been in a drinking establishment in Chicago for years." He had also visited the Green Door Tavern but he was not prepared to share that fact with the man sitting across from him.

"Hmm." Detective Finch studied him with shrewd eyes. "Well then, let me explain. If you order a root beer, you get a beer, usually house-brewed. You should try it. They make a good one here."

Beer was not Cabel's drink of choice, but his first cautious sip was quickly followed by a deeper one. It tasted of malt and barley and something else, something that gave the beer a pleasant, distinctive flavor. He nodded in appreciation and understanding before he drank some more. "So what am I served if I ask for soda?"

"First they'll ask you what flavor. Grape is for gin, winterberry is for whisky, strawberry is for sherry. You get the idea."

"And if you don't know which flavors are used by a specific establishment?"

"Just make up something that begins with the letter of the drink you want, they'll figure it out."

Cabel smiled, then asked, "How do you order a soda if you want a soda?"

Detective Finch laughed. "There are a few actual soda shops in the city. The storefronts with the green doors or shutters usually serve alcohol and the others serve the legal stuff. Every once in a while we find out about the wrong kind of soda fountain when a tourist walks into the station and reports getting something different from what was ordered."

Smiling, Cabel finished his beer and set the glass aside. His smile faded. The time had come to discuss Jim's case. "Detective Finch..."

"Greg, you can call me Greg."

"Okay, Greg, I came to the station to tell you about what I found in Amanda Channing's apartment, though perhaps the police from the other precinct already told you." He waited but received no response. "I don't understand why you couldn't talk with me. And why pretend I was someone else? What's going on?"

"I was with another detective. He outranks me and he already knew what I'm about to tell you. Your parents, aunts, uncles, or whoever they all are, have gotten the investigation closed."

"You mean they had you taken off the case?"

"No, though not from lack of trying on your aunt's part." He sipped his beer as he studied the patterns carved into the tabletop by bored patrons over the years. Cabel had a sense that the young man was fighting to contain a strong emotion, anger probably, though little of it showed in his face. "No," the detective said again, "I mean what I said, the investigation is closed. I'm not to ask questions, interview Jim again, seek out Miss Channing's family, nothing."

Cabel shook his head. "That can't be right. Surely Jim's parents want to know what happened to their son."

The detective's dark eyes, cold and unyielding rose to meet his. "I have been told by my superiors that your family wants this investigation closed, and they have the influence to get their way in this matter."

"I still don't understand. Why would they want it closed when nothing's been resolved? Even if the girl was the target, Jim almost died as well. Don't they want to know who did this?"

"Apparently they think they already know." He sighed. "Your cousin calls you Cabe, may I?"

"Sure."

"Okay, Cabe, you've heard your aunt and uncle at the hospital. They've been repeating the same thing since Jim was shot, that you are behind the attack against your cousin to get him out of the way so you can return to the family business."

Greg was right, Cabel had heard these words before, but believed he had grown immune to their power. Instead, a black rage grew within him and he struggled to control it. "But…"

"Your uncle said that you have a connection to Capone through the Charades Club, you know that," Gary continued, unaware of the dark effect his words had on Cabel. "He told me, and I'm sure anyone else who will listen, that you used this connection to try and have your cousin killed at a time when you had an alibi. He's been consistent in this story and, even though there's no proof, some people believe it. My boss explained that your family wants to handle the matter themselves rather than have this 'private matter on public display' I think are the words he used."

Cabel barely noticed as the waitress replaced their empty glasses with fresh ones. He didn't reach for his beer, knowing that his shaking hands would reveal too much. Before the war, he hadn't known rage, or how to kill, but both were now a part of him. Five years ago that rage controlled him, but never again. He drew a few deep breaths before reaching for his glass. Yes, his aunt and uncle had made the same accusations in the hospital, but he had thought they had said it to hurt him, not because they believed it was true. Maybe he'd been wrong. He shouldn't care what they thought, what others believed, yet he did.

"Detective…"

"I've asked you to call me Greg."

Cabel nodded. "Sorry, Greg. You probably don't care, but I had nothing to do with what happened to Jim or Miss Channing. It wasn't me."

"I know."

Those two words, spoken with absolute certainty, had Cabel raise his eyes to meet those of the man across from him.

"The problem I have with this situation is that the people who should want answers instead want the investigation shut down. The one who shouldn't want me to find the truth, the one supposedly behind the shooting, is the only one who is upset that the matter is closed." He picked up his beer and drank it down a few inches then looked at Cabel. "I know I'm young but I've earned my place on the detective squad because I'm good, especially at getting a read on someone. I think that your aunt, your uncle, your father even, know more than what they've told me about the shooting. And as for you, you have your demons, no surprise there, but you had nothing to do with what happened to your cousin."

"Thank you," Cabel said, pushing the words past the lump that had formed in his throat. Detective Greg Finch may not be able to help him find the answers Jim needed, but he believed that Cabel was innocent, a gift beyond measure.

"So you said you stopped by the station because of what you found in Miss Channing's apartment. What did I miss?" Greg asked, shifting the conversation to somewhat safer waters.

Cabel almost smiled, remembering that he had a bone to pick with the detective over his cowardice in the face of the flower parlor. Over the next several minutes he explained to Greg what he had learned from Mrs. Marshall, the break-in at Miss Channing's apartment, as well as what he had found there. The detective listened intently, asking questions, and studying the photo that Cabel had found hidden in the hat brim.

"I didn't see Miss Channing's body under the best of circumstances, and she's older now than she was when this picture was taken so I can't be sure, but I think this is her and perhaps a sister." He tipped the photograph so as to see it better in the uncertain light of the bar. "From everything she told your cousin about herself, she isn't from this area and it's the first time she's been this far west, but I recognize the place where this photograph was taken. In fact, I'm sure I've been there. I just can't think where this is at the moment."

Cabel nodded, having had the same reaction to the photo. "I don't know how I'm going to tell Jim, but I'm wondering if he knew anything real about his Miss Channing at all."

Greg looked from the photo to Cabel before handing it back. "I don't envy you that conversation." He sighed and rubbed his hands across his face. "However, there is a bit of good news in all of this, I think. Whatever your family knows, they aren't worried about Jim's safety even with you on the loose and supposedly able to strike again. Also, given all of the questions surrounding the girl and her actual identity, I would guess that the initial impression was accurate. Someone followed the girl to the speakeasy and killed her. She was the target, not your cousin."

This had been the detective's assumption all along and the break in at Miss Channing's apartment supported that belief. Still having Greg repeat it now and with such certainty helped ease Cabel's mind. "I hadn't thought of it that way, but I hope your right." He shook his head. "I still don't understand why, if they are convinced I'm guilty, they don't want me arrested. I would think my aunt, especially, would be very happy to see that happen."

"Probably, but I'll have to leave those speculations to you." He pulled out a pocket watch and checked the time. "I need to leave. I have a wife and a baby, a little girl, waiting for me at home." The bright smile that lit the detective's face made him seem younger, more vulnerable. His smile faded and his eyes became hard once again. "I can't keep the investigation open. I won't risk my job over this case." He looked at Cabel who nodded in understanding. "Still if you need something, let me know. I might be able to help."

He stood and Cabel joined him, tossing money on the table to pay for the drinks, a small token to express a larger gratitude.

Once they reached the street they shook hands. Greg Finch looked at Cabel with sadness and regret. "I'm sure you already know this, but you need to find out how your family's involved in this mess." He gave a small salute, then turned and walked away into the cold night. Cabel stood looking after him for a moment before pulling up the collar of his coat against the rising wind and went in search of a cab.

CHAPTER 10

Cabel was a few yards down the hospital corridor from Jim's room when he heard shouting. Nurse Adams reached the doorway just steps ahead of him and disappeared inside. From the threshold he watched the nurse, hands on her hips, chastising Jim and his father. Both appeared contrite, but the look in their eyes said that they would resume their argument the moment she left. All three of them noticed Cabel at the same time, with very different reactions. Jim's face lit with pleasure, Uncle Frank scowled, and the nurse eyed him with assessment, trying to determine if he would help or hinder the problem.

"Cabe, you're just the man I wanted to see," Jim said, motioning for Cabel to join him near the bed.

"We don't need him here. This is between us. His presence will just make things worse." Uncle Frank crossed his arms over his chest and glared at both members of the younger generation.

"If I hear one more raised voice, I am canceling all visiting hours for the rest of the day." Nurse Adams held up a hand to ward off their protests. "While I'm pleased that Mr. Jim is feeling well enough to express himself so vehemently, he is not the only patient on this ward. Rest is the best healing medicine we have and if any of you impede that process for the other patients I will have you two removed." She pointed a stern finger at Frank and Cabel. "If that isn't enough, I will cancel visiting hours for tomorrow as well." Jim nodded sullenly and leaned back against his pillows. Satisfied that her message had been received, the nurse left the room, closing the door behind her.

Frank turned to point an accusing finger at Cabel. "See what you've done?"

"I had nothing to do with this, as you well know." Cabel hadn't meant to say the words aloud, yet in that moment he realized that he was tired of being the family scapegoat. He would not deny his past mistakes but these new accusations must stop.

His uncle must have sensed this new resolve for he took a step back and mumbled, "Perhaps."

"I'm sorry my father is unwilling to offer an appropriate greeting but I'm glad that you're here." Although Jim lay propped up by the pillows, his color had improved and a sense of strength and vitality had returned. His cousin was healing.

Cabel smiled. There were other concerns, there always were, but Jim's wounds were mending and the world seemed brighter. "You're looking better today."

"That's because I'm feeling better. Who would have thought that a row with my father would have such restorative properties?"

Cabel laughed, he couldn't help it.

"I think your cousin should leave now so we can finish our conversation." The authority in Frank's voice was diminished by the fear in his eyes.

"His name is Cabel, remember? My cousin, your nephew, heir to the family company." Jim leaned forward, wincing at the pain this movement caused. "You don't care about what happened five years ago. You thought Uncle Edward had it coming. Most of us did." He silenced his audiences' protests with a slash of his hand. "Let's have a moment of honesty, if that's possible. Your dislike of Cabe is because he's a better businessman than you, and so am I when it comes to it. You and Uncle Edward play your games and compete over nothings while Cabe, and now me, keep the company profitable and growing. I'm ashamed at how we've treated Cabe. We are done with it. I need his help while I'm recovering, if he's willing, and if you or Uncle Edward do anything to impede this process, I will take the matter before the board." Jim lay back again, tired but resolved.

Frank sputtered. "The board would never condone having this, this person back in the company."

"Yes they would. You know it and so do I. If you want to test the issue though, please feel free to do so, but what if they want Cabel back as head of the company full time?"

"No," Cabel said. "I don't want that." He was lying, and he suspected Jim knew it, but within the lie was the truth. He couldn't go back. No matter his success, his years of hard work, the rumors of his attack on his father would persist, something to live down or explain away at every turn. He loved the company, would do anything to help further its success, even if that meant staying away.

"See, he doesn't want to," Frank said. "You can't force him to do it."

Jim studied Cabel a long moment. "We both want the same thing, Cabe, to keep the company strong. I guess I understand if you don't want to come back and, to be honest, it would be difficult for me. I like being the one in charge, looked up to, successful."

"Jim."

"No, Cabe, let me finish." He leaned against the pillows and closed his eyes a moment. When he looked at Cabel again, his mouth was set with determination. "The last few months I was distracted by Amanda and not paying as much attention as I should to some of the details of the company. I have to wonder what mischief our fathers managed during this time and shudder to think what trouble they will get into during my absence." A sharp glare cut off Frank's protests, and then Jim's focus returned to his cousin. "I need you. Right here, right now, I need you. Our grandfather's company needs you." His eyes grew sad. "I know this is a sacrifice for you, but it's one for me as well. Even though we spoke a few months ago and your intention was clear, I have lived in fear of your return to the company from the day you left. People like you, respect you, and you're good. I'm afraid I'll be found wanting by comparison."

He smiled then, and Cabel's heart hurt to see it.

"Jim, there are others who can help you, men on the board, business associates. It doesn't have to be me."

"It does, though." Mischief returned to Jim's smile. "Even having been away, you know this company and, more importantly, you know our parents. You're the only one who could keep them in line."

Cabel thought about this while Frank sputtered in the background. Edward and Frank were part owners of the company, as were Cabel and Jim. The fact that the brothers stepped aside, leaving the day to day running to Jim, was a matter of convenience for them. It was the prestige and wealth of the company, rather than the business itself, which they enjoyed. So Jim had stepped forward and proven himself to be the right Evans for the job. The board had confidence in his abilities, both to keep the company running smoothly and to keep Edward and Frank away from anything that could prove damaging to the bottom line. Still the brothers were owners and no one would gainsay them if they wanted to make changes. Without either he or Jim in charge, disaster was almost inevitable.

He nodded in defeat and Jim smiled with satisfaction.

Frank grew quiet, his eyes darting nervously between his son and his nephew. Swallowing hard, he took a step back. He glared at Cabel. "Your father won't like this. He won't allow it."

"He won't have a choice," Jim said, every bit the president of Evans Manufacturing. "Until I can resume my duties, Cabel will run the business."

Cabel watched his uncle stomp out of the room before turning back to his cousin. Jim seemed weaker and paler than a moment ago, but pleased as well. "Jim, I'm not sure I can do this."

"That's okay. I am."

CHAPTER 11

"Mr. Evans, it's so good to see you again." The woman who greeted him as he entered the executive floor of Evans Manufacturing was older, perhaps fifty, and held an air of quiet efficiency. Her face tugged at his memory as she looked up at him expectantly.

"Judith," he said, relieved that he'd recalled her name. "Judith Walker."

The woman beamed with pleasure. "I'm honored that you would remember me." She nodded with satisfaction then gestured for him to walk beside her. "Mr. Stanford Jr. is in the library and asked to speak with you once you arrived."

So it had begun. Cabel's stomach, already knotted from the stress of walking into the company's building, twisted further.

They arrived at the dark wood door that opened into the library. Mrs. Walker stepped back and nodded for Cabel to enter before returning to her post in the reception area. Alone in the hallway, Cabel grasped the doorknob and met his past.

Christopher Stanford Jr. rose from his chair and crossed the deep carpet to meet Cabel halfway across the room. Those actions showed respect, something that he hadn't expected. As they shook hands, Cabel studied the older man's face but could find nothing there but genuine pleasure.

The last time they had met was at the board meeting where Edward Evans had pushed his son too far and nearly died from the subsequent beating. Many of the details of those moments were blurred, though Cabel did remember throwing his father onto the carpet and hitting him until someone had pulled him away. He couldn't imagine anyone who had been present that day would be happy to see him again.

The attorney now seated across from him hadn't changed much in the last five years. His hand-stitched suit with its subtle pinstripe was conservative but something in its cut managed to convey a modern sensibility. His father had cofounded the firm of Owen, Stanford, and Mills and had sat on the Evans Manufacturing board of directors since its inception. Upon the father's retirement his very capable son had assumed that role.

"You've changed since last I saw you," Christopher said, studying him carefully. "There is a calmness about you that wasn't there since the war."

Cabel flinched at the assessment. "Given the circumstances in which we last met, I don't think that would be difficult to achieve."

The attorney allowed himself a small smile. "True, but it goes deeper than that. To be honest, you're looking better than I expected."

At a loss as to how to respond, Cabel nodded.

"I wanted to be here to welcome you back. Many other members of the board, myself included, appreciate that you've stepped forward to take over Jim's role while he is recuperating."

"Really?" Cabel decided that now was the time for him to learn the truth about how he was viewed by the executive staff. Jim and the company deserved his best efforts and to do that he needed to know exactly where he stood. "To be honest, I'm surprised. From what I've seen and heard Jim is doing a magnificent job as president of the company. I would suspect it could manage a few months without his daily participation."

"True, Jim has represented the company well, especially since his meeting with you in July." He smiled in response to Cabel's stunned face. "Yes, he told me about it and how you helped him to trust his own instincts, even if they went contrary to the wishes of his father and uncle. Because of you, he truly became the president of this company."

"I don't think I did anything, not really. It was all Jim."

"You're wrong. You gave Jim confidence at a time when he and the company desperately needed that confidence, and the leadership that went with it. He was able to avert an ill-advised project that your father and uncle had started. I was against it, as were most of the board members, though the elder Evans men have a few cronies who will pass anything they wanted done. Still as long as Edward and Frank kept Jim malleable to their schemes, there was no way to stop them. Then Jim spoke with you and he stopped the project and brought the board back under control. You underestimate the gift you gave your cousin and this company."

Cabel hesitated as he considered Christopher's words. When he had met Jim for the first time since his exile, he had been surprised that his cousin had become the leader of the company. Surprised and a bit jealous as well. Although he wanted the company to succeed, a small, mean part of him had hoped that it couldn't, not without him, his grandfather's handpicked successor. As he and Jim talked that night, about the company, about their past, he realized that Jim had come into his own, both as a man and as the company president. He had been proud, and sad. His family, his company, didn't need him anymore.

Returning to the present, Cabel looked at the corporate attorney and said, "I'm glad if I was able to help Jim in some small way back then. I'm here, now, to help him again, but I need you to be honest with me. What kind of cooperation can I expect?"

Christopher nodded in satisfaction, as if Cabel had passed a test. "You have my full support, and the support of all of the board members except Joseph Nelson, Martin Sawyer, and Allen Porter. From what I have experienced, the sole purpose of their membership is to support your father and uncle. They have already contacted me to protest your return, however temporary that may be."

Cabel nodded. "What about the staff, especially here on the executive floor. Will they work with me or against me?"

"There will be two camps, three really as I think this through. First, there will be the ones who know you from before your absence. They are still very loyal to you and will support you in any way they can. It's true," the lawyer said in response to the involuntary shake of Cabel's head. "You have always been liked and respected. As for the incident... Most who were here at the time thought your father got what he deserved. Not that you didn't go too far, but then given your war service, no one was really surprised by that either. You do have friends here."

Cabel shook his head again and blinked hard to stop the tears that threatened to fall. He had expected anger, resentment, and even hatred, but not this. His heart warmed at the attorney's words, yet a dark inner voice, born in the blood and death of the French trenches, whispered that he didn't deserve such loyalty.

"There is the second group," Christopher said, returning to the matter at hand. "They are loyal to Jim. They love and respect him, would do anything for him. Of all of the groups, this is the one that will be the most problematic for you. There are some who will support you because Jim asked them to. Others might not, if they think you are here to take his place. Tread carefully and you will manage.

"The third group should come as no surprise, the ones loyal to Frank and Edward. They will show a united front against a common enemy, you in this instance. However, they are very like the brothers themselves, willing to turn on each other if there is a prize to be won. Regardless of the situation they will not help you and may go so far as to sabotage you where possible."

Cabel sighed. "So with the addition of Jim's group, nothing's really changed."

The attorney nodded. "Exactly." He glanced at his watch, then stood. Cabel stood as well. They walked to the door and Christopher once again offered Cabel his hand. As they shook, he said, "I wanted to meet you today to prepare you for what you could expect and also to remind you that you are also a good businessman and there are many here who will help you. You aren't alone."

"Thank you."

"Telephone me if you need me."

With that, the attorney left the room, leaving Cabel to his fate.

IIII

The business offices of Evans Manufacturing were located on two floors of the Monadock Building on West Jackson Avenue. Too far inland to catch even a glimpse of the lake, the building still had its own personality and style that had made it a Chicago landmark almost from the moment it had been erected. Now Cabel sat in Jim's office, once his own, and tried to concentrate on the information in front of him.

Jim's secretary, Katherine, had greeted him with harried relief and suspicious reserve almost an hour earlier. Originally she had led him to a small, unused office on the floor below, promising to set it up as his workspace. Cabel gently but firmly led her back to the executive floor and to Jim's office, explaining that the room held most of what he needed and it made sense for him to work there. She wasn't happy, but she complied.

Now he wondered if she wasn't right to settle him into a different location. The office was filled with memories of his past, and the past was something he avoided as much as possible. After he returned from France, damaged in ways that could not be seen, he had thrown himself into the company, a lifeline against the darkness. In this office he had found success, satisfaction even, and a purpose. His seeming normality, the calm façade, hid the cracks and fissures that ran too deep to repair. In this office he had hoped to find himself again, and he did after a fashion. But it also served to remind him of how much was lost, of what life could have been like if he had never gone to war. In the end he had broken.

Forcing his thoughts from their unproductive meanderings, he returned to the task at hand. Recent company financial and production reports were spread across the desk. The company was thriving, and Cabel had to tap down the jealously that began to float to the surface. Jim led the company well, keeping their grandfather's legacy alive. He had exceeded everyone's expectations of him and lived up to the potential that had once been reserved for Cabel.

A knock on the door interrupted his thoughts, if not his work. Katherine bustled in without waiting for Cabel's permission and brought yet another stack of documents to set on the already overflowing desk.

"Please place them on the table in the corner. I'll get to them as soon as I can."

Katherine nodded and did as she was told, though each step was brittle and grudging.

As soon as she finished, she hurried toward the door.

"Please, Katherine, take a seat for a moment. I think there are some things we should discuss."

She faced away from him a moment longer, as if gathering herself into the pretext of a pleasant demeanor before turning and taking the seat across from him, hands folded in her lap, the picture of compliance.

He let her sit a moment, knowing she was young and angry. Despite her training, he doubted she would hold her tongue much longer.

"You shouldn't be here. You don't belong here. Not anymore." She gasped and covered her mouth with her hand, but too late for the words had already escaped.

Cabel stifled a smile. "You're right, you know. And you're wrong too." He let his words hang in the air between them, a truce of sorts. "I am not here to take Jim's place. It's clear from every file you bring me that he's earned it. I'm proud of him."

Katherine offered a tentative smile.

He smiled back. "Jim is younger than me, not much, but enough that he was more of a nuisance than a friend when we were children. We lived next door to each other, summered together in Michigan, but we had separate friends and interests. We didn't really compete for anything and we were happy."

"Of course you didn't compete for anything. You'd already won before Mr. James even had a chance." Her quiet words resounded with truth. "You were the eldest grandson, your grandfather's favorite. Mr. James couldn't change that and he didn't want to play the games your father and his played with each other. He saw how they were, and he didn't want to be like that. He loved you too much."

The secretary's words carried him to the past. He saw Jim as a child, a boy, then a young man. How easy it had been to overlook his cousin's hurts and sacrifices. Jim had been so young when Cabel had gone to war. Afterward nothing had penetrated the walls he had erected to keep his nightmares in and the world at bay. The risk Jim had taken in asking Cabel to return to the company was greater than he had appreciated. His cousin put the company ahead of his own interest. His selflessness proved that he was the rightful president and Cabel could now fully accept that truth. There was a twinge of pain somewhere in his soul as the dream of returning to the family business died once and for all. Yet with it came the birth of the possibility of something new, as yet unknown but exciting. What had started as a mere daydream in St. Joe now felt tangible. He had work to do for Jim and the company, but for the first time in many, many years, Cabel looked ahead and saw the glimmer of a future for himself.

Katherine sat across from him, her fingers clenched around a file in her lap, probably afraid she had overstepped her bounds. She had, but he was grateful to her nonetheless. Still he had to ask, "How do you know all of this about Jim? Did he discuss this with you?"

She shook her head. "No, I'm just good at listening and filling in the missing pieces. I don't always get things right, but I usually come close."

Cabel nodded, now understanding why Jim had chosen this young, impetuous woman for his secretary. She was organized, skillful, and loyal. More importantly she looked beyond the obvious and drew insightful conclusions. Unless she left to marry and have children, she would mature into an even greater asset.

"I hadn't thought about Jim and I in quite the terms as you describe, but you're right. I had always assumed that Jim didn't like the business world and so he made other plans."

She shook her head and lowered her hazel eyes to her lap. "I don't know. He's never said. But I think he decided that he would never have a true place in the company so he went his own way." She raised her eyes again to meet Cabel's. "Then you left and he stepped forward."

"Is it what he wanted? Is he happy here?" Cabel wondered why it never occurred to him to ask.

She smiled, but there was sadness there too. "Yes, he's very happy here, though I think he's always regretted how it came about. Sometimes I wonder if he thinks he's just holding your place until you decide to return."

And that returned them to the present.

"Since you've been honest with me, I will return the favor." He took a deep breath as he tried to decide how to say what was in his heart, what her honesty a moment ago had helped him to accept. "I would love to return to the company." He raised his hand at her gasp. "But I don't belong here anymore. It was a dream of mine, I won't lie to you, but I never thought it could happen. Now I sit in my old chair in my former office and realize that it isn't mine anymore. Every report you bring me, every spread sheet, shows me just how capable Jim is. Not competent, not qualified, but truly an exceptional businessman. I am both jealous and very, very proud."

He leaned forward across the desk to capture her full attention. "Right now Jim needs my help to keep things running smoothly until he is ready to return. I plan to do whatever I can for him, though from what I've seen, there isn't much to do. He has it all well in hand."

"There are a few things coming up that will need to be addressed: contract renewals, some shipping problems, and two new companies bidding to become suppliers," she said the words grudgingly, not entirely ready to trust him. "Those things can't wait."

"Good. We'll manage that together and I'll be sure to get Jim's approval before anything is finalized."

The girl nodded.

"I promise you, I will leave as soon as Jim asks me to, and I won't make any changes without his full knowledge and support. Besides, there isn't anything here I would change. The company is in great hands and I will return it to him in the exact condition that I found it. But until that time, I need your help."

She considered his words before nodding. "I will do whatever I can."

"Good." He felt the tension ease from his shoulders. "There are a few things you could do to help me right now. First, I need to prioritize this information into what I need to know to keep things running smoothly over the next month or so and what can wait."

"I can do that." Her smile was a bit sheepish. "I've probably inundated you with more than you needed, but I can help whittle it down and bring you copies of the contracts that are up for renewal."

Cabel could read people, or at least he could before he had isolated himself from the world. The skill was there, not as dormant as it had been few months ago, but still a bit rusty. Even so, he sensed that he had succeeded in transforming an enemy into an ally. The truth had a way of doing that.

"The second thing I need to know is if there are any problems, anything that Jim might have been concerned about or perhaps unaware of that should now be addressed."

Her hesitation was all the confirmation he needed.

"I know he's been distracted with Miss Channing and I can't help but think that my father and uncle might have used that distraction to their advantage."

"I think that's possible." She stopped as her loyalty to Jim warred with her promise to Cabel. "He was so in love with her and she was so beautiful." Her voice turned wistful. "I didn't see them together often, but she stopped by the office on two occasions to meet him for lunch. I was sure I was meeting his future wife. They were so happy."

In spite of the questions Cabel had about Miss Channing's motives, his heart ached for Jim, for what might have been. "So it is possible that my father and uncle took advantage of the situation, but do you know to what end?"

Katherine shook her head. "The problem is, you see, that they are completely autonomous. They don't really do anything for the company directly, but they have a staff and keep themselves busy, mostly entertaining clients. From what little I've heard, they had a plan to start a new branch of the company but Mr. James put a stop to that."

"So they might have used Jim's relationship with Miss Channing to resurrect this project?"

Katherine nodded again.

"I don't see how. They would need full board approval for something like that."

"Yes." She was thoughtful for a moment, still not ready to fully trust him. Finally she said, "I was in the hallway a month or so ago and happened to be reaching a corner just as Mr. Edward and Mr. Frank were coming the other way. Mr. Edward said that he had found what they were looking for in the bylaws, something about a way to get around the board. We reached the corner at the same time and they stopped talking. I didn't think anything about it at the time, but now I have to wonder what it was about."

"I see. Can you find the most current copy of the board of directors' by-laws for me?"

"Of course."

Now it was Cabel's turn to hesitate. He didn't want to ask but he needed to know. "How are my father and uncle taking my return?"

"They're not happy, and I know that they've tried to get the board against you, to keep you from coming back. Other than a few of their friends, everyone else would rather you be here than your father or uncle in charge again." She leaned forward, her eyes kind but resolved. "What some people say is that while your father ran the company it faltered, and there was a great fear that it would close. Then you came back from France and fixed everything. Those people are now loyal to Mr. James, but they think he was wise to have you step in rather than leave his and your father in charge."

Cabel couldn't remember fixing anything, just doing what needed to be done so that both he and the company could survive. During that time he had lost his relationship with his fiancée, Elizabeth, and eventually with his family and even himself. Yet through it all, the company continued and prospered. This, at least, he had accomplished.

"I understand," he said at last. "And thank you for your honesty. I'll need that more than anything, until Jim returns. Now, if you could find me those by-laws, let's see if we can discover just what my father and uncle are up to."

CHAPTER 12

Cabel found the lake calming and, after the last few days at the company offices, he would have preferred to take a ship back to St. Joseph, Michigan, rather than go by train, but early November was a time of unpredictable weather and sudden storms. More than one ship had sunk in years past when their owners, focused on profits, had forced captains to sail in late autumn when caution dictated the ships remain docked. While the lake was deep enough to accommodate the large vessels, it was shallower than the ocean. When caught in high waves, ships could literally be smashed against the lake bottom. At the moment Cabel felt something like that himself, which is why he decided that he would be better served by a long weekend home than one spent in the city. But he would go by train.

He had informed his housekeeper, Marta, that he would be returning home but not the exact time. A cold wind whipped his hair and tore at his clothes as he stepped from the train. The small brick station was deserted except for the station master who stayed snug and warm inside. After the train pulled away, Cabel looked toward the lake. Past the track of the rollercoaster and beyond the Shadowland Ballroom, the water churned dark and gray, reflecting the ominous sky. Sand blew in drifts across the roads near the shore, making them impassable. Once the storm blew over, crews would be out to shovel it away, just as they would with the snow that would fall in the coming weeks.

There were no cab drivers willing to risk becoming stranded in the sand drifts which meant he had to walk to the top of the bluff. Although there was an easier path near the river, Cabel chose the closer, steeper stairs that would, hopefully, allow him to arrive home before the rain fell.

Marta greeted him at the doorway and was quick to take his bags before moving him into the parlor where a roaring fire warmed the room. She bustled out and returned moments later with a tray filled with coffee cups and a plate of sandwiches.

"Dinner will be at seven, but I thought you might be hungry now and this will tide you over." She beamed and stood expectantly in front of the small table where she had placed the tray. He stared at her confused until he realized that there were two sets of cups and plates laid out in front of him.

"Would you care to join me?" he asked.

"If you don't mind. I'd like to know about Jim's recovery and how you're getting along, being back home in Chicago."

He smiled at her as he accepted a cup of coffee. Taking a sip, he considered her words. "I'll have to return to the office, you know, but by spending time in the city and near my family I've realized that this is home." The statement held the truth and everything that went with it, sadness and joy and a bit of hope. Chicago held his past and Jim's future. He needed to find his own life and St. Joseph was a good place from which to start.

"I have to say, I'm of two minds about that." She sighed and handed him a small plate of corned beef sandwiches. "I know it's been hard for you since the war, but it's like you buried a part of yourself with Jon Warner back in France."

He nearly choked on his coffee. Looking into her careworn face, he saw the sadness in her eyes and felt a pang of guilt for being the cause of it.

"You've been better the last few months, and Jorge and I had hoped that you were ready to get on with life again. You're not yet thirty, still a young man. It's time you found yourself a nice girl and started a family of your own."

Cabel smiled at his housekeeper's fantasy. How could he care for a wife and children when nightmares and memories haunted him awake or asleep? Then there were the incidents, ones he never spoke of, when he relived moments of the war as if it had never ended. These were the worst and caused him to fear for his sanity. How could he inflict this madness on innocents? This was the reason, one of them at least, why he had broken his engagement to Elizabeth. She deserved so much more than he could give.

She must have seen the doubt in his eyes. "Cabel, your grandfather fought in the Civil War and was changed by it as well. Granted, he had taken a wife before he left to fight, but he came home and made a life for himself. It's time you do the same." With another sigh, she leaned back in her chair. Her smile turned rueful. "I'm so very glad that Jim will recover and that you are helping with the company until he is well enough to go back to work, but I've also worried that you would go to Chicago and never come back again. I've enjoyed having you here."

Now it was his turn to smile. "I have no plans to return to the city, I promise. Now let me tell you how Jim is doing and just what he's gotten me into." Settling more deeply into his chair, he told Marta about all that had happened, only leaving out the questions that had been raised about Amanda Chandler.

IIIII

The biting wind brought sleet and freezing rain, encouraging indoor pursuits. Cabel spent most of the day in what he had thought of as his grandfather's study, but which had slowly become his own. Metallic clangs echoed up from the basement as Jorge Voss and Walter Arledge worked to get the furnace running again. Walter's wife, Kaye, helped Marta in the kitchen, baking bread and pursuing other domestic activities. Anne worked alongside her mother and Marta while the youngest Arledge children had run of the house. Belinda was a sweet child of about eight or so, while the youngest, Nate, was more than a handful. He had been helping fix the furnace until there was a loud bang, followed by a few choice words, and with that the boy was sent upstairs to be among the "womenfolk," much to his dismay. Cabel had pointed out to Nate that he was also upstairs, but apparently pushing about papers at a desk was not a manly enough pursuit to qualify as work by the opinionated boy.

If he closed the study door, Cabel would have the quiet he needed to focus on the documents he had brought home. The problem was that having young Nate here, he felt more comfortable being able to listen to the rhythm of the house. The boy had a knack for breaking things and getting into trouble, even when it would have seemed impossible to do so. While not as peaceful as it would be if the door were closed, Cabel felt it better to be forewarned, if not forearmed.

He would have gotten more work done if he had stayed in Chicago. In addition to reviewing the contracts coming up for renewal he also needed to purchase a few more business suits and shirts, as well as a suitable winter coat. The wiser course would have been to remain in the city, but he needed a break from the stress of his less-than-happy family reunion and the business that forced them together.

In the three days he had been in the office, his father and uncle had found varied and insidious ways to let him know that he was not welcome. Meetings were held but not placed on the formal schedule so Cabel learned of them as they were occurring or after the fact, making him seem inept, at least to some of the staff. Memos went missing and some information was denied him altogether, though he had already taken steps to assure that these issues were resolved.

While the subterfuges ranged from annoying to upsetting, there were a few bright moments. His father, Edward, had scheduled a lunch meeting with a contractor only to be stood up because Cabel had unknowingly made an appointment with the same man at the same time, but at a different restaurant. The man was smart enough to realize that there was a conflict, not only in the schedule but also within the management, and had chosen to meet with Cabel rather than with Edward. Cabel had already been favorably impressed with the man, and that only increased when he learned the entire story upon his return to the office.

In spite of that small, unwitting success in the war with his father and uncle, their bitterness and the lack of support from much of the staff had worn on him. His brief return to St. Joseph was the salve he needed.

He sighed and stretched, rising to throw another log on the fire burning in the dark brick fireplace on the other side of the room. Although a few clangs of the radiator were followed by wisps of warm air, it was clear that the furnace repairs were incomplete.

Crossing back to his desk he saw the package of clothing he had found in Amanda Channing's apartment sitting on a small table in the corner of the room, an unwelcomed reminder of the second task Jim had set for him. As he studied the package, he wondered once again what his father and uncle had done while Jim was distracted with Miss Channing. Now was the time to find out.

He dug through his leather business satchel until he located a slightly tattered copy of the company's by-laws. Few changes had been made to them over the years with the most recent amendments implemented about four years ago, presumably while Frank was heading the board. Picking up the thick document, Cabel started at the beginning and had to wonder if the lawyers charged by the word rather than the hour.

Two hours later, including a break for coffee and a snack, Cabel discovered what undoubtedly Edward and Frank had also unearthed. He leaned back in his chair and closed his eyes as he considered all of the ramifications of what he learned. A few moments later he realized he wasn't alone. Looking toward the doorway, he found young Nate standing there, hands on his small hips, shaking his dark head in derision.

"You seem to take a lot of naps, especially for not being a grandpa or anything," the boy said, a look of profound disgust on his face.

Cabel sat up straighter. "I wasn't napping."

"I know. You were just resting your eyes, right?" He shook his head again and turned away, clearly not accepting an excuse he was well familiar with.

Cabel fought against the impulse to follow the boy down the hall to defend himself. He also found that he was smiling. Six-year-old Nate saw the world through a child's eyes and judged it accordingly, a source of both humor and frustration.

The small interruption had helped Cabel's mind to clear and he now saw the steps he needed to take to address the problem. Putting pen to paper, he detailed a plan to uncover the secret plots his father and uncle had hatched.

IIII

Although he had intended to stay in St. Joseph a few more days, he decided to return to Chicago on Monday. No one would be expecting him and maybe that surprise could be used to his advantage.

He had called ahead and spoken with Katherine, asking the secretary to meet him at a nearby restaurant for an early lunch. A harsh November wind blew across the lake, reminding him that he needed a warmer dress coat. He arrived at the restaurant to find Katherine huddled inside the entryway, sheltered from the cutting wind but not the cold. Her smile seemed genuine when she caught sight of him. He opened the door and ushered her in ahead of him. They were seated in a booth and ordered quickly.

Once the waiter had left them, Cabel took out his notes and studied them a moment as he tried to determine how to begin.

"You found it, didn't you? You found whatever it was that your father and uncle found in the by-laws," Katherine said, both excited and a bit concerned.

"Yes, I think I did and I have an idea of what they're up to, but I'm going to need your help."

She nodded as she accepted a cup of coffee from the waiter.

Another was placed in front of Cabel and he took a warming sip. "I found a rule in the by-laws that allowed the president to authorize the pursuit and evaluation of smaller projects without full-board approval, if those projects were related to existing business activities of long standing."

Katherine considered this for a moment then began to nod. "Your father and uncle wanted to start a new arm of the company, retail stores like Sears Roebuck recently opened, but Mr. James stood against the idea and the board agreed with him. Do you think they're trying to keep this project going behind Mr. James' back?"

Cabel nodded. Christopher Stanford had mentioned this project last week, had been glad that Jim had stood up to his father and uncle to stop it from going forward. The endeavor was doomed from the start. This was clear to everyone except the elder Evans men.

Edward and Frank had decided that if Sears Roebuck could go from catalogue sales to retail stores, Evans Manufacturing would open stores as well. Their scheme ignored several issues such as the fact that Evans Manufacturing made parts that went into other people's products so there would be nothing to sell. Then there was Sears and Roebuck itself, Evans Manufacturing's biggest client. If there were any hint that the smaller company was attempting to compete with the larger one, the business relationship would end, severely damaging Evans Manufacturing's bottom line. The company might survive the loss of its largest source of sales, but that loss would be devastating and require significant work to reestablish financial stability. Cabel felt weary, imagining the fight that lay before him if his father and uncle had used Jim's distraction to resurrect the project.

"We think we know what Edward and Frank are planning, but we need to confirm it and discuss the situation with the full board."

The two spent the remainder of the lunch reviewing Cabel's plan to uncover the secrets that others were trying to keep hidden.

CHAPTER 13

Cabel stepped from the cab that had taken him to his aunt and uncle's home in the Gold Coast neighborhood of Chicago. He would rather have met Jim at the hospital, but it had taken three days to find proof of his father and uncle's treachery. By then, his cousin had been released into the care of a private nurse at his parent's home. No one at the office had been told of the change. This was Cabel's first inkling that his father and uncle knew what he had learned and they were attempting to keep him from speaking with Jim. They couldn't. As much as Cabel wished to be someplace else, he had made a promise to his cousin and had a commitment to the company. The time had come for Edward and Frank to tell Jim what they had done.

Now he stood in front of Frank and Eunice's home, prepared to face yet another specter of his past. His own parent's home stood next door and his grandparents' home had been the next house over. Strangers lived there now. Cabel gave a small, depreciating laugh when he realized that the people who lived in the house in front of him were strangers of another sort, as were those who lived in his parents' home. He had no place here, yet he had no choice but to continue up the walkway.

The house had changed little over the years. Three stories high, made of gray stone, it had a small porch and an abundance of windows. Flowers had been planted in regimented rows lining the walkway but they were withered now as winter neared. The doormat welcomed visitors to the house, though Cabel knew it wouldn't apply to him. He lifted the heavy brass knocker and let it fall with a resounding clang.

A curtain twitched at a downstairs window before an older woman in a serviceable black dress answered the door. Looking over his shoulder, she said sternly, "You are not welcome in this house and the owners ask that you leave at once."

"I'm not here to see my aunt and uncle. I'm here to see my cousin."

"Mr. James is not receiving visitors at this time. You must leave now or we shall call the police."

Cabel laughed, he couldn't help it, and felt some of the tension ease from his shoulders. "I can't imagine my aunt would allow such a gauche display as having the police here. What would the neighbors say?"

The housekeeper's mouth opened in surprise at Cabel's lack of respect for this threat of the law. Thoughts flitted across her face like pictures on a movie screen—shock, disgust, and anger. She knew he was right but didn't like the challenge to her authority, limited though it may be.

"I know you expect me to leave, but I will not do so until I have spoken with Jim."

Her glare of pure hatred would have stopped a less-determined man. No wonder his aunt employed her. But he *was* determined.

Reading his resolve in his eyes, she reverted to social norms. "I'll see if Mr. and Mrs. Evans will receive you. Please wait here a moment."

The door began to close but Cabel, anticipating such a move, shoved his foot forward to block it. "I'm sorry but I won't wait outside. Either you let me in or I will come in without your leave."

"How dare you?"

"You would be surprised at what I would dare for Jim's sake."

They stood another moment in quiet standoff until she relented, opening the door wide and standing aside. He nodded his thanks before stepping into the marble-floored foyer and removing his coat and hat, which she took and hung on a nearby mahogany stand.

"Is he finally gone, Matilda?" his aunt's shrill voice called from the parlor.

The housekeeper's eyes held a bit of fear and Cabel suddenly understood the awkward position he had placed her in.

"Don't worry," he said. "I'll handle my aunt."

Matilda's eyes narrowed in suspicion but she turned toward the kitchen instead of the parlor, leaving him to deal with what he had wrought.

"Matilda?" his aunt called again.

Cabel didn't need her voice to find his way to the parlor. The house was a mirror image of the one he had grown up in. Although he had spent much time in both houses, he realized that he had never been comfortable in either one. It was Jon's house that had felt like home and Jon's mother who had sheltered him from the cares of the world.

Bile rose in his throat and he fought to swallow it down. He had promised Jon's mother that they would both come home, but that promise had been made by a boy inexperienced in the ways of war and was shattered by the shell that had exploded near the trench, killing his best friend and many others as well. He had tried to write to her, this woman whom he loved as a son loves his mother, but words could never convey the depths of his despair or guilt. So he hadn't written and had avoided her and all of Jon's numerous sisters since he had returned to Chicago.

With a mental shove, he brutally pushed the past back where it belonged. He had enough to face in the present. Taking a deep breath, he focused on his father's deceits, letting a bit of anger take the edge from his nerves. He straightened his tie, gripped his case more firmly, and stepped into the parlor.

"Matilda, why don't you answer me?" An earsplitting shriek followed the question when Eunice Evans saw who had invaded her home. "Get out. Don't you know you're not welcome here?"

"I know, but I need to speak with Jim."

"You can't. He's upstairs resting and I won't have you causing a relapse. He almost died because of you."

Fury burned bright at her lie, but he refused to give into his demons. Cabel closed his eyes as his anger and hatred for this woman ran unchecked through his soul. Rage washed over him then flowed away, cleansing him of the stain of familial relationship. When he opened his eyes he saw only a desperate woman who feared not for her son's health, but that he would learn the truth. Until this moment, Cabel hadn't realized how much he wanted to use that truth to punish his family, to make them experience the same shame and loss that he lived with since the war and all that followed. Now he felt detached from her, from his parents, and uncle and this separation brought peace and a measure of freedom.

He saw Eunice Evans through a stranger's eyes and pitied her.

"I told you to go before I call the police."

"So your housekeeper informed me, but I doubt you'd want the scandal so I let myself in anyway." He stepped further into the room. "If I can't see Jim then I should speak with Edward and Frank. Are they here?"

Eunice glared at him.

"Why don't I make myself comfortable until they return, shall I?" With a confidence he hadn't known in years, Cabel sat in a chair near the fireplace and set his case on a nearby table. Ignoring the angry woman standing near the piano, he opened his business case and removed several files and a small notepad on which Katherine had written a concise outline of Edward and Frank's duplicity.

"Is he finally gone?" Frank called from another room.

Cabel looked up at Eunice's sour face, waiting to see what she would do.

"No. He's still here and now he knows you are too. You'd better come and talk to him."

Frank stomped into the parlor, stood with braced legs and pointed toward the door. "Get out."

"No."

Frank's eyes widened and his face flushed. "Young man, I told you to leave."

Cabel considered his options, then nodded and rose. "As you wish. I had hoped to keep this matter between us, for Jim's sake as well as the company's, but I will call a full board meeting instead." He sorted the files and slid them back into the case as he listened to Frank sputter in the background.

"You have no cause to call a board meeting."

He turned. Frank's complexion had changed from florid to pale. "As acting president of Evans Manufacturing, I can and will call a full board meeting. I wanted to handle this matter differently, but you leave me no choice."

"There is no reason to involve the board. We've done nothing wrong," Edward Evans said as he strode into the room. He had no limp and carried the cane under his arm until he came to a halt next to his brother. The cane tip dropped to the floor with a thud and Edward leaned heavily against it, as if for support. He gazed at his son with loathing.

Cabel met his father's eyes, knowing his own revulsion was there for this man to see. Edward had betrayed Jim and the company and could no longer use guilt to manipulate him.

"I disagree and find that there are several issues that require board review." He took a step toward the archway that led to the front of the house. "I will have my secretary inform your staff as to when the meeting will take place, but I expect it to occur no later than tomorrow afternoon. Good day."

"Wait," Edward commanded. "I don't think you realize just how strong my position is on this matter."

"Our position," Frank added.

"I think I do." Cabel turned to his father. Eunice sat rigidly in a chair while Frank hovered behind her. Edward stood in the center of the room as if on a stage, sure of his role and the part everyone else would play in the drama he scripted. He was about to learn that Cabel would no longer speak the lines assigned him. "I have read the by-laws and the resolutions you had drawn up."

"Jim signed those documents. We didn't forge his signature."

"Shut up, Frank," Edward said over his shoulder. Looking back to his son, he added, "Jim agreed to our project. There's nothing you can do about it."

"You took advantage of his distraction with Miss Channing to get those documents signed."

"Of course we did," Frank said, "but it doesn't matter. Jim gave us the authority to go ahead with our retail stores and there is nothing he or you or the board can do about it now." He moved from behind his wife to stand beside his brother. "We're still finalizing the details, but we've got most of it worked out."

Cabel shook his head. "The fact that you have little or no stock to put in these stores and we're likely to lose our biggest customer over this venture doesn't concern you?"

"Let us worry about the stock. As for the clients, they are Jim's problem not ours," Frank said.

"You really don't care if your project destroys the entire company, do you?"

"You and Jim are supposed to be the great businessmen, I'm sure you'll figure out a way to save the business." Edward pointed a shaking finger at his son. "This is really your fault. My father chose *you* over me to run the company. You weren't old enough yet, but it was only a matter of time. When you chose to start working for the company rather than go to college, I knew I needed to act."

Cabel felt numb. His father's voice still reached him but the words were muted, as if they traveled a great distance before being heard.

"America had decided to join in the fight against Kaiser Wilhelm and I saw my chance. I sent you off to fight in that war so that the board would have time to recognize me as the rightful heir. Instead you came home and they turned their backs on me. Now they will realize their mistake."

A few months ago, Jim had warned him just how much Edward envied Cabel. His cousin had used the word "hate" but Cabel hadn't accepted it. Now the truth could no longer be denied. Cabel stared at his father and felt nothing.

"I thought they realized that mistake five years ago," Eunice added.

"True." Edward almost smiled. "But now we'll put both you and Jim in your places. Frank and I will finally receive the recognition we deserve. I hated living in my father's shadow and then yours. I won't live in Jim's as well."

"Do you believe that destroying a thriving business to serve your own purposes will give you respect?"

"We aren't going to destroy the company, we're going to expand it," Frank said. "You'll see, you'll all see. Edward and I are excellent businessmen and we will take Evans Manufacturing to the next level, compete with Sears Roebuck on a national stage. We have the vision you and Jim lack, but our success will prove to everyone that we should have been the heirs to the company."

"My brother's right. This new venture will go forward. There will be a few challenges but if you are as good as everyone thinks, then you and Jim can sort it out. In the meantime we're going ahead with our plans and you really can't stop us," Edward said.

"We'll leave that to the board, but what I would like to know is why you kept working on this project? Approval was denied in August."

Frank and Edward looked at each other, then at him. They hadn't expected this question.

Cabel spoke into the silence. "You couldn't have known Miss Channing would move to Chicago and capture Jim's affections so…"

Eunice gasped and put her hand to her heart. Frank paled and he tugged at his necktie with a shaking hand. Edward had gone still, like a soldier listening to a sound, trying to determine if it meant the enemy was near.

Cabel took note of these reactions while something Jim said floated up to his consciousness. *It was as if she was made just for me.* The truth hit so hard he doubled over as if someone had landed a solid punch to his stomach. When he could breathe again he raised his eyes to his father. "You hired her."

CHAPTER 14

For a moment no one spoke, as if shocked to hear this truth spoken aloud. Eunice shook her head and Frank shuffled his feet, refusing to look at Cabel. Only Edward seemed undeterred.

"If you hadn't interfered this wouldn't have been necessary." He glared at his son. "As with everything else, this is really your fault."

"Stop. I refuse to allow you to continue to lay the blame and responsibility for your atrocities at my feet." With those words Cabel straightened. Regret and self-loathing retreated as he faced these men, knowing that their hatred could no longer touch him. "You hired this girl for Jim to fall in love with and..."

"No. Jim did *not* love that floozy." Eunice rose from her chair, her body shaking with anger. "She was just a distraction, nothing more."

"She did her job too well," Cabel said. "Jim wanted to marry her."

Eunice shook her head and fled from the room, tears falling as she ran. Once again he felt pity, not for her, but for Jim. How would his cousin react when he learned the truth? He turned to Frank and Edward. "Is that why you had her killed, because Jim planned to marry her?"

Frank sputtered and shook his head.

"We had nothing to do with that," Edward demanded. "What kind of men do you think we are?"

"I think you are the kind of men that would send one son to war and hire a would-be fiancée for the other to serve their own ends. I almost died in that war, Jon Warner was killed. Murdering the girl when she became inconvenient is exactly what you two are capable of."

Edward paled and clenched the knob of his cane. "I never meant for you to die. The war was supposed to be quickly won. You were going to be an officer, come home a hero. I was afraid you wouldn't be gone long enough. Instead…"

Cabel didn't want to hear any more. He turned to Frank. "Whose idea was it to hire this girl?"

"Mine," Frank spoke to the floor. "I had a friend out east whose nephew was going to inherit half of the business my friend and his brother had built. The boy had done nothing, deserved nothing, but was going to get half. The girl was hired to distract his nephew while my friend worked with a lawyer to limit the boy's control of the company."

Cabel felt lightheaded as he recalled the newspaper article about Jefferson Banton. "Did this young man kill himself?"

"Yes," Frank whispered.

"And you hired the girl anyway, knowing what she had done before?"

"It wasn't her fault that the boy was weak. I knew Jim would never be so foolish." He crossed his arms over his chest, raising his chin to meet Cabel's eyes for the first time since the conversation had begun.

"So you hired her and she accepted this employment?"

"No. Not at first." Edward took up the story as he sat on the sofa. "I wrote to Frank's friend and he put me in touch with the girl through one of the private investigators she used as intermediaries. The, ah, incident with the young man had become problematic for her. There had been a photograph of them together in the society section of the newspaper a few weeks earlier and she felt it prudent to move to a different city. We offered to help but she refused, said she didn't like the area and wasn't interested." Edward turned to his brother. "But later she contacted you."

Frank sighed. "I received a telegram. She had been offered a second job in Chicago and decided she would accept them both. I guess the money she was to be paid overcame her earlier reluctance." He shook his head. "I almost said no, I should have said no. I was concerned that she wouldn't be able to do what we needed her to do if she was working for someone else at the same time, but you're right. She's very good at her job."

"I'm sure whoever else hired her killed her," Edward added. "No one else wanted her dead."

"There's the boy's family from out east and others she's helped scam out of inheritances or business ventures." Cabel looked at the two men in front of him. "I could think of several people who might want her dead, including you."

"But we told you, we had nothing to do with her death."

Cabel almost laughed, but the truth hurt too much. "You've told me many things, most of them lies. I can't believe anything you tell me."

Edward rose. "Cabe, Son."

Cabel flinched. For years he would have given his life to hear his father speak to him like this, but now...

"I understand why you might think badly of us, but I promise you we only hired the girl to distract Jim while we sorted out the new company," Edward said.

"You what?"

All three men turned to find Jim standing in the doorway leading to the foyer and the stairway to the second floor. Wearing a robe over pajamas and slippers on his feet, Jim looked like a small boy who had just learned that Santa Clause wasn't real. Cabel wanted to protect him, to comfort him, to weep for them both.

"Cabe, what did he mean, that they hired her?"

Cabel stared at his cousin, unsure what to say.

As the silence lengthened, understanding dawned. Jim's expression shifted from confusion to disbelief and finally horror.

"No. Amanda loved me. I loved her. We were going to be married." He fell against the wall. Cabel rushed to support him, putting an arm around his waist to take some of Jim's weight. "It isn't true, is it? Please, Cabe, tell me."

"I'm so sorry. I didn't know until a few moments ago, but yes, they hired her to serve as a distraction while they restarted their project."

"What?" Jim turned to his father and uncle. "You did this for a business deal?"

The men neither answered the question nor denied its truth.

"Get me out of here, Cabe. Take me somewhere, a hotel, somewhere, anywhere but here."

"No, Jim, please..." Frank stepped forward.

"Now, Cabe."

"We need to get you dressed first."

Together the cousins went upstairs leaving their fathers behind.

CHAPTER 15

"You were right to bring him here." Marta whispered as she eased the bedroom door shut. "I've already called Dr. Lewis and he'll stop by to check on Jim to see if he needs anything more than bed rest."

"Thank you." The words were inadequate for all his housekeeper had accomplished since he had called to tell her he was bringing Jim home. She had arranged a car to meet them at the train station and had called the mayor's office to make sure that the roads were cleared of sand. The room next to Cabel's had been aired and the bed made with fresh linens. A fire warmed the room in addition to the heat from the now-functioning furnace. Both Walter and Jorge waited at the house to help Jim up the stairs and into bed. Although Jim's health had improved, the departure from his parents' home and the train ride to St. Joe had overtaxed him.

Together Cabel and Marta went downstairs before they separated, she to her kitchen and he to the telephone in the hallway. His first call was to Christopher Stanford to learn where matters stood with regard to Frank and Edward. Cabel had telephoned the lawyer from the train station before leaving Chicago, telling him what he had discovered and the confessions that his father and uncle had made. Christopher promised to look into the matter. Now Cabel needed to know what steps had been taken.

"Cabel," Christopher said when he answered the phone. "I'm glad you spoke to me before you left the city. I immediately drove to your office and found your father and uncle emptying the contents of several filing cabinets into boxes. They were not happy to see me."

"I'm sure they weren't." Cabel wished he could be shocked that Frank and Edward would return to the office after the confrontation that morning, but doubted that the two men could do anything to surprise him again.

"I refused to let them remove anything from the offices, speaking on your behalf as acting president." Christopher gave a chuckle that turned to a sigh. "Your father used his name, his place on the board and the family to rally the staff against me, but most sided with you, Jim, and the company. Because the files they were taking had to do with Evans Manufacturing, Frank and Edward were forced to leave them behind."

"They won't give up so easily."

"No, but don't worry. I left a few of my legal clerks at the office to assure that the files remained on the premises. With your permission, I'll have them begin to review those files. If we can find proof that they intended to use company resources to start a completely independent venture, we will have what we need to remove them from the board and their positions in the company."

Now it was Cabel's turn to sigh. "I never meant for this to happen, to force them out."

"Cabe, you've done nothing wrong. In fact, you've done everything to protect the business and your cousin. Don't feel guilty over what happens to your father and uncle. From what you've said it will be less than they deserve. And please trust that I will keep their more shocking indiscretions from becoming public knowledge."

"Thank you."

Christopher went on to explain in great legal detail what papers would be drawn up and actions to be taken to assure that

Frank and Edward would be removed from the company. In the meantime, the lawyer was drafting an injunction to keep the elder Evans men from the corporate offices until all relevant matters could be settled.

Cabel thanked him again and placed his second call to Katherine who told him that the other company officers and primary staff had reacted to the situation professionally and with some relief. The business had become more divided than Jim and Cabel realized and the current situation had brought the fissure to light. While no one on the staff, Katherine included, knew the extent of Frank and Edward's betrayals, they knew enough and took the situation personally. More telling, many of those working directly for the elder Evans men either submitted letters of resignation or asked to be reassigned to other departments. Cabel would address those matters personally when he returned to the office on Monday.

The final call had been to Detective Finch. Unable to reach him, Cabel left a message at the precinct asking that Greg call him as soon as possible. Maybe the new information he had would allow the police to reopen the investigation into the shooting.

After replacing the earpiece of the telephone, Cabel walked into his office and sat behind his desk. He found a piece of paper and wrote a note to ask Marta to get a telephone extension installed in the office, one of the standing models with the new rotary dials, not a wall-mounted one, so he could place calls from his desk rather than standing in the hallway.

Thinking of Marta, he smiled. She had a knack of anticipating his needs as was evident from the fact that she had left his business case conveniently near his chair. He removed the files, stacking them on the polished surface of his desk. As he did so, he questioned the necessity of the third call he had made. He knew all he needed to about Amanda Channing. She was an employee, not a girlfriend, and her death had nothing to do with Jim. She had enough sins in her past to ensure a range of potential murder suspects including her other client and whoever their target had been. If Jim hadn't been with her when she was killed, he wouldn't have been injured. In all likelihood, he also would never have known what happened to her after she died, presumably under a different name. Maybe that would have been a blessing.

"I haven't been in this room in ages."

Jim stood in the door, wan but steady, as he surveyed the study. His smile was genuine as he stepped into the room, noting the details. "It looks the same as I remembered it." He gave a small laugh. "You look enough like Grandfather that for a moment I thought it was him sitting behind the desk."

"Sometimes I feel like an imposter in here," Cabel admitted as he stood and gestured for Jim to join him on the leather couch in front of the fireplace. "I had been back for months before I could even open the door and that only happened because Marta tricked me into it."

"I didn't trick you," she said, appearing in the doorway carrying a tray that she set on the table in front of the couch. "I merely asked you for some architectural drawings of the house. It's hardly my fault that they were kept in here." The twinkle in her eyes belied her aggrieved tone.

"I'm sure you did what was necessary," Jim said.

She smiled at him before she left the room, closing the door behind her.

"Be careful," Cabel said. "You never know what she might decide is necessary for you."

"True, but at the moment I've got other things to concern myself with." Jim's hands shook as he selected a ham sandwich from the platter on the tray.

Cabel poured cups of coffee before picking up a sandwich of his own. They ate their snack in companionable silence until the last bit of ham and cheese had been devoured. Jim's appetite was good and his color improved as he ate. Cabel hoped that this meant that the shock of what had transpired that morning would not cause a setback in his recovery.

Jim refused to wait until the following day to review the papers that Cabel had brought with him. By mutual agreement, they moved from the couch to the desk. Cabel pulled a chair next to his own so that they could look at the papers together. The desk was huge and easily accommodated them both sitting behind it, as well as the many files spread across its surface.

A granite rock that served as a paperweight glinted under the lamplight and caught Jim's attention. He picked it up and turned it in his hands, watching the gray-black flecks in the pure white stone sparkle as it moved. "I remember finding this in the park along the bluff. I couldn't have been more than six. I gave it to Grandfather, telling him it must be a diamond because of how it sparkled. He never corrected me. I hadn't realized he kept it all these years."

"Grandmother also kept a selection of the odd gifts we'd given her as boys. She displayed them on the parlor mantle," Cabel said. "They were hard to see amongst all of her bric-a-brac, but she'd kept them just the same. I think they both cared for us more than they would show."

"Think of what they would say if they saw us now."

Cabel found the thought depressing. They would be proud of Jim, who had stepped forward and ran the company as well as the best of them. He also believed that while both grandparents would have understood the effects the war had had on him, they would be very disappointed to see how weak he had been in the face of it. Shaking off these sad thoughts he turned to the matter at hand.

"Let's see what mess our fathers have made for us to clean up."

They sifted through the papers Jim had signed over the last few months. With each untidy signature scrawled on unread purchase authorizations or project approvals, Jim berated himself as a fool. "Look at this one. I signed it when I was hurrying out the door to meet Amanda for lunch. Dad stopped me in the hallway and wouldn't let me leave until I signed this supposedly urgent contract renewal." He rested his elbows on the desk and put his head in his hands. "That happened over and over again. They would delay me with legitimate problems until I was running late and then would slip these other things in for me to sign. I should have known they were up to something. They never took such an interest in the day-to-day operations of the company before."

Cabel gave Jim's shoulder a squeeze. "It is pretty amazing what they can accomplish when they're motivated," he said by way of a joke and was rewarded with a small smile. "Remember, they planned this, all of it. You didn't stand a chance."

The pain in Jim's eyes when he looked at Cabel was almost impossible to bear. "I'm not sure which is worse, that they could do this to me or that she would." He looked away as he blinked tears from his eyes. "All I can think is that you never would have been fooled like this. You would have figured it out."

"Can't you see how wrong you are? They did do this to me, or something quite like it, five years ago. My father wanted me gone from the company and knew that the war had changed me." His voice caught. "He found my weaknesses and exploited them until he pushed me too far. He just hadn't anticipated becoming injured in the process."

Jim shook his head. "It isn't the same. They used a girl to distract me. You never would have fallen for such a ruse."

There were confessions Cabel didn't want to make, but Jim needed to hear the truth. "Have you forgotten? I had ended my engagement to Elizabeth. I couldn't be with her without remembering Jon and how he died." He cleared his throat to dislodge the lump that had begun to form. "The war had damaged me in ways that I cannot explain. Although I could function within the business, my father knew I was too broken to seek out any type of attachment to a woman. No, he would never have considered such a ruse with me. Instead he just kept pushing me, undermining me, criticizing me until it became too much." He gave his cousin a small smile. "At least, unlike my father, no one ended up in the hospital because of your mistake."

"Except me, and a girl died as well," Jim said harshly.

Cabel jerked as if slapped. How could he have forgotten? "Jim, I'm sorry. I didn't mean..."

"It's okay, Cabe." Jim took a deep breath. "I understand what you meant. I didn't kill Amanda and I don't think our fathers did either. But someone shot her because she came to Chicago, because they hired her."

"No. Someone else hired her, as well. I told you that. Her death had nothing to do with you."

"I couldn't protect her. She died in my arms. Her death had everything to do with me."

CHAPTER 16

Exhausted from a day of calming employee fears and addressing board member and client concerns, all Cabel wanted to do was return to his hotel and rest. Instead he found himself standing in front of his childhood home, knowing that his next action would likely bring disaster, but he had no other option.

A bitter wind swirled leaves in his path as he mounted the steps. Cursing his promise to Jim, he raised the door knocker and let it fall. A young woman in the expected high-necked black dress and simple white apron answered the door. Although she hadn't been employed by his parents when he'd lived in the house, she knew who he was. With a polite smile and downturned eyes, she opened the door wider and gestured for him to step inside.

"Shall I take your coat?"

He nodded, as he unwound the scarf before handing it and his hat to the maid who placed them on a bench with his newly purchased winter coat. Disconcerted at being treated like a visitor in the only place in the city he could claim as home, he completed these formalities before stepping into the parlor.

His mother stood near the fireplace, hands clasped in front of her, a gesture he knew from childhood but only now realized sent a subtle but direct message that she wished not to be touched. Firelight glinted in her blond hair, styled to emphasize her large blue eyes and perfect features. Only her smile, polite and distant, kept her from being beautiful, though others might find her cool demeanor enhanced her loveliness.

Did she hate him for what he had done to his father, her husband? She hadn't spoken to him at the hospital despite the more-than-five years which had passed since they'd last seen each other. Perhaps the drama of the others had kept her silent, but there was no one to interrupt them now and she had nothing to say.

"Mother," Cabel said. "You're looking well."

Her lips smiled, though her eyes remained distant. "Thank you, dear."

He waited but she had nothing more to offer.

A memory surfaced too quickly to catch and tamp down. As a child he made a game of making his mother speak to him, not to a group or him and his father, but to him alone. Her voice was melodious and to Cabel it seemed as if she sang her words rather than spoke them. Getting her attention had been difficult, but to have her speak was the prize. There had been a list, he recalled, because he had kept track of how many words she had uttered for him, gifts begrudgingly bestowed and sometimes stolen. Ten, the most he had received in one encounter had been ten. "Thank you, Cabel. The scarf is lovely and quite thoughtful."

He couldn't recall when the game had stopped, when he understood he would never truly have his mother's love or devotion. At some point he hadn't needed it anymore because Jon's mother had filled that void in his young life.

With a slight shake of his head he focused on the present and the woman before him. "I'd like to speak with you about Amanda Channing. Did you know what Father and Uncle Frank had done?"

Her mouth twisted as though tasting something sour. "No. Your father does not involve me in business affairs."

Cabel stared at his mother, wondering what it would take to break through the gauze she had wrapped around herself. "He might have considered it business, but I can assure you that Jim had a different experience of the situation."

His mother looked at the fire a moment before drifting to a chair and lowering herself onto its seat with the easy grace of a charm school graduate. Perfection accomplished, she turned to her son and waited.

"So you didn't know?"

"Cabel, why do you worry yourself over this?"

"Jim needs to know the truth of who she was and I promised…"

Her gaze turned deliberately vague. She still had nothing to offer him.

"I'm sorry to have troubled you." He turned to leave.

"Eunice would like to know if her son is well."

Cabel couldn't help but count her words, the habit had become ingrained. Ten words and they weren't for him, but for his aunt. "He continues to recover. Marta takes good care of him."

"She would like him home again."

Cabel stepped to his mother's side and knelt beside the chair. "You do know what happened. They hired a woman to distract Jim so Father and Uncle Frank could do as they wished with the company. Aunt Eunice knew, the entire time Jim was falling in love, she knew it was a lie." His anger rose as he spoke and she flinched from the emotion. He stood and looked down at the top of her head. A small ache settled in his stomach as he realized another binding tie had frayed to nothingness. "Jim will come back to Chicago and the company, as soon as he's able. I doubt he'll return to his parents' home."

She gave a small nod. "What is it you want to know?"

Cabel stopped in the doorway and looked back at his mother in surprise.

"I don't know if I can help you, but I would like to try," she said softly.

"Why?" He wished he could have stopped the word, but it was too late and the question held too many meanings.

"Because you are my son, of course." Her sad smile held a bit of honesty and he was taken aback. "I know I have not been a warm mother to you, but the reason is not of your making. There are things I never meant to speak of, but perhaps you and I shall do so, only not today."

She rose and walked to him, touching his arm lightly before drifting beyond his reach. He turned to follow her progress.

"I need to know how Father communicated with Miss Channing, how he paid her. I understood from what he said that there was an intermediary. I must speak with him."

Margaret Evans paused in the arched doorway, a picture of beautiful loneliness. She nodded once and spoke over her shoulder, "I will send word to you at your office should I discover the answer." And then she was gone.

Cabel stared at the place she had been. He had forgotten to count the words, but then that no longer mattered. She would help him because he was her son. Perhaps some ties were too strong to break even if they were made of gossamer threads.

CHAPTER 17

November winds pushed him down the street with relentless insistence, almost shoving Cabel past the doorway he sought. The grimy windows were dark, attesting to the truth of the closed sign that hung on the battered oak door. Despite this evidence that the private investigator was not there, Cabel knocked.

Traffic rumbled along South Michigan Avenue a half-block away. This was Cabel's first visit to the Levee District that lay west of the lake and south of Printer's Row. Although he'd never visited this Chicago South Side neighborhood, he knew it by reputation. A red-light district since the mid-1800s, its vices had expanded to booze, drugs, and gambling since Capone had annexed it as part of his empire. Grimy pawnshops and grubby diners shared the dirty street with soda fountains whose owners made no effort to comply with prohibition laws and a clientele who didn't care.

Sandwiched between a barber who did a brisk business in hair tonic and a clothing store with mannequins that managed to appear embarrassed by their poorly made attire, Cabel found the address his mother had sent to his hotel. The business' door had been handsome once upon a time, carved of oak with an arched glass window. Little remained of the faded gold-and-blue letters that had been painted across the now-filthy glass, yet a shadow of the words "Jacob Martin, Investigator" could still be seen in its surface.

Cabel knocked again before grasping the knob. It resisted a moment before turning with a grudging moan. Even then Cabel had to use his shoulder to force the door open.

"Hello," he called as he pushed his way into the office. Weak light streaked through the grime-coated windows and gave the room an odd, underwater atmosphere that momentarily distracted Cabel from the chaos within. Papers lay strewn across the floor. Overturned chairs and file cabinets were flung about as if in anger. Glass from broken picture frames crunched beneath his feet as he took a tentative step. The sound reminded Cabel of the horrors he had witnessed a few months earlier at the Charades Club, an upscale speakeasy owned by Capone. That night he had been caught in the middle of a gun battle between rival gangs, and a woman he'd known since childhood had died in his arms. He drew in a deep breath, hoping to push the past away. Instead, the smell of death filled his nostrils and dragged him to hell.

His ears rang from the mortar blast that had flung him across no-man's-land. Men screamed in pain. With the air knocked from his lungs he couldn't join them. Slowly his breath returned and carried with it the stench of death. A moment passed before he realized he lay atop a mound of bodies. He opened his mouth to scream but vomited instead. Crawling to the edge of the small pit that the blast had tossed him into, he prayed for the souls of those beneath him. English, American, French, or German, he couldn't tell in the dark but it didn't matter. They deserved better than to rot in this hole, but he could not help them. He could barely help himself.

Something sharp struck his ribs and he groaned.

"I told you he was drunk." A harsh voice cut through the darkness. "I saw him stumble out of that door over there."

"He looks like a swell. Let's roll him while he's too corked to know."

Cabel felt a tug on his coat but couldn't find the energy to resist.

"You leave that man alone."

"Really, Mack? What will you do if we don't?" the first voice asked with a sneer.

"You'll never buy from me again, or your father, either."

"You leave my old man out of this."

"I will if you leave this poor man alone."

Another sharp jab to the rib, then footsteps shuffled away. "I won't be forgetting this," the harsh voice grumbled.

"Neither will I," said the other voice.

Cabel tried to open his eyes but pain stabbed like an ice pick into his brain. Someone knelt beside him.

"Don't worry about them hooligans, they're gone now," the man spoke quietly, kindly, as he ran his hands over Cabel's torso. "Your ribs are bruised, but I don't think they're cracked. Can you sit up?"

An arm supported Cabel's shoulders and slowly he was able to sit. Weak from the effort, he sat on the dirty sidewalk while his rescuer knelt patiently beside him. After another minute of rest, he nodded and the arm returned, supporting his back while Cabel rose to his feet. His legs wobbled but held, and slowly he shuffled along where he was led. He didn't dare open his eyes for fear of the pain and the nausea that still lurked nearby.

"Step up, just here."

Overhead a bell tinkled as a door opened and Cabel stepped up. Strong, antiseptic odors assaulted his nose, harsh but somehow pleasant. Aftershave, he realized as he was settled into a chair.

With a practiced hand, the man Cabel guessed was a barber, placed a warm towel over his face and soon the *thwap*, *thwap* of a sharpening razor could be heard. With no energy to fight, no desire to object, Cabel submitted to the ministrations of the man who had saved him from the boys on the sidewalk.

The warm towel was replaced with the tickle of the shaving cream brush and the woodsy smell of soap filled the room. The barber knew his trade and the blade whistled across his cheek without hesitation or cut. Cabel focused on these things, using the mundane as a talisman against the darkness.

A soft cloth wiped the last of the soap away and a pungent, musky aftershave was patted over his face and neck.

"Would you like a trim while you're in the chair?"

Cabel nodded and let the snick of the scissors further calm him, yet he knew he couldn't take refuge in the barbershop much longer. Taking a deep breath, he opened his eyes. The pain in his head increased, but not as much as he feared. Slowly his eyes grew accustomed to the brightly lit shop. Mixed in with the bottles of lotions and creams, the razors, straps, and other paraphernalia of the shop were large bottles of hair tonic of a color and style he'd not seen before.

"I had a brother who served in the Great War," the barber said. "Took a toll on him, it did." Their eyes met in the mirror before the man turned back to his work. "Loud noises, unexpected ones, were hard on him, would send him back to the war." The scissors paused. "He said it was like the time travel stories we read as boys, only it took him back to the worst of it. After one of his spells he would be sad for days. One day he didn't want to go back no more so he hung himself in our parents' shed."

"I'm so sorry." Cabel forced the words past stiff lips.

The barber shrugged philosophically, though his eyes held pain. "I was at the shop door, keeping an eye on those boys out there, when I saw you stumble from the office next door. The look on your face reminded me of Brian's, standing with one foot here and the other back in France."

Cabel closed his eyes and swallowed the bile that had begun to rise. How aptly put, yet so inadequate to describe the cruel tricks his mind played.

"Did you have business with Jacob?"

"Jacob?"

"Jacob Martin, the investigator?"

"I had some questions for him."

"He hasn't been around for a few days, not unexpected in his line of work, but usually I'd see him by now. I am surprised he'd leave his office open. He was particular about keeping it locked."

Cabel began to shake.

"Here, now, nothing to worry about, I'm sure. Have a sip. It'll help calm your nerves."

The barber turned the chair so that they were facing each other and handed Cabel a small bottle of the unusual tonic the man stocked. With unsteady fingers, he unscrewed the cap, releasing the pungent smell of alcohol, and not the medicinal kind.

"Don't worry. I brew the whisky myself in the basement with a recipe handed down from my grandfather. You won't go blind, I promise."

Raising the bottle to his lips, Cabel took a sip. Smokey and rich, he could almost taste the Ireland in it and decided he should try a bit more. The whisky performed its magic and soon even the pain in his head became a memory. With some reluctance he recapped the bottle and returned it to the barber. "One of the best I've ever had," he said.

The barber smiled. "It's nice to have it appreciated. Too many around here aren't educated enough to know when they have something special."

Cabel smiled in response, then grew serious. "How well do you know the man next door?"

"A bit," the man shrugged and turned away to fuss with putting his scissors away. "He comes in from time to time but we aren't exactly friends, if you know what I mean."

"You probably won't be happy to hear this, but I think something's happened to this man and I need to let the police know."

"What? I can't have the police here."

"I understand, but I think that Mr. Martin may have been killed in his office. The smell, you see..."

"Oh."The barber's eyes widened with sadness and understanding. He flipped the open sign on the door to closed then pulled an old crate from under a counter. "Are you needing to call right away or can I have a few minutes?"

"Take your time. I want to reach a specific detective first, if I can, and I'll keep him away from your shop if possible."

"Just give me a few minutes and I'll be ready," he said, packing the bottles into the crate.

Cabel rose from the chair. His vision wavered a moment then cleared as the past receded. He watched the barber a moment before grabbing the nearest bottles and handing them over for crating.

"I'm Cabel Evans," he said as he passed another bottle that was then efficiently wrapped in brown paper.

The man kneeling on the floor smiled up at him. "I'm Mackenzie Donahue, Mack to my friends."

"It's a pleasure to meet you, and thank you for your kindness."

"'Tis nothing. Here, help me with that door back there, will you?"

The narrow door at the back of the shop opened to a small, untidy office. Mack walked to the far wall, pushed aside some empty boxes with his foot, balanced the box on his knee, and pressed on a knot of wood in the paneling. A wide section of the paneling swung open on silent hinges to reveal a small landing and a flight of stairs that led down into darkness.

"Push that button, there," Mack pointed with his chin.

Cabel felt along the wall until he felt the button and pressed. Bare bulbs illuminated a steep staircase and Mack carried the box down with the dexterity of long practice. After a moment Cabel followed.

A gleaming still stood against the far wall of the large brick room at the bottom of the stairs. Bags of grain and sugar lay on nearby pallets as did boxes of empty jars and several large canisters of fuel. Shelves held a sample of various sizes of filled jars, each affixed with a hair tonic label. Sealed crates and boxes were stacked neatly against the far wall, which had a large ventilation grate set near the ceiling and a new metal door, complete with several latches and a heavy lock.

While Cabel perused the room, Mack had set down the box he had brought downstairs and checked the low fire under the still. Nodding in satisfaction he looked back at Cabel. "I'm trusting you with my secrets."

"I promise they are in good hands." He looked around with curiosity. "This looks more like the basement of a house than a business."

"That it does because that it is." Mack smiled as he sat on a low stool near the still. "Much of the land on which the city is built is rather soft. Sometimes buildings settle and are torn down or rebuilt. The lowest levels are either abandoned or completely forgotten." He looked around the room with pride. "When I bought this place the last owner didn't know this room was here. I started to dig down, planning some—let's call them renovations, when I nearly broke my leg falling through the ceiling."

"Fortuitous."

"That it was, my friend, in more ways than I knew." He nodded toward the metal door.

Cabel thought a moment. "Tunnels?"

"That they are. The big ones in the Loop are still used to carry coal and deliver goods to the businesses and such. That's what these were for too back in the day, but the trains stopped running, so now they're used for something else."

"Illegal?"

"But what else would it be?" Mack started back up the stairs and Cabel followed.

When they reached the little office Mack resettled the boxes in front of the hidden door and then nodded for Cabel to follow into the shop. He rearranged the remaining bottles on the shelves to fill the gaps where the whiskey had been. "My neighbor started using my door down there a few months ago. Didn't think he knew about it, but there you have it." Mack's face turned solemn. "Guess he was a better detective than I thought."

"Did he say where he was going or who he might be meeting?"

"Now, my friend, if a fellow's going into Capone's underworld, it's best not to ask too many questions. For sure it's a dangerous place to be but, depending on your purpose, it's safer to conduct business below than above." He looked around the shop and nodded in satisfaction. "There's a telephone at the corner drugstore. Just don't buy their gin or you might go blind."

"Thank you for your help," Cabel said as he held out his hand.

"'Tis nothing. Oh, and if you find out what happened next door, let me know, will you? Jacob and I weren't friends, but he was a good enough man. Shame what happened to him."

Cabel nodded then left the shop.

CHAPTER 18

Less than twenty minutes later, Detective Finch met him near the drugstore. "Looks like a place where they probably sell bath-tub gin," he said by way of greeting, nodding toward the grimy shop windows. "I trust you're too smart to buy it."

Cabel nodded but couldn't relax into an easy banter. They walked down the street, toward the private investigator's office, toward the body. Each step felt like a burden.

The detective eyed him closely. "Odd, you look a bit scuffed but with a nice haircut."

A smile pushed its way past his anxiety. "I had a rough time in the private investigator's office and fell down, I think. A couple of teens thought I was drunk and tried to take advantage of the situation, but the barber next door took care of me."

"Kind of him."

"It was. He had a brother in the war and I guess he recognized… Well he knew what to do."

Finch nodded. They passed the barbershop and stopped in front of the investigator's office. The door stood slightly ajar, but it didn't look as if anyone else had been inside.

"You said you didn't see the body, right?"

"No, but I know the smell." Cabel swallowed. "The light is poor in there, I didn't turn the switch, but I guess you'll find a body behind the desk. It was the only place I couldn't see."

"Okay then. You wait here while I have a look around."

Cabel nodded and leaned against a light pole. Five minutes passed, then ten. People passed him and stared at the well-dressed man, probably wondering if he was a patron of the Levee District's many brothels. Tired of the stares and angered by his cowardice, he pushed himself away from the pole and started toward the office. Finch should have been back by now.

They nearly collided in the doorway.

Finch held a large manila envelope in his hand and gestured for Cabel to turn around. They returned to the pole and faced one another.

"You said on the phone that your father and uncle hired the dead girl to distract your cousin and all of this was over a business deal."

"Something like that, yes."

"That explains why they didn't want her murder investigated. It had nothing to do with you and everything to do with them."

Cabel nodded. He knew that, and Jim did too, but hearing Finch say it eased a tension he hadn't been aware of until it was gone.

"There is a body, behind the desk like you thought. I checked the victim's pockets. His wallet was still there and it had a few bucks in it as well as some papers. It looks like the dead man is Jacob Martin and my guess is he died a few days ago. Shot, first through the kneecaps and then in the head. Whoever did this was looking for information, not money."

"If the man was tortured, then whoever did it destroyed the office. I guess they found what they were looking for."

"I think you're wrong."

Finch looked at him a moment, then at the envelope in his hand before turning his gaze back to the office. "After I saw the body, I couldn't understand why whoever killed him would take apart the office like that. No reason to do that if the guy told the killer what he wanted to know." He shook his head. "I think there were two of them, killers I mean. There are shoe prints in the blood."

Cabel shuddered. "Maybe one set of prints is mine. Maybe..."

"No, the prints were near the body and you never went that far into the room. Besides, the blood is dry." He pulled out a pack of cigarettes, offered one to Cabel who shook his head. Finch nodded, lit one himself and stood a moment, his eyes always moving, watching the rhythm of the street. With the instinct of the criminal, most recognized him for what he was and found excuses to cross to the other side of the road.

"Anyway, I think the poor investigator lied and the killers didn't realize it until after he died so they took the office apart looking for whatever they came for." He held up the envelope. "Martin must have suspected something like this might happen. I found a gun in a holster made from leather straps nailed to the underside of the center drawer of his desk. Smart precaution in his line of work, he just couldn't get to it in time." He shook his head. "Found this taped next to it." He looked at the envelope again. "I opened it, that's what took so long. There's a lot of information in here about the girl."

"Amanda?"

"That's one of her names, yeah." Finch shifted his weight. "The thing is, if I leave this here, the detective assigned to this case will probably ignore it. The girl's murder case is officially closed and there's no reason to think that this file is connected to what happened here."

"But..."

"Just listen." Finch finished his cigarette, dropping it to the street and grinding it out with the toe of his shoe. "This murder isn't an official matter yet, but as soon as it is every inch of the office will be searched. I'm sure the envelope will be found and while I believe it's related to Martin's murder, I doubt anyone else will. No one knows what you told me about your family's involvement with the girl, and your father has powerful friends, which means no one ever will." He sighed. "I should leave this here if for no other reason than the last man who had it was murdered." Finch handed the envelope to Cabel. "Promise me the same thing won't happen to you. I like you and don't want to be responsible for your death."

Cabel tried to take the envelope but the detective refused to release it.

"I'm not joking. Promise me you'll be smart, careful, and that you'll call me again if you need help."

"All I can promise is to do my best not to get killed, but some things are out of my control."

Finch gave a small smile, shrugged and let go of the envelope. "True, but have a care. Some answers aren't worth dying for."

Cabel nodded. He'd heard these words before, spoken by Walter Arledge while Cabel was searching for his daughter's killer.

"What will you do about Jacob Martin?"

"I'll have someone call in an anonymous tip. He won't be left here too long."

"What about us? Don't you think people will mention that we were here?"

"In this neighborhood?" Finch laughed. "It would be bad for their illegal enterprises. Besides, the murder happened days ago. That's what the police will focus on." He sighed again. "I still don't know if I'm doing the right thing, giving you that."

"You are. Jim needs to know who killed Amanda and I need to know if it's related to what my family is up to. It's unlikely, but I need to be sure."

"Well good luck and let me know what you find." The detective held out his hand.

Cabel shook it. "I will, and thank you." He stood and watched as Finch strode down the street and turned at the next corner before returning to the barbershop to warn Mack that more police were on their way. Then he walked back to Michigan Avenue to flag down a cab, the envelope like a Pandora's box in his hand.

CHAPTER 19

The Tiffany lampshade scattered prisms of color across the envelope that lay on the leather-bound blotter. Most of the employees of Evans Manufacturing had gone home as night edged near. The offices were quiet but not deserted as Cabel studied the envelope on the desk. Standard in shape and color, larger than needed for letter correspondence but one used regularly to send larger documents. The corners showed some minor wear but there was no writing or other marks on the outside. The flap had once been sealed but was now sliced open, presumably by Detective Finch.

Picking it up by the corner, Cabel tilted the envelope, spilling its contents onto the blotter. A few papers did not fall out, so he reached inside and gently released them from the envelope. He found he held four newspaper clippings with neat, handwritten notations of which paper they were from and the dates they were published. Each contained a photograph of a young couple taken at a social gathering. Cabel held the photos under the light to see them clearly.

Each young man looked dapper and happy in various styles of formal wear and every young woman appeared lovely and demure. The men were different from photo to photo but upon closer inspection Cabel realized that the girl was the same. The hair styles were slightly different and he suspected the colors were as well, though it was impossible to know for certain from the black-and-white photos. In each photo the girl either tilted her head slightly away from the camera or used her hat to cover part of her face. If he had seen the photos in newspapers, at the time they were published, he wouldn't have noticed that the girl was the same, but studying them together left no doubt.

The names were different as well, Abagail Carter, Amelia Croft, Aubrey Clayton, and Adelaide Connors. Although she stayed on the east coast, she varied her locations as well: New York City, Philadelphia, Boston, and Baltimore. For over two years she carried out her masquerades and deceptions, and these were only the ones that Jacob Martin had discovered. In the most recent of the clippings she posed with Jefferson Banton, the young man who killed himself. Cabel had to wonder if she cared that her actions caused such misery.

Setting the newspaper clippings aside, he picked up a pair of photographs. The first one showed Amanda, he needed to call her something, posing in front of the same background as the photo he found in her apartment. She looked to be about seventeen, and instead of the younger girl, she posed with a boy. He seemed to be a few years older than Amanda, perhaps twenty or so. Their arms linked around each other's waists and she smiled up at him. Here was love; here was the truth of the girl.

The young man stood in profile to the camera, his hat casting a shadow across his face. He looked down at Amanda and seemed pleased but aloof, as if he enjoyed his conquest of the girl but did not fully share her affections. Cabel turned the photograph over and found the penciled words "House of David, July 17, 1920."

The House of David, no wonder the setting looked so familiar. This odd, religious sect owned a great deal of land in Benton Harbor, Michigan, and their amusement park, orchestra, band, zoo, and baseball teams drew visitors from all over the country. As a child Cabel had visited their park, though he'd always preferred the smaller but familiar Silver Beach in St. Joe.

Amanda could have been a tourist or a resident of the House of David. He needed to see the other photo of her he had found in her apartment so he could compare hairstyles and clothes but from what he remembered, they were different. Unfortunately he'd left it in Michigan with the other items he'd found. It didn't matter right now. With luck she was more than a visitor and he would find some answers.

Setting that photograph aside, he picked up the second one, a candid shot of Amanda dressed in clothes similar to what he had found hidden in the stove of her apartment. She wore her hair differently and the thick makeup around her eyes made her appear older than she had in the newspaper clippings, more experienced somehow. The photo captured Amanda as she ran up the steps of what looked like a brick apartment building. Cabel flipped the photograph over and found an address was written in pencil on the back in handwriting more masculine than the writing on the other picture. Cabel stared at the address and guessed it was located not too far from the private investigator's office, though he'd need a map to be certain.

Turning the photo back over, he stared at the building, and the girl who had played her parts so well. Maybe the key he had found would open the door to the apartment building and Cabel felt frustrated that he had also left it in Michigan. Marta could send it, but he needed to talk to Jim about what he had found. The weekend would be soon enough for the journey.

The two photos joined the stack of newspaper clippings and Cabel picked up the last item on the desk, a small ledger that could easily fit in a jacket pocket. The cheap brown leather cover had no embossing or other marks indicating ownership. From the wear along the edge it appeared to be fairly new but well used.

Cabel opened the book and found that it had been divided into two distinct sections, each with notations of funds taken in and paid out, as well as a retainer kept by the detective. He studied the numbers a moment. Oddly, only one of the two clients appeared to have paid Amanda for her services. Who would she have worked for without pay? He suspected that Jacob Martin had known the answer to that question and wished he could speak to the man now. The private investigator probably wasn't the one whom his father had originally contacted but the man clearly served as a go-between for Amanda and her employers here in Chicago.

Both sections of the book also had notes written in a code or shorthand of some kind. Each entry was dated, as were the financial notations, but the dates on the notes and payment didn't always match. From the photo it was clear that Jacob Martin had followed Amanda on at least one occasion, maybe there were other times as well. Had he done this on his own or was there a third party involved who paid him to spy on Amanda? Maybe he had followed the girl at the behest of the people who hired her. Had this activity gotten him killed or had Amanda's other employer wanted to sever his last ties to the girl?

Cabel rubbed his tired eyes. The items from the envelope created more questions but also held the possibility of finding some answers. The prospect depressed him. Everything he learned about Amanda caused more heartache to Jim and that would likely continue. And then there was the murdered private investigator. At least one person had a secret worth killing for. He needed to know who else had employed Amanda and why.

A light tapping startled Cabel from his thoughts. "Come in," he said, glancing up as Kathleen opened the door and walked in carrying a sheaf of papers.

"I saw the light shining under the door and guessed you were still here," she said as she crossed the room and set the papers on his desk. "I know you have a full schedule tomorrow so I stayed a bit late to finish these contracts."

"Thank you." Cabel picked up the documents and set them on top of the newspaper clippings and photographs, hoping the sharp-witted secretary hadn't noticed them.

"My goodness, I haven't seen this since secretarial school," Kathleen said as she picked up the notebook that still lay open on the blotter. She looked at Cabel. "This is written in shorthand, did you know?"

He shook his head. "I wondered, but no, I hadn't realized."

"That's why you're the boss and I'm the secretary." She smiled at him then returned her attention to the book. "What exactly is this?"

Cabel hesitated. Katherine's loyalty and discretion were not in question, but he doubted Jim would want his secretary involved in such a private matter.

Katherine gave him a quick smile before setting the notebook on the desk. "I'm sorry to be so nosy. It's none of my business."

"It isn't, no," Cabel said, "but I need help. I can't decipher this thing but it sounds like you can." He gestured for her to sit.

She settled herself into a visitor's chair before picking up the notebook again. "Yes and no. This is shorthand, but there are two kinds. The person who wrote this, a man I suspect from the handwriting, is using the Pittman version. Most correspondence courses and some secretarial schools teach this method. The school I attended taught the Gregg method which is what many of the schools have switched to. Most of the secretaries here use the Gregg method but a few of them use Pittman."

"So you can't translate this for me."

Katherine laughed. "We call it transcribing, but yes, the two versions are different, but similar enough I could manage most of this without too much trouble and I'm sure one of the girls in the office could loan me her Pittman book if I find something I can't decipher." Her smile faded. "This has something to do with Amanda Channing's death, doesn't it?"

Cabel nodded. "It does." Still he hesitated. He leaned forward, looked into Katherine's clear blue eyes and made his decision. "And I am trusting in your loyalties to Jim beyond your position as secretary within this company."

She nodded. "I would do anything to help him. What do you need?"

As concisely as possible Cabel told her what little he knew of Amanda Channing's past, her role in Jim's life, and the fact that someone else had hired her for second job that she was doing at the same time she was with Jim. He explained about finding the private investigator murdered in his office and how he came by the notebook. Though he wanted to exclude the role that his father and uncle had played in the matter, the information was likely contained in the notebook and he decided it would be better for him to tell her the truth on this issue. Some things, like the key he had found and the photographs, he held back, but he told her what he thought she needed to know to transcribe the notes.

Katherine's eyes never left his face as he spoke. She didn't interrupt, take notes, or react in any visible way. She had tears in her eyes when he finished.

"Poor Mr. James."

Cabel nodded. "Amanda's death was difficult for him but with this..."

"Yes, this is different." She looked out the window and into the darkness. "Which is worse do you think, Miss Channing's betrayal of Mr. James or his father and uncle's?"

"I've asked that question myself, but find I don't have an answer. Maybe there isn't one."

She turned to look at him again. "There is still one thing I don't understand. What is your role in this?"

"I had nothing to do with hiring that girl or killing her, if that's what you're asking," Cabel snapped.

Katherine's eyes widened. "No, that's not what I meant. I'm so sorry." Tears gleamed but didn't fall. "I never thought... I mean I might have before I met you, but now... Oh, dear." She drew a handkerchief from her skirt pocket and dabbed at her eyes.

"Katherine, I'm so sorry."

"No, I understand, given how I treated you when you first arrived." She sniffed again and put the handkerchief away. "I guess I knew that you were helping with the company, dealing with your father and uncle over business matters, but why were you at the private investigator's office?"

Cabel smiled. "A reasonable question," he said, but one he didn't want to answer. He looked at the young woman across from him, sad, anxious, and smart. Pretty, too, he realized with a start and wondered if Jim had noticed. "This past summer I helped a man learn who had murdered his daughter. Jim has asked me to do the same with regard to Miss Channing and that search led me to the private detective's office."

She nodded while she considered his words then looked at him. "Do you know? Are you closer to the truth?"

He shook his head in disgust. "No. I learn things, I find things, but it all leads to more questions than answers." If Katherine were to become more involved she deserved to know all that he had discovered. Handing her the rest of the contents of the envelope, he said, "I found a few things in Amanda's apartment and I left them in my office in Michigan, but here is what I found today." He gestured to the papers on his desk.

She looked at the small stack, then at him. "Can I take these with me? It's getting late and dark, I need to get home."

Cabel hesitated but resigned himself to the truth; Katherine was a part of this now, as much as he was. "Of course." He returned them to the envelope and handed it to Katherine. "Get your things and I'll order you a cab." He waved away her protests. "You stayed late because of me and even longer because of this mystery. The least I can do is see you safely home."

After she left he put on his coat and hat, picked up his business case and went to the elevators to find her waiting. Once they reached the street he waved down a cab, placed her in it, and gave the cabby enough money to assure that he could drive the girl anywhere in the city and have enough left for a decent tip.

His coat collar turned up to protect against the brutal wind, Cabel prepared to fight his way the few blocks to his hotel, cursing himself for not purchasing a bottle of hair tonic.

“Cabel. Cabel Evans.”

He turned to find Christopher Stanton rushing toward him.

“I’m so glad I caught you before you left. We have a serious problem on our hands,” the lawyer said.

CHAPTER 20

"I'm still looking into this, but it appears that your father and uncle can continue with their business venture."

"First, they destroy Jim and now you're telling me they might be able to dismantle the company as well?"

Christopher Stanton shrugged and leaned heavily on the small table of the hotel bar where they had retired to discuss business. The only drinks on the menu were near-beer and sodas so there were few other patrons, which afforded them privacy. Still Cabel would have traded the quiet for something stronger to wash away the bitter taste of his fear.

"Regardless of how it happened, Jim did sign the papers giving the elder Evans men permission to continue this project. The board cannot intercede in the matter."

"What can I do to stop them? Something must be done or they will drag the entire company down with their folly."

"I understand that," Christopher said. "Unfortunately, under the bylaws Jim can't revoke his approval. What he can do is limit the scope of the project and assure that company resources aren't diverted beyond that narrow scope. As his proxy, that task would fall to you. I am having the papers drawn up as we speak."

Cabel toyed with the soda straw in his glass, wishing he were back in the Irish Pub with the odd sense of humor. "Even if we can limit their project to opening only one store, that could be enough to have Sears and Roebuck break their contracts with us. Evans Manufacturing could still lose everything."

"I agree."

"Why don't we have a meeting with our contacts at Sears, explain the situation."

"I've considered that." Christopher's shoulders slumped as he eyed his near beer with distaste before pushing it aside. "The problem is that we can't explain this, not really, without airing a lot of dirty laundry. Fortunately, the business community has a favorable impression of Jim. If they realize he was distracted..."

"Manipulated."

"It won't matter. He's young and some people already questioned whether he had the maturity to be the president of Evans Manufacturing. The fact that your father and uncle would prefer to socialize rather than attend to business allowed your cousin to step forward. While the elder Evans men don't want to work, they do want to step outside their father's shadow and yours to some degree. I think the fact that Jim also proved to be more capable in running the business drove them to decide to strike out on their own."

"What I don't understand is why they don't make a complete break with Evans Manufacturing," Cabel said. "They have the connections to get investors of their own to start their business. Why do they need to take down our company to build their own?"

"They have the connections, yes, but after what happened with the production problems and the lawsuit, many people won't trust them with their money."

"I'm sorry, what lawsuit?"

The lawyer looked surprised for a moment, "Oh, of course, you were...away."

Away, in hell, fighting for his life, there were a surprising number of ways to describe war. "So what happened while I was away?"

Christopher sighed and looked into his glass as if he also wished it held something stronger. "After your grandfather died,

Edward and Frank were angry that you were left with the bulk of the shares, a public humiliation as far as they were concerned, even though no one outside of us at the law firm and your family knew. Evans Manufacturing is a family-held company, not a publicly traded one, so only a few people on the board of directors knew, but it still stung."

Cabel remembered. The death of his grandfather had been painful, but being ostracized by his father had hurt even more. At fourteen, he hadn't understood the implications of what his grandfather had done through his will or why his father and uncle had reacted as they had. His grandmother, devastated by her own grief, had managed to keep the family together. Cabel and his father had never had a close relationship, but after James Cabel Evans had died of a heart attack a chasm opened between them and now he understood why.

"Your father and uncle took over the running of the company while you were too young to take control and before you inherited your shares you were sent off to officers training and then the war." Christopher looked at Cabel. "I know everyone thought that once America entered the war it would be over quickly. Still I question what prompted your father to push you to enlist, to become an officer."

"Lately I've wondered that myself." Cabel nearly choked on the words, surprised that he'd said them. He had wondered, but now he knew. The truth would haunt him, but it also freed him of his guilt.

Christopher only nodded. "Jon's family didn't want him to go, you know, you either for that matter. Lily was so angry with your father for setting everything in motion. She knew you would go since your father demanded it and knew her son would do the same because you were more like brothers than friends. You were one of her children, as far as she was concerned, and she didn't want either of her sons going to war."

Cabel swallowed hard and blinked away the tears that threatened to fall. He loved Lily Warner more than his own mother and he was to blame for Jon's decision to enlist. Although he never asked Jon to join, Cabel was relieved that he would not go into battle alone. Lily had lost her only son in that war because of Cabel. A piece of him died the day that Jon was killed. Knowing that Lily must hate him as much as he hated himself was a weight Cabel carried in his soul.

"You can't blame yourself," Christopher said as if understanding where his thoughts had led. "She doesn't. Her husband wanted Jon to go to war as well. Everyone thought it would be over so quickly, you see. No one expected..."

"How do you know her?" Cabel swallowed again.

"Her husband's company is a client of mine and she has her personal business with us as well. I see her on occasion and she asks after you. I know she'd love to see you."

Cabel shook his head. He hadn't been able to write her when Jon died, couldn't bear to see her when he'd returned home without her son. How could he face her now?

"Mothers are odd creatures," Christopher said in a quiet voice. "They love the children in their arms but pine for the ones who are missing, even if they don't realize they're lost." He cleared his throat. "It appears that we've wandered from our topic. Your father and uncle became president and vice president of the company after their father's death and things went well for several years. After the war began, Evans Manufacturing experienced a business boon. The government needed all manner of parts and machines and many companies stepped up to fill the orders."

"That seems straightforward enough," Cabel said. He'd rather discuss the mess of his own family rather than the grief of Jon's. "We've always produced quality parts which other companies used in their products. Evans Manufacturing should have thrived under these conditions."

"You underestimate the power of greed," the lawyer said. "Edward and Frank decided to save some money and increase profits by using an inferior and less expensive raw material to manufacture certain types of bolts and screws. This violated the contract with the government and the companies subscripted to manufacture parts for airplanes. The defective parts failed and Evans Manufacturing was stripped of its contracts. The government filed a lawsuit. Eventually the need for the parts your company manufactured outweighed the failure. The government dropped the lawsuit and the contracts reestablished, though Evans Manufacturing had to replace all of the subquality pieces as well as submit to intermediate inspections to assure that this didn't happen again."

"That's not possible. I would have heard. Someone would have told me." Cabel's mind reeled at the implications. "This would have damaged our reputation with our existing customers. How did the company survive?"

"Evans Manufacturing was inundated with contracts and demand exceeded production capabilities. Edward subcontracted this project to a smaller company and worked through them to manufacture the bolts. When the problem came to light, Edward blamed the other company, which went bankrupt. This shielded Evans Manufacturing to a great degree."

Cabel thought this through. "But what you're saying is that my father and uncle knew about this, profited from it?"

The lawyer nodded.

"And we still had to pay the government for the defective parts and some significant fines as well. I don't remember seeing an outlay like this on the books after I came home. I might have been distracted by my experiences overseas but I would have noticed something like this."

"That is a bit of a mystery. Edward said he would handle the matter and somehow or another he did. There is nothing in our files. He clearly didn't want whatever was done to rectify the situation to be common knowledge."

"I'll see what Katherine can dig up."

"I doubt you'll find anything at the office. Your father played this very close to his vest. However, as a significant shareholder in the company and the man who will have a controlling stake once the trust has ended, you have a right to know."

Cabel sighed. "I need to talk to my father again."

"Yes, I'm afraid you do."

IIIII

Unable to convince Christopher to join him for dinner and unwilling to venture into the cold night, Cabel ate a solitary meal in the hotel's restaurant. Although early, there were more patrons than he expected. A passing waiter explained that the hotel occupied the same block as a few theaters and jazz clubs and many people stopped in for a light meal before heading to their destination.

The same waiter gave Cabel a woeful look as he took away the dinner plate. Though the steak had been grilled to perfection and the whipped potatoes were buttery and light, Cabel's appetite diminished as he considered how close his father and uncle had come to destroying the business in the past and worried that they might yet succeed.

He tipped heavily to compensate the waiter for his disappointment and pushed himself away from the table. Crossing the lobby, he had reached the elevators when he heard someone call his name. Turning, he searched the crowd until his eyes settled on Elizabeth.

The hotel lobby faded. All he could see was Elizabeth Gish, the girl both he and Jon had loved. Beautiful, witty, charming, and wise, she had loved them both in return, unwilling or unable to choose between them. Elizabeth had waved to them both as their train left the station and stood beside Cabel when he returned alone, damaged in ways beyond understanding. She had done her best to love him despite the changes the war had wrought. As she stood before him now, he wondered how his life might have been different if he had let her.

She rushed forward and hugged him tight, placing a small kiss on his cheek. Stepping back, she held his hands, her eyes searching his before they widened slightly, as if in pleasant surprise.

A man stepped forward as well and placed a territorial arm around Elizabeth's shoulders. She looked up at the man and beamed. "This is Cabel Evans. I know we've spoken of him." She turned to Cabel. "This is my husband, Henry Lassiter."

The men shook hands, assessing each other as they did. Henry Lassiter wore an expensive evening suit and wool coat with a fur collar so he clearly had the means to care for Elizabeth. A youngish man, probably near Cabel's own age, Henry had a serious air about him except for the small wrinkles at the corners of his eyes which indicated that he smiled often, at least under different circumstances.

As they stepped apart, Cabel's eyes returned to the girl he'd once loved, the woman who was now someone else's wife. Her blond hair was still bright and the light blue satin evening gown perfectly matched her eyes. She wasn't as slim as he remembered though it wasn't until she placed a hand against her abdomen in the protective gesture of women since the dawn of time did he realize that she was pregnant.

Henry slid his arm around Elizabeth again and held her tight as if afraid that Cabel would snatch her away. And part of him wanted to though he knew he had no right. He had pushed her away, afraid that the darkness within him would consume them both. Seeing her radiate with happiness, he knew he had made the right decision, though his heart ached. He realized that he was staring again and the moment had turned awkward. He hoped to lighten the mood by asking, "Is this your first child?"

"Our second," Elizabeth said with a smile. "Our oldest, Jon Henry, is home with the nanny while I enjoy my last evening out before I've become too big to be seen in public."

Cabel's heart twisted as he heard the child's name, both in the loss of his best friend and the joy of knowing he wasn't forgotten and never would be. "And what about this one? Have you chosen some names?"

"Stuart Andrew, if it's a boy," Lassiter said, "after my father."

"And Lily Anne if it's a girl," Elizabeth added. "You know Jon's mother was more affectionate with both of us than our own parents. My mother is furious that I won't name a child after her but…" Her eyes darkened with unpleasant memories. "Anyway," she said brightly, "I am not saddling my daughter with the name 'Agatha' so that is that."

"You've made the right choice I'm sure." He tried to smile but his own memories made it difficult. Swallowing his emotions he shifted the conversation to safer ground. "And what do you do for a living, Mr. Lassiter?"

"Call me Henry, please, and I am in banking."

"He's being modest. Henry is a junior partner at the Franklin Bank on Adam's Street." Elizabeth looked up at her husband with pride and genuine affection. "I think he'll make partner soon."

Henry blushed and shrugged, "I don't know about that but I do my best." He cleared his throat. "I know Evans Manufacturing uses First National, but if you ever want to try a bank that's a bit more conservative, please come and see me. You could also speak with your mother about the bank as she has an account with us."

"I will." Cabel struggled to hide his surprise. His mother seemed so dependent on her husband for everything that he couldn't imagine her having her own account.

"Well, it was a pleasure to meet you," Henry said, "but we need to rush along I'm afraid. We have theater tickets and Elizabeth should have something to eat before the performance."

"Of course, and I enjoyed meeting you as well." Cabel realized he spoke the truth. Elizabeth was well loved and well cared for, as she deserved to be.

Elizabeth reached up and hugged him again, whispering in his ear as she did, "Please visit Lily Warner. She loves you so and doesn't blame you for anything that happened. She needs you, Cabe."

She stepped away and took her husband's hand. Together they walked toward the restaurant engaged in companionable conversation.

Cabel turned toward the elevators. His heart ached with longing for Jon, for Elizabeth, for the future he would have had if not for the war. And for the bottle of whiskey he should have purchased while he had the chance.

CHAPTER 21

Dry leaves clung to the dead vines that covered the brick wall, the same one that Amanda had posed in front of with a girl, and later a boy. Cabel held the photos up for comparison and there was no doubt that they were taken at the entrance to the House of David Amusement Park in Benton Harbor, Michigan. Tucking the pictures back in his coat pocket, he walked across the frozen ground to where he had parked the Model T he had borrowed from Dr. Lewis earlier in the day. Several months ago the doctor had helped Cabel discover who had murdered Kittie Arledge. That same person was also responsible for the deaths of the two young men who had vied for Kittie's affections, though that wasn't the motive. Dr. Lewis' involvement in Cabel's erstwhile investigation had been the first of several relationships that had drawn him back into society.

Now Cabel stood at the brick archway entrance to the House of David Amusement Park, the dismantled rides and boarded sales booths a testament that summer was long past. He cranked the car and drove down the rutted dirt road toward the Shiloh Mansion, the seat of this odd religious sect.

Although he had rarely visited this amusement park as a child, he had been fascinated by these long-haired men who played baseball and music and the pretty women who sold their wares to the many park visitors. As he drove toward the administrative and residential complex he realized that at least one new mansion and several additional outbuildings had been built since he'd last been to the House of David. How could a religion that required its members to practice celibacy, even those couples who were married, grow at such an astonishing rate? He knew the Davidites ate only fruit and vegetables, believed that God would return to earth in their lifetime, and that their bodies would rise from their graves. This is why the men did not cut their hair or beards, so that they would enjoy one thousand years of paradise on earth when this jubilant event occurred.

He parked the car near the mansions and stepped into the cold. Despite his numbing hands, Cabel paused to admire the architecture and craftsmanship of the Shiloh Mansion. Gabled and with porches above and below, it was really two mansions connected by a second-story walkway. The site was impressive, as was the knowledge that at least three other mansions were also built on this property. Despite its odd teachings, the House of David was a prosperous group with industrious members.

A young man pruned the trees which lined the path. He gave Cabel a wary smile and simple directions to the administrative side of the mansion. The interior held simple yet elegant furnishings. A large portrait of their founder, Benjamin Purnell, dominated the foyer and greeted visitors with a stern countenance. His white suit and wide-brimmed hat were in stark contrast to his long dark hair and beard.

"May I help you?"

Cabel turned to find a young woman with anxious hazel eyes and dark brown hair standing before him. Her unadorned dress was an unbecoming shade of yellow that couldn't diminish her loveliness.

"I hope that you can," Cabel said, extending a hand in greeting. "My name is Cabel Evans and I'm here to see if anyone can help me identify someone from two photographs taken in front of the amusement park.

The girl shook his hand then quickly stepped away. "My name is Clara Babcock and I need to ask, are you a reporter?"

Taken aback, Cabel said, "No. I'm just trying to learn the name of a girl in some photographs and hoped I would find some answers here.

"Okay then, I'll help if I can. You need to understand that we have thousands of people who visit our park every year, so I doubt anyone can assist you. Still come with me and we shall see what can be done."

She led him through a set of double doors which opened into a large work space. Several women of varying ages sat at desks answering phones, typing on machines, or writing in ledgers. They kept their eyes to their work but Cabel had the impression that they shared Clara's anxieties. This sense of tension surprised him. Although he had not visited the amusement park in years and had never been to the compound proper, the House of David had a reputation as a cheerful group anxiously awaiting God's return. What had changed?

Clara Babcock continued through the room, glancing over her shoulder to assure that Cabel followed. They walked down a long hallway, passing several open doors. Each small office was occupied by either a man or woman engaged in some manner of business. Although Cabel had no idea the specific nature of their jobs, he had seen this type of activity many times in his own offices in Chicago. No, Jim's offices, he reminded himself with a slight shake of his head.

They reached an empty room and Clara entered, taking a seat behind the desk and gesturing for Cabel to sit across from her.

"Let's see them then," she said, holding out her hand to accept the photographs.

He slid them from his pocket and handed them to the girl.

Her smile froze as she looked at the pictures. She looked up at him with concern in her eyes. "Which person are you asking about?"

"The older girl here," he said, pointing to the photo of the two girls. "And I think it's the same girl here." He touched the photo of the girl and young man. "Do you know her?"

Clara stared at the photos as if mesmerized. After a moment she looked at Cabel. "Yes, I believe I do but I'm not sure I'm the person you should be speaking with." She stood and rushed to the doorway. Looking back, she asked, "Is Ada okay then? Does she want to come back?"

"Ada?"

"Ada Cummings, the girl in the photographs."

Cabel hesitated.

"Yes, I see. I best get Mrs. Marigold."

Ada Cummings. At least Cabel had a name to give to Jim, no real comfort but the truth would have to be enough.

Moments later, a woman walked briskly into the office and seated herself behind the desk. Gray was the word that came to Cabel's mind when he looked at her. Hair, eyes, clothing, even her demeanor, everything was gray as if she were in mourning. The only thing colorful about the woman was her name.

"I'm Marigold Peabody," she said by way of introduction. "Most of our members call me Mrs. Marigold, as you may. Clara told me that you are Mr. Cabel Evans and you've come to ask about Ada. May I inquire as to your interest in her?"

"First, let me say that I came here with photographs of someone my cousin knew as Amanda Channing. She died and we've been unable to locate her family. These photographs, which were found in her apartment in Chicago, show her standing in front of your amusement park so I came here to learn what I could."

"Hmm." Mrs. Marigold studied the photographs. Her polite smile congealed into a scowl when she looked at the photo of the young man and woman. She pushed the photos across the desk, face down, and crossed her arms over her meager chest. "I can confirm that the older girl in the photographs is Ada Cummings. The younger girl is her sister, Hazel, but she and her mother left the compound a few months ago to return to their family in Kentucky. Before you ask, I have no idea how to reach them. If that is all, I'll have Clara see you out."

Mrs. Marigold started to rise but Cabel shook his head. "I'm afraid I do have more questions, several in fact."

The woman glared at Cabel but returned to her chair.

"When did Ada leave the House of David and do you know why she left?"

"I would have to check our records but I believe she left about six or seven years ago, just after she turned seventeen. We were all very upset and saddened as she had lived here since she was nine years old. She was cheerful and productive, and had a knack for knowing what she needed to do to make the people around her happy. I had watched her grow up and expected more of her than her risking her soul and defiling her body by running away with that boy."

"The one in the picture?" Cabel asked, turning it over and turning it to face Mrs. Marigold.

"Yes, him. I don't know his name. Just that he worked at a nearby cider mill and began to visit the park on a frequent basis."

Cabel picked up the photo of Amanda, he couldn't yet think of her as Ada, looking adoringly at the boy whose face was turned from the camera. "Did he come to the park specifically to see her?"

Mrs. Marigold shrugged. "I couldn't possibly know. We have hundreds of people living and working here and I don't think anyone really paid much attention to one visitor until he became a nuisance."

"How did he do that?"

"That boy would distract the girls as they worked and wouldn't leave them alone. Sometimes I think he liked the challenge of attracting the attention of girls sworn to celibacy rather than actually caring for any of them. In the end, he persuaded Ada to run off with him. Her mother and sister were devastated. We all were, really. She was one of ours."

"Are you sure there is no way for me to contact the family? Did they write to each other? Are your, um, members allowed to receive mail?"

"Of course our brothers and sisters receive mail." She shook her head at his stupidity. "Before you ask, we have over seven hundred members and I can't possibly tell you if Hazel or her mother received letters from Ada. I doubt her mother did because she would have told someone, but Hazel may have. As you can see from that picture you have, she had a misguided trust in her older sister."

"What about letters from her family? I'd like to let them know of her death."

"I've said I don't know who the Cummings may or may not have written to or received letters from." She leaned forward and said, "Ada has been dead to them for years. The knowledge that her earthly body has also died will bring them no comfort or understanding."

Cabel looked down at the picture of the two sisters and held it up for Mrs. Marigold to see. "What of her. Surely she would like to know what became of Amanda."

The older woman's eyes flashed. "Her name is Ada and we do not speak of this family and do not know where to find them. If you truly came to learn about Ada, then you have what you came for. If you are here for more nefarious reasons, well either way, this meeting is over."

She stood and walked to the door, moving as if she'd been starched as stiff as his collars. He followed her down the hall and through the open work area. Several women eyed him curiously before returning to their tasks. When they reached the entrance, Mrs. Marigold turned to him and said, "Please understand that we do God's work. We try to keep our children on the path to salvation, but each must choose their own way. Ada chose hers, as have others, and now our group faces greater challenges."

"I'm sorry, but I don't understand."

She studied him with her shrewd gray eyes and gave a bitter smile. "Then you are one of the few in this county living in that blessed state of ignorance." She hesitated a moment. "I didn't ask how Ada came to know your family or how she died. To be honest, I think it might break my heart and it is already in such pain." She blinked away the tears that had begun to gather, then squared her shoulders and looked into Cabel's eyes.

Though he didn't understand its source, he recognized despair and felt helpless in its presence.

"I can't help Ada, but I will pray for her soul, and her family. I think I will pray for you as well, for the path I believe you have chosen is a difficult one."

"Thank you," he said, "both for the assistance and for the prayers." He and God had not been on speaking terms since the war. In fact Cabel had begun to doubt the existence of a divine being, for there was little grace to be found in the horror and death of the battlefields. Still the woman's prayers were sincerely offered and he would accept them as the gift she meant them to be.

Marigold Peabody studied him again, a brief smile played on her lips as if she knew his thoughts. With a final nod, she turned and walked back to the office area.

Cabel stood a moment to watch her leave; her shoulders slumped under a heavy burden he did not understand. Putting on his hat and coat, he braced for the bite of the harsh wind that would greet him when he opened the outer door. Once outside, he braved it a moment longer to look again upon the mansion. He could not accept many of the tenants of this sect, but he had great respect for its followers' sincerity and commitment.

The cold engine took several cranks before it sputtered to life. Cabel jumped into the cab and jostled along the hardpacked road toward home. He now knew Amanda's true name and a bit about her family, but would this information help Jim heal or add new depths to his pain?

CHAPTER 22

Cabel returned the car to Dr. Lewis then walked the few blocks home. He arrived to find Jim sitting on the couch in his office, sipping a cup of coffee in front of a blazing fire.

His cousin studied him a moment, then his eyes widened. "You've learned something about Amanda, haven't you?" Hope, love, and sadness flickered across Jim's face until only grief remained. He blinked a moment then gave a false, bright smile. "Come and sit with me. I want to know whatever you've learned and how it will help you with our investigation."

Cabel joined Jim on the couch. Marta bustled in with a tray laden with a coffeepot, cups, and a plate of cookies. Cabel rose and took the tray, placing it on the low table in front of the couch. Marta filled cups for herself and Cabel, topping off Jim's as well, before settling into the deep leather chair next to the couch. For a few moments they sipped coffee and munched gingerbread cookies as they watched the fire burn.

Jim broke the silence when he turned to Cabel and said, "I know you want to protect me, cousin, but I need to know what you've learned about Amanda."

Few words were needed to share the enormity of what he had discovered. Pulling a handkerchief from the sleeve of her dress, Marta dabbed the tears from her eyes while Jim stared into the flames.

"How sad, but at least we know her true name. Will you be able to track down her family?" Marta asked.

"I'll have some people look into it as soon as possible, though I don't know how much luck they will have. Still I'll do my best." Cabel watched Jim as he spoke the words but his cousin appeared to be lost in his own thoughts, ignoring the conversation.

"I hope that poor girl or her little sister weren't part of the horrible things happening at the House of David," Marta added.

"You know what's going on over there?"

Marta looked at Cabel in mild reproach. "If you'd read something beyond the business section of the paper, you might learn a thing or two about people instead of just profits and losses." She refilled Cabel's cup and then her own, glancing at Jim with sadness before returning to the conversation.

"A few months ago, Benjamin Purnell was accused of being a child molester. He and his followers claim that it's all lies told by people who left the order or girls seeking attention." Marta stared into the fire a moment. "I find their religion strange and I could never accept Benjamin Purnell as a true profit of God, but that doesn't mean he did what he is accused of."

"True. Some people want to think the worst of those they don't understand. It helps to justify their prejudices," Cabel said.

"That's possible, but there could be something to the charges. From what I've heard from my cousin, who lives in Benton Harbor, there was a pattern you see. Over the years, some women with young daughters were sent back to their families, children and all, with no explanation and nothing but the clothes on their backs."

"But they all work," Cabel began.

Marta shook her head, "Yes they work, they work very hard, but they do it for the benefit of God and the House of David. No one receives wages, just food, clothing, and shelter. And when they join the sect they are expected to give up all of their worldly possessions, aren't they? If they leave, they do so penniless."

Cabel couldn't imagine choosing such a life, but perhaps his faith wasn't strong enough to surrender to another's concept of God.

"Part of the problem is that they're so secretive. No one really knows what happens over there, just that families with girls tend to leave more often than those with boys." She began to gather the cups and plates. "Some say that there are tunnels under the Shiloh Mansion where he forced himself on the girls, claiming it was part of a religious ritual. Others think that people are jealous that the Davidites are such good business people. The case is going to trial next week, so I guess we'll know then."

Marta left with her tray, pausing in the doorway to look at Jim, tears gathering in her eyes.

Not wanting to disturb his cousin, Cabel sat at his desk. A stack of local newspapers sat on the corner where Marta left them each day. When he lived in St. Joe, Cabel would read the local business section, ignoring the rest as he moved on to the *Chicago Tribune*, which he purchased from the young paperboy, John. Now that he spent so much of his time in Chicago, the local papers were completely neglected, as was the paperboy. Cabel made a mental note to ask Marta about the child, who had come to her attention over the summer, and to purchase a paper from him tomorrow morning.

That decided, Cabel skimmed through the local *Harold Press* and found several articles that confirmed what Marta had told him. Knowing Jim would want to read them for himself, Cabel set the columns aside. Who was this girl who had been born Ada Cummings and died as Amanda Channing, with so many other names in between? What had it been like to live at the House of David and were the stories about Purnell true? Had she been a victim of abuse and is this why she left, or did she choose to leave simply because she loved the boy in the photograph? Too many questions and it troubled Cabel to know that most would go unanswered.

Of all the things he had learned today, the one that bothered him most was Marigold Peabody's statement that Ada had always seemed to know just what she needed to do to make the people around her happy. Had she learned to be this way in order to survive in the commune or was this subtle manipulation a natural part of her personality?

"You will find them, Amanda's family," Jim said, his voice rough and low.

"Of course." Another impossible promise, but one he would somehow keep.

Jim nodded, then turned to speak with Cabel over the back of the couch. "How many names did she have, do you think?"

Cabel reached for his business case and retrieved the file that contained the papers Detective Finch had found in the murdered private investigator's office. Jim joined him at the desk and together they looked at the newspaper clippings. Cabel had seen them before but his cousin gasped when he looked at the pictures of the girl, same yet different, in each one.

"Abagail Carter, Amelia Croft, Aubrey Clayton, Adelaide Connors." Jim read the names as he studied each photograph. "And these are just the ones we know of, right? Well, I guess we can add Ada Cummings and Amanda Chandler to the list as well." Bitterness tainted his voice.

"We don't have to go any farther," Cabel said. "We know her name and we'll find her family to let them know she died, but we can stop at that."

"But she didn't die, did she? She was murdered, shot dead in my arms." Jim's voice broke. "And somehow none of this matters." He shoved the clippings aside. "She was Amanda, my Amanda. I don't care about her other names, her other lives. I loved her, still do." Tears fell on his cheeks, but he didn't wipe them away. "I need to know the truth."

Jim rushed from the room. Cabel heard quick footsteps on the stairs followed by the slam of his bedroom door.

He gathered the scattered papers and placed them back in the file along with the photos he had taken to the House of David. There was another picture, one he hadn't shown to Jim or Mrs. Marigold. Amanda dressed not as Amanda, rushing up the stairs of an apartment building in Chicago. Cabel turned over the photo and reread the address written there, then retrieved the package of Amanda's things from the office closet. The key he needed was still lodged in the toe of the cheap, black shoe. Although it looked quite ordinary, he hoped it would unlock more than a door.

Next week would start with a critical board meeting and who knew what would happen to his schedule from there. He would go back to Chicago tomorrow and spend Sunday afternoon visiting the apartment of this professional chameleon.

CHAPTER 23

The bitter November wind forced Cabel to hold his hat on his head as he made his way to the address written on the back of the photograph he'd found in Jacob Martin's envelope. The taxi had dropped him at the corner of 19th Street and Dearborn, just a few blocks west of Jacob Martin's office.

Yellow and brown leaves swirled around his feet when he paused in front of the four-story walk-up he sought. Few cars parked along the street and no one was about this cold, cold day. Cabel walked up the concrete steps and opened the apartment building door. The small lobby was bare except for the metal mailboxes that lined the wall. He read the names on them until he found one labeled "A. Cort." Given Amanda's pattern of using the initials A and C, he guessed he'd found the right box. He didn't have the key to open the box and read her mail, but it did identify her apartment number, 3C.

Cabel climbed to the third floor. From the landing he could see the four apartments, two facing 19th Street and the others at the back. He pulled out the key to insert it into the lock of apartment 3C when he realized the door had been broken. It still hung on its hinges so the damage wasn't obvious until you stood next to it, but clearly someone had gotten here before him.

Uncertain what to do, he stood a moment then turned when he heard the door to the neighboring apartment squeak open. A young man with a pale face and oddly shaped eyes stared at him a moment.

"Are you a friend of Miss Alma's or are you one of the bad men that are looking for her?" the boy said with a slight lisp.

"My cousin was a good friend of Miss Alma's. My name is Cabel Evans."

The young man studied the outstretched hand a moment before a childlike smile spread across his face. He flung his apartment door open and gripped Cabel's hand, shaking it vigorously. "My name is Billy and I live here with my momma. Her name is Beatrice and she works at the Cullerton Hotel. That's where she is now. She just serves drinks even though the law says you shouldn't, but she doesn't take the men upstairs like some of the girls do. She has to work like that 'cause my daddy left when I was a baby. He said he didn't want to be around no imbecile son or the stupid woman who done give birth to him, so he left." Billy paused for a breath. "I'm good with my hands and my momma doesn't have to pay all the rent 'cause I fix things around here. So I'm not so dumb, am I?"

"No, I'm sure you're not," Cabel said, now understanding the childlike behavior of this young man. "Do you know if anyone is in her apartment right now?"

Billy shook his head. "Some mean men came here looking for her, pounding on the door and waking everyone up, but they had guns so no one said nothin' cuz we was too scared." Billy's eyes were huge. "They came back a few days later and knocked down the door and looked in her apartment. She wouldn't like that at all." He paused to take a breath. "Those men left and haven't been back since. Another fella came by after that, asking if anyone had worked for Miss Alma, but I didn't say nothing to him. It was our secret. But then I got worried that Miss Alma wasn't back but figured she was scared of the men. I know she was going to move soon and that made me sad but maybe these bad men are why she's leaving. I fixed the door up so it wouldn't be so bad when she came home. She's real nice to me, Miss Alma. I couldn't clean up all the mess inside, but I'll help her when she gets back. I like helpin' Miss Alma. Do you know when she'll be back?"

Cabel's heart cracked a bit at the sight of Billy's eager face and then a bit more when Billy's smile faded.

"She's coming back, isn't she?" he whispered, eyes filled with tears.

Wanting to lie but knowing he couldn't, Cabel said, "I'm sorry, Billy, but no, she isn't. She died a few weeks ago and…"

Billy's howl of despair drowned out the rest of Cabel's words. The boy flung his hard, compact body against Cabel, sobbing as if his world had ended. Given how the young man must view the world, perhaps it had.

Cabel let the boy cry, handing him a handkerchief when the tears slowed.

A hand touched Billy's arm. Both men turned to find an old woman standing there. "Come now, Billy. Stay with me until your mother gets home. We can listen to the radio. You'd like that, wouldn't you?"

Billy nodded and allowed himself to be led down the hall to one of the other apartments. He shuffled inside before the woman looked at Cabel and said, "He's not supposed to talk to anyone he doesn't know so when I heard voices out here I listened at my door to be sure he was all right." She shook her head. "He has no common sense but a huge heart. I think Alma did too in her own way. That poor woman. She was nice to Billy, but I can't say I'm surprised she's dead, not with the man she was seeing and who he works for."

"Who was she seeing?" Cabel asked. He didn't want to know this woman's information, but he needed to know. Jim needed the truth.

The old woman held up a hand. "If you don't know, I suggest you leave and stay well away from here."

"But I need answers."

"Then I'll pray for you, like I do all fools who wander into danger despite all warnings." She closed her apartment door. A few moments later the sounds of music drifted through the hall.

Knowing he didn't have the luxury of heeding her warnings, Cabel walked back to apartment 3C and jimmied the door open. The contents of the tiny sitting room lay in broken shambles across the floor, a scene not so different from the one he had found at the Northside apartment of the woman he still thought of as Amanda.

Then he had felt the weight of Jim's grief and worry over who had killed the woman he loved. Now he waded into the mess of this second apartment, leased by the same woman under a different name, and felt disgust. She had used Jim with a cold calculation, just as she had assuredly used the other man she had been hired to distract. Hired but not paid. That fact, like a sore tooth, bothered him in a dull yet constant manner because it made no sense given what he had learned of this woman.

Whoever she was, Amanda hadn't deserved Jim's love or Cabel's efforts to find her killer. Though in truth if everyone received what they truly merited for their sins, he would be buried in a French grave and Jon Warner would be alive, married to Elizabeth, and perhaps have a son named Cabel. Shaking his head, he reminded himself that it didn't matter. He had made a promise to Jim, and he supposed that even Amanda was allowed some measure of justice.

He surveyed the mess and noticed a smashed pile of packing crates in the corner. She had succeeded in distracting Jim. Maybe her other job had ended as well and she planned to leave but had been killed instead. He doubted there were answers here but he would try.

Stepping over a broken footstool and a smashed crate, he wondered if there was anything left to be found. Did the men who searched the apartment know she was dead or simply missing? And who was the one who returned later? Had he hired Amanda or was he the man she targeted? These questions danced with the specks of dust that swirled in the light from the windows but the answers remained in the shadows.

Even through the destruction, it was evident that Amanda's furnishings were cheaply made and of modest content. He could identify the remains of a loveseat, chair, and small table. A lamp lay shattered nearby, as did a small figurine. Kicking aside a clump of cushion stuffing he found a wicker suitcase that looked as though someone had stomped on it. He knelt down and pried it open but found nothing to reward him for his efforts.

The small bedroom had also been roughly searched, with the cheap, gaudy dresses ripped from their hooks and flung aside. The mattress had been cut open and the small vanity lay smashed on its side. A broken bottle of inexpensive perfume added the cloying scent of roses to the wasteland. A cheap hat crumpled in the corner once again brought to mind the other apartment and how clever Amanda had been when it came to hiding secrets.

The small kitchenette lay on the other side of the sitting room and held only a dented hot plate for cooking and a small icebox that someone had shoved over. Spoiled milk puddled beneath it, adding a sickly stench to the scene. The cabinets and drawers had been flung open, their meager contents dumped on the floor. There was no convenient oven for her to hide anything.

A small closet served as the pantry, but as with the apartment near Addison, there was little in the way of foodstuffs. A piece of paper stuck in a glob of jam caught Cabel's attention. He knelt down to pick it up. It was a receipt for four months' rent in the name of Alma Cort. She had leased it the week before she had rented the Northside apartment from Mrs. Marshall.

He looked into the pantry as he rose and noticed something odd. Stepping over the jam, he went into the little room and maneuvered himself to his knees so that he could reach under a low shelf in the dark corner. His fingers strained until they touched metal. Cabel dragged his treasure into the light. The metal pie safe was pale cream with bunches of cherries painted on the sides. He carried it to the kitchen counter before opening the hinged door.

A brown paper package lay inside. On top of it lay a piece of paper with an odd, hand-drawn picture of a crescent moon with a line above and below. The drawing meant nothing to him but, since Amanda kept it, Cabel believed it might be important. He folded it into a small square before tucking it into his coat pocket.

Turning his attention to the package, he found it to be nearly identical to the one she hid in the other apartment. He felt deep anger for this professional liar, but he realized that Amanda understood men. Few of them would think to look for something hidden in an oven or on the floor in a dark corner of a near-empty pantry.

He used a kitchen knife to cut the twine and found what he expected to see. A fashionable, expensive day dress that she would have worn as Amanda and a pair of matching shoes lay carefully folded within the brown paper. Cabel looked in the toes of the shoes and checked the pockets of the dress but there were no helpful keys, notes, or other clues to be found. She had been smart, he realized, to have one outfit of the other personality in each apartment. If her plans changed unexpectedly, she could still play her necessary roles.

Cabel gently refolded the dress and wrapped it and the shoes back in the brown paper, not bothering with the twine. He'd take them back to his hotel, knowing at some point Jim would want to see what he'd found.

He left the apartment, tugging the door back into place as best as possible. The music from the radio in the front apartment drifted into the hallway and he hoped Billy had recovered from the sad news of his friend's death. Cabel sighed. One more innocent was mourning the death of a woman who didn't deserve such consideration.

In the lobby he took a closer look at Amanda's mailbox and found that it too had been broken into and was now empty. Cabel felt dejected as he left the building. He had another name to add to the list of Amanda's aliases but no idea of what to do next.

As he reached the sidewalk, a car pulled up alongside him and a gun was shoved through the open window.

"Get in."

CHAPTER 24

No other words were spoken. Cabel stared at the gun then looked into the cold, flat eyes of the man who pointed it at him. "Comply with the order or die," those were his choices. Cabel opened the back door of the car and slid into the seat. They were racing down the street before the car door closed.

The second man in the front seat turned, assessing his captive as if deciding where to shoot first, then motioned with his gun for Cabel to give him the package. He handed it over, expecting the man to unwrap it and ask questions. Instead, he put it on the floor near his feet then gazed out the window with a bored expression. Cabel wasn't fooled. Both the driver and his companion were tense, though he didn't know if it was from worry or excitement.

After Cabel's encounter with Capone, he had made an effort to educate himself about the gangster. They were in his territory and these men were probably in his employ. His hands began to shake so he stared out the window and began to identify everything he saw, a bench, car, or lamppost, anything to keep his mind grounded in the present.

They drove south for a few blocks before turning east toward the lake. There was no marker indicating that they had left the Levee District and were now in the Near South Side, but it was obvious all the same. The buildings were better kept and the hotels appeared to conduct legal business.

They stopped in front of the Metropole Hotel. Both men exited the car and the driver opened Cabel's door, gun plainly visible in its shoulder holster. They escorted him to the lobby where men with machine guns eyed him suspiciously.

"Is he in?" the driver asked.

Someone grunted an affirmative.

"Call up and let them know we're coming. The boss is going to want to talk to this sap." The driver grabbed Cabel's arm and shoved him toward the elevator. The lead ball of anxiety in his stomach grew heavier with each floor they passed.

Several armed men met them on the fourth floor. One stepped forward and patted Cabel down, searching for hidden weapons. When the man signaled that Cabel was unarmed the rest of the group relaxed. The driver grabbed his arm again and marched him down the hall until they reached room 418. The door cracked open and a brown eye assessed them. Apparently satisfied, the guard opened wide and hauled Cabel to the center of the room.

Al Capone ended a conversation before turning to see who had entered. His eyes widened in surprised recognition. Taking the cigar out of his mouth, he said, "Well, if it isn't Mr. Wrong-Place-Wrong-Time." The men in the room laughed but Capone and Cabel didn't join them.

Capone turned to the driver and asked, "Where did you find him?"

The driver told this story, emphasizing his cleverness. There wasn't much to tell but Capone hung on every word. When the driver finished, Capone nodded. "Good work, Ricky."

The man beamed with pride until Capone nodded toward the door. "You and Floyd get back to the Cullerton. I'll let you know when I have something else I need you to do." He turned to Cabel, the driver forgotten. The mob leader walked to a large padded chair and sat. A footstool was hastily shoved under his raised feet. He motioned for Cabel to step closer. "You look better than the last time I saw you, still pale but steadier."

Cabel nodded but didn't speak.

Capone smiled and pointed at Cabel with his cigar. "This is a shrewd one. Smart too. If he lives long enough some of you could learn a thing or two from him." He turned back to Cabel. "How did you know Alma Cort."

"I didn't."

The men laughed and this time Capone joined in, shaking his head in disbelief. "You just happen to show up at the apartment of a woman I'm searching for? One I've promised a one-thousand-dollar reward to the man who brings her to me alive? And you say you don't know her?"

"Yes. But I do know that no one will collect the bounty from you. She's dead."

"She's what?" The ice in Capone's voice froze every man in the suite. He stood and walked toward Cabel, who fought against the urge to back away. Soon they were nearly nose to nose. "Tell me."

Cabel faltered, unsure of where to begin.

Capone stared at him a moment, then sighed. "I've seen that look on your face before. Someone get this sap a chair. I have a feeling this is going to take a while." He returned to his seat. "And let's clear the room. No, not you, Fratti. Sit back down and we'll see if you'll go home to your family or get fitted for a wood suit."

Feet shuffled as several men filed out. A few moments later the door closed and only Capone, Cabel, and four other men remained. A hard chair was placed in front of Capone's throne. Cabel sat and looked up at the most dangerous man he had ever met.

Capone nodded. "Start at the beginning. I'll tell you when to stop."

"My father and uncle wanted to distract my cousin so they could maneuver around him on a business venture. They hired a girl my cousin knew as Amanda Channing to be that distraction." Cabel continued, telling Capone everything he had learned about Amanda/Alma, ending with his men grabbing him off the street outside the apartment on 19th Street.

Throughout the rendition, Capone's eyes never left Cabel's. Unnerved but determined, he didn't look away until he had finished.

The gangster nodded and studied the glowing tip of his cigar a moment. Cabel nearly sagged in relief.

"Louie, look through those old papers, about two weeks back, and see if there's anything about a girl being shot in front of the Blue Diamond Club." For several minutes the only sound in the room was of newspaper pages being turned.

"Here it is, Uncle, just like he said," A youngish man with dark hair and easy manners stepped forward and handed Capone the paper. The mobster read the article, grunting as he finished, then tossed the paper aside.

"She's been dead all this time," he said more to himself than the men in the room. With a wave of his hand, the gangster motioned for someone to come forward. A man who looked more like a clerk than a gangster came into Cabel's view, visibly shaking from head to toe. "I guess you were right, Fratti. You weren't stealing my booze. The girl and whoever hired her set you up as the fall guy."

Fratti nodded.

Capone sat back in his chair and smoked his cigar, blowing its smoke toward the ceiling to join a thickening cloud. The ticking mantel clock was the only sound in the room. As the minute grew to two, then five, Cabel felt his nerves stress nearly beyond bearing. The distant booms of exploding shells and the rat-a-tat-tat of machine gun fire filled his mind. Fighting to stay in the present, he grasped onto a single image, the red tip of Capone's cigar.

With a grunt and nod, the gangster leaned toward Cabel. "Here's my dilemma, Mr. Evans. What you've said is completely plausible, probably even true."

"Lay off," said a portly man seated near the window, his brown eyes wide with shock.

"Pipe down, Jake. You don't know this sap, but I do." Capone turned his attention to Cabel. "Oh yes, I know you very well."

The man's smile made Cabel's stomach clench.

"After our meeting at the Charades Club, I decided to check you out, see if you were hinky or on the up and up. Here's what I learned. You were supposed to be the next leader of your family's business until the war messed with your head. Still you did right by them until you used your father as a punching bag. You disappeared for five years, came back to live in your house on the bluff in St. Joseph where an elderly couple takes care of you."

Cabel felt lightheaded.

"Oh yes, I know all about them and how they are the only family you care about, except your cousin Jim. Do you understand what I'm saying?"

"Yes," Cabel forced out.

Capone studied Cabel a moment then nodded. "Good. I need you to know who will be hurt if you aren't square with me. See, I'm going to tell you what Alma Cort did and to do that, you'll learn more about my business than anyone outside of my gang. Well, anyone who's still alive."

Jake gave a nasty chuckle.

"I could just leave now," Cabel said standing. His legs shook but he needed to protect the people he cared about.

"You could try, but you won't make it off this floor alive. Then what will happen to your cousin and the family business? What about your housekeeper and her husband? You leave, you die. You tell anyone about what you learn here today, what you will learn from this job you have, well, we'll start with the old couple and work our way to your cousin."

Cabel sat, his eyes never leaving Capone's.

"Smart. Now, let me tell you how this Alma doll helped someone steal my booze." He was yelling by the time he finished his sentence. He relit his cigar and puffed in silence. After a moment he visibly relaxed and leaned back in his chair. Except for the gun on a table near his right hand, he could have passed for a father about to tell his son a bedtime story.

"First, you need to understand a few things. Winter's coming and that means it's more difficult and dangerous to get booze and beer in from Canada. We fly the beer in by seaplanes that land on a small lake in Wisconsin where I own a house and a lot of land. Most of the booze comes from the Canadian distilleries across the river from Detroit. With the coppers patrolling the lake, it's safer to drive it here than bring it by boat."

Cabel knew this last bit, having stumbled across the information a few months earlier while trying to solve a different murder. He decided not to enlighten Capone.

"The thing is, the planes can't land on a frozen lake and the river gets too icy and dangerous to cross, so I have to stock up on supplies to hold me and my customers until spring." He shrugged. "We still have my breweries and distilleries in Cicero, but people like the other stuff too. Since early September, we've been bringing in extra crates of Canadian booze and beer to see us through the winter."

"Kind of like squirrels," Fratti added.

All eyes turned to the sallow-skinned man, who paled further at finding himself under the scrutiny of these powerful and dangerous men.

Capone studied him a moment then smiled. In a soft, menacing voice, he said, "That's right, Fratti, but someone was stealing my nuts, weren't they? And you helped."

"No, I didn't. Not on purpose."

"Shut up." Capone turned away in disgust and focused on Cabel as he picked up the thread of his story. "We store some of the booze in the basements of my clubs in the Loop and some of it in the tunnels under the Green Mill, a bar on the North Side. I'd like to keep more of the stock there, but it's in Moran's territory so we don't want to make it too tempting for him to reclaim it, understand?"

Cabel nodded. "Keep the product in different places so if one is raided, the whole stash isn't confiscated."

"Product." Capone grinned. "I like that. The thing is there is one place where we store most of our winter product and that's in the tunnels under the Cullerton Hotel. There's over twenty-five miles of abandoned rail and service tunnels down there. From those tunnels we can deliver booze to almost anywhere in the Levee without coming above ground. It's safer for us and the speakeasies. The cops don't see a thing." His smile hardened. "The thing is that there are coal delivery tunnels and others that have been there forever, so long that no one remembers them. There're also sunken rooms, even whole houses that people have forgotten about. One was used as a brothel, back in the day."

The men in the room chuckled but Capone's eyes showed no humor.

"We don't know where some of these tunnels are or where they lead. Even the tunnels we use all the time have hidden rooms or unused passageways and many of them have above-ground accesses that pop up in the oddest places."

Like the rediscovered basement below a barbershop, Cabel realized.

"We use that to our advantage," Capone said. "This time of year, when we have more deliveries than usual, we mix up where we take the booze underground so the police don't get suspicious. Fratti," the mobster gestured to the man, who flinched, "met up with this girl at Lucky's, just a couple of blocks from here. She said she was waiting on a fellow who never showed so Fratti here buys this doll a drink. They get to talkin' and then Fratti decides... what was it you said?"

Fratti cleared his throat. "It was like she was made just for me."

Capone saw Cabel flinch. "What's wrong?"

"My cousin, Jim, met Amanda the same way. They were at the theater and Amanda lost her escort so Jim took her to the box he was sharing with friends. Later, he told me that it was like she was made just for him.

"And what did that mean?"

Cabel shook his head. "I'm not sure. Just that she liked the same things he did and enjoyed the same music. They liked to go dancing at the clubs and I know he introduced her to his parents. She was beautiful, upper class, and very distracting."

The gangster grunted then turned to Fratti. "Is that how she was with you?"

"Oh no," he said. "She liked dog races and gambling, stuff like that. She wore dresses that made sure a man noticed her… Anyway, she didn't mind if I had a wife and we met at her place to, you know…"

Cabel closed his eyes. This woman had betrayed Jim on more levels than he had imagined.

"She wasn't around all the time. Said she had to visit her mother who lived over in Michigan or stay at a friend's place for a few days. I guess that was when she was with your cousin."

Cabel nodded. "Possibly."

"Well, she was good at her job. Too bad she didn't tell me what she could do or I'd have hired her myself," Capone said. "While she was distracting your cousin, she was getting information from Fratti here. He was in charge of the delivery and storage of the booze and is a lot smarter than he looks, if he thinks with his brain that is. He arranges the dates and times, which storage rooms and tunnel accesses we'll use, the whole shebang. Anyway, he told his new girlfriend where and when all of my booze deliveries in the Levee would happen. Information she passed along to someone else. Whoever it was, I want him found so I can take my time and kill him slowly."

CHAPTER 25

Capone's icy rage silenced the room. His breathing grew ragged and his eyes burned with hate. "Someone hired this girl to get close to Fratti so he could glom my booze, and if things had gone as planned we might not have discovered it for weeks. Still worse, he made me look like a fool in front of these men," he gestured to the others in the room. "If Moran finds out about this, he might think I'm weak and make a play for my territory." He looked at Jake and another man who sat cold and deadly by the windows. "My own men know better, don't they?"

"Sure, Snorky," Jake said.

The second man nodded. Capone stared him down until he said, "Sure, boss."

"That's right," Capone said, still staring at the second man. "I am the boss. You stick with me and you get rich. You go against me and you die."

"Understood," the man said with more deference.

Capone grunted in acknowledgement of the confirmation of his status. He turned back to Cabel and asked, "Can you imagine what it means, that someone knew when and where we'd be bringing the booze into the tunnels?"

Cabel thought a moment. "Your delivery would be well-guarded, so anyone who wanted to rob you wouldn't want to stop the truck or take it on the road."

"True."

He thought about the tunnels and understood. "If the shipments were large, it would take a lot of men to bring it down and store it. If you knew beforehand where that would be you could find a forgotten nook or make a hiding place to stash a crate or two and no one would notice. With enough deliveries, that could add up quickly."

"I knew you were smart. See, Fratti here, he stayed above ground with the truck and counted the crates as they were taken below, to make sure that they matched what we paid for. If someone had a hiding place along the route between the tunnel entrance and the storage room, no one would notice a case or two slipping away and Fratti wouldn't know it was missing."

Cabel nodded. "So how did you find out?"

Capone gave a humorless laugh. "Cognac. Not the crap from Little Italy in Arkansas. I buy that stuff too, but this was different. Aged. French. Almost impossible to get and expensive as hell, but I'd been working on my connections for months. I finally had a shipment arranged through Canada. I'd waited for this deal a long time. Twelve crates at eight hundred dollars each with twenty-four bottles per crate. A lot of money to pay for booze even for me, but I knew I could sell it for ten times that much. That's how rare it is here and I'm the only one in the Midwest who could get it.

"I had a special storage room with a new metal door and a padlock with one key." He fished in his vest pocket and pulled it out, his face turning sour. "I made sure I was at the Charades Club that night, having dinner with the mayor, so no one would know that a special delivery was taking place. Didn't want to be here until the booze was locked up."

Just in case the police stopped the truck or saw the crates being taken underground, Cabel realized. Capone risked the arrest of his men but not himself.

"I couldn't wait to get my hands on the cognac," Capone continued. "Everyone knew that I was going into the tunnels later that night, grab a few bottles, and then lock the rest up until the holidays. People tend to splurge when they're celebrating, especially on New Year's."

"How much was stolen?"

"All of it," Capone roared. He stood and began to pace. "I should have gone back to the Levee after dinner like I planned, but there was a great band playing at the club and some new girls we wanted to try. We didn't leave until morning. I had my driver bring me straight to the Cullerton so I could grab those bottles but when I opened the door the room was empty."

"How?"

"Someone knew which room we were using and what the plan had been. They found an old tunnel that ran parallel along the back of the one with the storage room." He stomped back to his chair and sat. "I think they planned to dig from the old tunnel over to the cognac room but found part of an old house instead. The guys who built the old tunnel just bricked it over, which made it real easy for the thieves to go through that room and knock down the wall of my locked room." The gangster leaned forward and yelled, "They carted the whole lot out the back and we haven't seen it since."

No one spoke.

"The location of the room was a secret. I had the new door installed on it the same time as some of the others. No one knew which one I'd use or how we'd bring the crates down. So, Mr. Evans, it's obvious these bastards had a lot of time to plan. Probably knew everything nearly as soon as I told Fratti. Now, what would be a smart question?"

"When did you first know when the cognac would be delivered?" Cabel responded.

Capone smiled. "This is why I like you. You're scared, and you should be, but that doesn't stop you from thinking." He relit his cigar, which had gone out as he'd paced. "I had the final delivery date in August and started making plans. A few weeks before Alma Cort showed up at Lucky's." He glared at Fratti.

Cabel waited several moments while the mob boss puffed on his cigar. Finally he said, "Anyone in the Levee might have heard about the cognac, but knowing to use Fratti, what kind of woman he would find attractive, and to be familiar with the tunnels?"

"Exactly."

"Now wait a minute," Jake said, "I still think Moran's men did this."

Capone smirked. "Really? And what do you think, Carlo?"

"Had to be an insider, one of the low-level guys in the outfit because they were hauling the booze. Anyone else wandering around in the tunnels would have been noticed."

"They could have been working for someone else," Jake said.

Carlo shrugged. "Maybe."

Knowing his question was dangerous, Cabel asked it anyway. "And you trust the men in this room?"

Capone laughed while the others yelled in protest. "Calm down, the sap here asks a good question." He turned to Cabel. "Jake was with me in the Charade's Club and Carlo joined us later. If they were part of this, they would have phoned to tell their people that I wouldn't be in the tunnels until the next day. My nephew, Louie—" Capone pointed a finger at the young man standing near the fireplace "—was visiting his family out in Chicago Heights that night and stayed there until the next morning. I spoke with his mother to make sure he was where he said he was.

"Fratti didn't know about the change in plans, just got the booze down into the tunnels. Carlo made sure the shipment was locked up and brought me the key. Only Jake, Carlo, and I knew I'd be coming down the next morning rather than that night like I had planned."

"But why steal it so soon?" Cabel asked. "As you said, they had a few weeks at least."

"Ah, Mr. Evans, they wanted to take it as soon as possible so they could get it above ground. Someone would notice a man hauling a crate of booze out of the tunnels, but not a bottle hidden in a boot or a bag. There were 280 bottles to be smuggled out. You need time to do that and not get caught." He sighed. "Fratti was the only one who knew enough for it to work. He had to convince me he wasn't the one who glommed the booze. I finally decided to believe him. Show him your hand, Fratti."

The man raised his left hand and Cabel noticed that his smallest finger was missing, the wound still red and angry. He swallowed bile to keep from vomiting on Capone's shoes. He looked up to find the gangster watching him.

"Since Fratti wasn't lying, I figured it was time to meet this Alma doll. I sent men to her apartment, which was empty, and then they searched the Levee for her. The glomming stopped the same time she did a runner so I figured she was in on it. I wanted her alive to find out who she was working for but I guess that isn't possible," Capone glared at Cabel. "I think the booze is still down in the tunnels but there're too many hiding places and I'm running out of patience. I've told a lot of my clients, wealthy people, about this shipment, getting them interested in the cognac, you know. I need to show them some soon or have people thinking I'm a liar."

"Why do you think it's still down there?"

"Because the plan changed, didn't it. The glommers thought they had a whole month to get the booze out, but I found it missing right away, didn't I? Since then I've doubled the security in the Levee and my men search any truck or car that seems like it doesn't belong. I have the men randomly searched for bottles. The gang thinks I'm worried about Moran or a petty theft, but I want to be sure that whoever stole my cognac won't be able to move it."

"Then we did the inventory," Fratti added helpfully.

Cabel wondered if the man's brains had become addled from living for two weeks in a state of constant fear.

"Good point. Why don't you explain to Mr. Wrong-Place-Wrong-Time what you've been doing while we've been searching for your doll?"

Fratti licked his lips. "I did an inventory of everything we'd taken in since September, which is when we start storing extra booze and beer." His eyes darted to Capone's then back to Cabel. "I found that the number of crates of booze we had in the storerooms didn't match what was taken into the tunnels."

"Tell the man when the glomming started."

Fratti paled. "A week after Alma and I started seeing each other."

"And how much was taken?" Capone asked in a toneless voice.

Fratti started to sway on his feet, "Forty six cases of booze in all, including some of the stuff we buy from the Irish barber."

"Forget about the barber. Explain to Mr. Evans why someone would take the booze and not the beer."

"You steal a bottle of beer you sell a bottle of beer. You steal a bottle of booze and you can sell ten or twelve drinks, more if you're stingy, make a lot more money this way."

"And they stole forty six crates of it," Capone yelled.

Fratti fainted.

Capone stared at the prone figure then turned his attention to Cabel. "Whoever took the booze started small, just two crates the first time then five, and then eight. I think they were testing out their system and we never even knew. I'm sure they had plenty of time to move most of that above ground, though there was a Canadian shipment of booze that came in two days before the cognac so those eight crates might still be around."

Cabel thought about the situation. "You have extra patrols down there, but you don't have men looking for the stolen crates?"

"Right now, only the men in this room know what was stolen from me." Capone's eyes glittered with hatred. "Other than Louie here, who normally works in the tunnels, I can't trust anyone else to search. It would raise too many questions."

"There're a lot of tunnels and it's taking a long time," Louie said. "I think I found a few places that were used for hiding some of the crates as they were being unloaded, but they must have been moved to a safer hiding spot later or taken above ground." He shook his head. "Before this, I had several guys I would have trusted to help me search but now..." He shrugged.

Cabel nodded in understanding. "When my father and uncle first tried to hire Amanda, or Alma, she refused the work, but a few weeks later she accepted. Apparently she had been hired by another person for a second job. The timing matches with your situation, but how would someone in a low level of your organization even know about her? Her targets were always rich young men and I'm guessing she got jobs through referrals. My uncle learned about her from a friend she had worked for. Would your people have those kinds of business connections?"

"Good question." Capone turned to Jake and Carlo. "What do you two think?"

The three men discussed the matter. Cabel tried to listen but soon became distracted by Fratti, who had started to moan and shiver. Having witnessed men in shock at the Front, Cabel knew the symptoms. Glancing around the room, he saw a blanket on the back of a couch and rose to get it.

"Sit down." Capone snapped.

Cabel pointed to Fratti then at the blanket.

Capone rolled his eyes but nodded his permission.

Once Fratti was wrapped in the blanket Cabel returned to his chair knowing there was nothing else he could do for the man. Louie stood nearby, watching Cabel's every move.

The men finished their conversation and Capone turned to Cabel. "I need to think about this question some more." He laughed, this time with genuine amusement. "If a sap had to walk into this mess, I have to say I'm glad it was you." His smile slipped away and his eyes went flat. "You made a promise to your cousin and that promise has dumped you into the middle of my business. Seems to me you find the girl's killer, you find my thief. Do that and you and your family are safe. Fail..." he shrugged, picked up his gun, and shot Fratti through the heart.

Cabel stared at the dead man then back at Capone, who nodded, pleased that his message had been received.

He said, "Louie, call downstairs and have someone take Mr. Evans to his hotel then make sure this mess is cleaned up."

CHAPTER 26

Cabel sat at the head of the boardroom table the next morning, drinking his third cup of coffee in a desperate effort to stay alert. The board was in the middle of one of its most important meetings in years and he struggled to pay attention. The war had raged through his dreams last night, making a mockery of what little sleep he had managed. Capone's threats and the gunshot that killed Fratti still rang in his ears. Despite these distractions, he needed to focus his attention. He reminded himself that at the moment he could do nothing about Capone, but he could protect his company.

"How could Jim have signed the papers and allow this to happen?" George Foster asked. "He's always done what's best for Evans Manufacturing and I can't believe he would have knowingly put the company in this position."

"That's irrelevant. He signed them and Frank and I are going ahead with our new business," Edward Evans said. "I know that others believe my brother's and my plans to be unprofitable and perhaps damaging for Evans Manufacturing." He paused to glare at his son. "However, we believe that those people are shortsighted, unwilling to see the possibilities afforded our company through the opening of retail stores."

"But..." George began.

"No. What you all fail to understand is that this matter is settled, regardless of how Jim came to sign these papers." Edward glanced at Cabel then back to the rest of the board. "My brother and I believe that our new retail stores will expand the reach of Evans Manufacturing and benefit each and every one of us."

"Perhaps you could elaborate on that position," Christopher Stanton said. "Evans Manufacturing is a privately held company and, other than the shareholders who are all members of the Evans family, we are paid a stipend to sit on this board and offer our expertise. Even so, your father, James Cabel Evans, structured this board so that we have certain legal authorities and responsibilities. Our decisions can only be overridden by 100 percent agreement of the shareholders. If the company fails, our personal and professional reputations will be damaged. You jeopardize more than your financial futures with this proposition."

"But that won't happen. You must trust that Frank and I know what we are doing." Edward said to Christopher, who shook his head in return. Edward turned away and addressed the board. "Your responsibilities will expand with the addition of the subsidiary company and so will your compensation."

"Yet we lose it all if this scheme goes as Jim and Cabel expect," George said. "Your leadership in the past has caused significant difficulties for this company, and your son and nephew present valid reasons not to pursue this new avenue of business."

"My son is an unstable man of questionable business talents and this is not a scheme but a viable and lucrative venture."

The men at the table fell silent as all eyes turned to Cabel. Edward Evans smiled with undisguised pleasure. Cabel answered with a genuine smile of his own. Frank and Edward had taken unconscionable actions over the years simply for personal gain. Cabel felt no loyalty or respect for these men and his father's words no longer held any power over him.

Edward's smile faltered in the face of his son's calm and in that moment he lost the last bit of authority he had struggled so hard to keep in his grasp.

"You know my objections to this venture, as does every man here. I will ask, both as your son and as acting president of Evans Manufacturing, that you desist in moving this project forward."

"You know I won't."

Cabel nodded. "Unfortunately, I do. In light of this, I have several propositions to make to the board at this time."

"It won't matter. There's nothing you can do to stop me," Frank Evans said, rising to stand next to his brother.

Cabel ignored them. "Gentlemen, as Christopher has explained, the elder Evans men found and exploited a loophole in the company bylaws which has allowed them to proceed with this otherwise-unsupported project. I now ask that you vote to amend those bylaws as recommended by our legal counsel to correct this oversight. All those in favor…"

The vote carried twelve to five, with Frank, Edward, and three of their friends opposing the change.

"Thank you. Next, I propose that the board accept the following modifications to the new venture."

"You can't do that," Edward stated, rising to his feet again. "This is finished and the board has no say."

"That isn't entirely true." Christopher said with a hint of anger in his voice. "There are many things this board can do and I recommend that we follow Cabel's leadership in this matter."

"What, then? What do you propose?"

"We limit the funding of the project to one store front and a thirty-thousand-dollar initial capitalization," Cabel answered.

Frank and Edward shouted objections. Cabel waited until they quieted before continuing. "This proposal will allow the project to prove itself before being expanded or discontinued."

"You can't do this," Frank yelled.

Cabel turned to Christopher to explain the position. "You have formed the company under the legal operations of Evans Manufacturing, utilizing its funds, staff, reputation, and relationships as part of this process. Although the board cannot stop you from going forward, it can advise and structure the process, which we shall do."

Edward glared at Cabel with pure hatred, raised his cane and pointed it at his son. "If you take this action, I shall remove myself from the company and force you to purchase all of my shares, and Frank's as well."

Frank looked up at his brother in shock, sputtering objections.

Cabel stood to face his father, the table and their past between them. "Father, this is a reasonable compromise that will allow you and Uncle Frank to show us all that opening these stores is a smart business move."

"But I shouldn't have to prove anything to you, or anyone else for that matter." He stood defiant with Frank tugging at his suit jacket, trying to get his attention. Edward shrugged him off, leaned forward with his fists on the table and said, "If you defy me in this, I will break from the company and take as much business as possible with me."

Cabel nodded. "That is your choice but understand this: you cannot use any Evans Manufacturing funds to start or operate such a business. Any company money you have used to date must be repaid since this project will no longer be under our purview." Edward shouted in protest but Cabel ignored him. Raising his voice, he added, "You cannot use any other company resources, though if staff members wish to resign their positions to work for you, we won't object." He spread his arms and said, "The choice is yours. Accept the challenge of demonstrating the financial viability and benefits of your venture to Evens Manufacturing or go your own way."

The smattering of applause from several board members surprised and pleased Cabel. Edward scowled.

"I will not accept an ultimatum from you, boy."

"Then accept it from us," George Foster said. "Cabel's proposal makes sense and is a reasonable comprise to an unfortunate situation."

"I agree," another board member added.

"Let's put this to a vote, then." Christopher stood. "All in favor of accepting Cabel's proposal to modify the new venture please raise your hands." The results were the same as before, twelve for and five against the proposal. "That's settled then." Christopher turned to Edward who shook with rage. "As Cabel said, stay with the company or repay the funds you've spent and go off on your own. If you want to sell your shares in Evans Manufacturing, I'm sure Cabel and Jim could finance a purchase but, under the bylaws, you must give them three months to do so. Let us know your decision.

"I believe that is all we need to address today. Thank you, gentlemen, for your guidance at this meeting. We are adjourned."

Edward stormed from the room with Frank following, slump shouldered, in his wake. Their friends hurried after them while the rest of the board members gathered their business cases and other belongings.

George Foster walked to Cabel's side and extended his hand. Cabel shook it, grateful for the man's support.

"This is such a messy business and I wish your father and uncle would see reason, not that those two have done so in the past." He sighed. "The problem, as I see it, is that regardless of their decision, they can cause a lot of trouble for this company. I hope you're ready for a war."

CHAPTER 27

George Foster's dire prediction followed Cabel like a death knell as he walked to his office. He opened the door to find Katherine sitting in the chair by his desk, a few pieces of papers in her hand.

"Rumors I've heard say that you had a rough board meeting," she said with a sympathetic smile.

"It was," Cabel said as he sat behind his desk and reached to take the papers from her. "I've been told that my father and uncle will make trouble no matter what happens at this point."

"That's probably true, but honestly, I think this was coming, one way or another, ever since Jim was made president of the company. Mr. Edward and Mr. Frank could accept that Jim was the man really in charge as long as they retained the titles of co-presidents, but when Christopher convinced them to make Jim's true position official, well..." She sighed. "I think they saw it as losing respect even though everyone knew the truth of who ran things here."

Cabel nodded, thinking of his aunt who wore the latest fashions despite the fact that they didn't suit her and of Edward and Frank who cared more for appearances than what was best for the family business. He turned his thoughts to Capone and the other problem that plagued him as he glanced at the papers she had brought.

"What is this?"

"These are the transcriptions from the notebook you found in Jacob Martin's office. Maisie finished them this morning and brought them to me. There was one symbol she couldn't translate and asked me to look at it, but it doesn't mean anything from a shorthand perspective. The investigator must have thought it was important because he wrote it down."

Cabel briefly scanned the four pages. As he suspected when first looking at the notebook, most of the information was about payments received and paid, but there were additional notes as well. He set them aside to read in more detail when he had the time. "What else is happening that I need to know?"

She fidgeted in the chair and his stomach clenched. "Mathias Trenton from the Sears and Roebuck's Purchasing Department called and asked for a meeting."

His head began to throb and he closed his eyes against the pain. He didn't need to be here, he reminded himself, this wasn't his company anymore. He opened his eyes to find Katherine studying, worry in her eyes. Biting back a sigh, he knew that she needed him here, as did Jim. "Call him back and find out when he's available to meet. But first, find out where he likes to dine and see if they have a table open, lunch, dinner, whatever fits in with Trenton's schedule."

She nodded and left, closing the door softly behind her.

IIIII

Several telephone calls later, including one to Jim, Cabel had a better understanding of what George Foster had meant; they were truly in a war against Edward and Frank. Three of Evans Manufacturing's primary suppliers of raw materials called to ask about order changes and Cabel had to make excuses for the confusion, apologize for the mistakes, and assure these companies that all was well. These were small problems designed to have the businessmen question his competency, not damage the company, and the effort seemed to be a success.

Cabel rubbed his hands over his face, tired from his encounter with Capone and the sleepless night that followed. Terror was a strong motivator, but was not conducive to rest. Jim, Marta, and Jorge were in grave danger, and the responsibility of protecting them had reawakened a darkness that had birthed within him during the horrors of battle. The war had damaged him and, although he had successfully fought against this beast within for nearly five years, it had broken free one terrible day. It took mere moments to lose his family, his place in the company, his self-respect. His long exile in New Orleans had served as penance and the last several months in Michigan had helped him heal. The darkness had slipped into the shadows but now it stirred again. He didn't know if he was strong enough to battle his demons, Capone, and his father all at once, but he had no choice but to try.

He took a deep breath and read the note that Katherine had slipped to him during his last telephone call. The lunch meeting with Mr. Trenton was scheduled for one o'clock at the Congress Hotel restaurant. Cabel checked his watch. He had nearly an hour until the meeting and the hotel was located across from Grant Park, just a few minutes' walk from his office.

Deciding that his mind might be clearer if he focused on something else for the next several minutes, he picked up the transcribed notes made by Jacob Martin. The pages, like the notebook, were divided into two sections. First was a list of dates from someone the private investigator identified as "Mr. Suit" that documented weekly deposits of three hundred dollars into a bank account.

Nauseous, Cabel set the papers aside. Most of the people in the building made between thirty-five and forty-five dollars a week, yet his father and uncle were willing to pay nearly ten times that amount to destroy Jim and serve their own ends. The first time he had looked through the notebook he had been more concerned about learning what he could about Amanda's true identity. This time the coldness of the arrangement was obvious and made him ill.

So much more was at stake now than there had been just a day before. He needed to put his feelings aside if he were to keep Jim, Marta, and Jorge alive. He returned to the tally. The investigator kept thirty dollars and transferred the rest to an account in the name of A. Collins at the Franklin National Bank. The deposits started about a week before Jim first met Amanda and ended the week of her death.

The second section of the ledger was kept for someone identified as "Slick," a name which would not help Cabel identify the man. At least he assumed it was a man. Unlike his father, Slick made only a single deposit of one hundred and fifty dollars and Mr. Martin retained all of it. Why would Amanda have worked for Slick without charging her fee? Was he someone from her past or someone who knew of her past and used that information to force her to work for him?

Interspersed among the financial data were tidbits of other information. Martin knew who Amanda was, had met her at the Lincoln Park Zoo to finalize their banking plans. With more skill than Cabel would have expected from the cheap office, the detective had followed her to both apartments and identified both of her marks. Jim was referred to as "the son" and the other he called "the organizer."

Martin had also tracked down Edward and Frank. Cabel wondered if the private investigator was planning to blackmail them later. Given the location and condition of the office, this arrangement with Amanda must have been a financial boon. Perhaps he hoped to extend the extra income after she had finished her jobs.

The notes on Slick documented that the detective had tracked this unknown person to the Levee District. There was an asterisk next to a notation that wondered if there was a possible connection between Slick and Capone. Martin also mentioned the barber, Mack, and using the tunnel entrance in the basement to track down some information. This was dated a week before the cognac delivery, ten days before Amanda's murder, and two and a half weeks before his own. Beside this notation was the symbol that Katherine and her friend couldn't translate: a dot within a circle.

Cabel took the paper he had found in Amanda's Levee apartment, he still thought of her by that name, and placed it next to the other. The symbols had nothing in common and there was no way to know what they meant. As he tucked the two papers into a file along with the transcribed notes, he wondered what happened to the package he had found in the apartment. Capone hadn't mentioned it and Cabel didn't remember seeing it after he'd given it to the driver's sidekick.

A knock interrupted his thoughts. Katherine peaked around the door. "You have fifteen minutes to get to your luncheon with Mr. Trenton."

"Thank you." Cabel put on his coat and hat, picked up his business case, and strode out to fight the next battle for the company's survival.

IIII

The brisk walk from the office to the Congress Hotel helped clear Cabel's mind of Capone, allowing him to focus on the upcoming meeting. With its gray and imposing edifice and its panoramic views of Grant Park, the hotel presided over South Michigan Avenue. Cabel hadn't eaten at its restaurant in years and would have looked forward to the experience if there weren't so much at stake.

He entered the lobby and wended his way to the restaurant entrance. A portly man with a dour expression stood near the maître d's stand. Cabel's heart sank. He walked up to the man and said, "I'm Cabel Evans. Are you Mr. Mathias Trenton?"

The man turned and studied Cabel from the top of his barbered head to the tips of his polished shoes. Apparently, he had passed the inspection because the man nodded but said nothing else until they were seated at a quiet table that would afford them some privacy to discuss business. They ordered quickly and Cabel forgot what he'd selected the moment the waiter walked away.

"So what the hell's happening at Evans Manufacturing?"

Cabel nearly flinched at the blunt statement but responded calmly. "We're having a generational disagreement over some business options, but are sorting this out as quickly as possible."

"So I've heard." He glared at Cabel. "You do understand that Sears and Roebuck is a national company and we contract with many suppliers across the country. Evans Manufacturing is just one of many who can meet our needs."

Cabel nodded, hoping his fear wasn't obvious to the powerful man who sat across the table.

"I knew your grandfather and have enjoyed a long and mutually beneficial relationship with your family's company, though that nearly ended during the war. Fortunately, you came home in time to right the ship so things went on as before.

"There were concerns after you left but your cousin filled your shoes very well. He was too young for this level of responsibility and made a few mistakes along the way, but he learned and he led. You were in much the same position when you returned from the war." He sighed. "I can't understand how James Evans' sons missed out on these excellent business instincts. However, I'm pleased that his grandsons are up to the challenges of managing his legacy."

"Thank you, sir."

"Before I forget to ask, how is Jim's recovery?"

Cabel smiled for the first time since Sunday afternoon. "Very well. He is currently living at my home in St. Joseph, Michigan, but I expect he'll be back in Chicago and at the helm before the end of the month."

Trenton nodded. "Good." He paused. "Will you be staying on as well?"

"No," Cabel said. "As you have already stated, Jim is doing an excellent job as president of Evans Manufacturing and he has earned the right to remain in that position."

Trenton leaned back in his chair and gave Cabel a thoughtful look. "A very wise and mature decision. Your continued presence could weaken Jim's authority and potentially create a situation where there would be a battle for control of the company. Or another battle I should say."

The waiter set plates in front of the two men, fish for Cabel, steak for Trenton. They ate in companionable silence until Trenton said, "So you've been tasked with keeping the company together until Jim returns."

Cabel nodded. His mouth too full to speak.

"That doesn't appear to be going well."

Cabel nearly choked. After taking a sip of water he said, "That's true. I hadn't realized, and neither had Jim, just what our fathers were planning and how far along they were in the process. We are sorting this out as quickly as possible. I just came from a board meeting where we severely limited their options."

Trenton's right eyebrow ticked up and this small gesture somehow conveyed the extent of the man's displeasure.

"Jim and I know their path is the wrong one and will do what we can to rectify the situation." Cabel hesitated to say anything more; not knowing what would hurt or help his cause. He took the risk and added, "My father has threatened to force a sale of his shares and remove himself from the company if we don't agree to his plans."

"And what did you say to that?"

"We would agree to those terms if this was his decision."

A small smile made a brief appearance. "That would be the best thing for the company, as well as for you and Jim." He nodded to himself. "Yes. That would be most acceptable."

The waiter returned to clear the plates and offer a dessert menu, which both men declined. Trenton paid the bill despite Cabel's attempts to do so. They walked through the lobby and onto the street when Trenton placed a hand on Cabel's arm.

"I believe you understand the precariousness of your situation but just to be clear, if Evans Manufacturing opens even one retail store, your contracts will be terminated and all ties with Sears and Roebuck severed." He tipped his hat then raised a hand to flag a cab.

CHAPTER 28

The Levee District seemed subdued early on the frigid Tuesday night. Only a few stylish flappers with their dapper dates hurried toward various clubs or bars which made little effort to disguise their trade.

Cabel sat in the back of a cab and watched the glittering world pass by. The day had gone much as the one before with telephone calls and meetings, working desperately to block his father's ambitions. One difference had been a note shoved into his pocket by a passerby as he walked to the office, a demand from Capone to meet him at the Cullerton Hotel this evening.

Tomorrow Cabel and Christopher Stanton planned to meet again with Edward and Frank to discuss Trenton's ultimatum. Cabel wondered idly if he would be alive to attend.

The cab driver dropped him off in front of the Cullerton Hotel. The brightly lit building should have been welcoming but somehow missed that mark. At first Cabel thought his own mood was the cause of this impression but then realized it was the building itself. Built in a large, low square, only four stories high, it seemed to squat on its corner of the Levee. There were large, decorative windows on the front façade but the ones he could see on the nearest side were small, narrow, and barred, even those on the upper floors. His shiver had nothing to do with the temperature.

The wide doors to the hotel stood open, armed men stationed at each. Capone waited somewhere within. Cabel ignored his survival instincts and entered the gangster's domain.

Dark paneling and crystal chandeliers lent an air of respectability to the room, as did the tasteful furniture scattered in groupings throughout the lobby. The sounds of drunken revelry coming from another room and the scantily clad women who lounged near the check-in counter dispelled that impression immediately.

Louie rose from a chair to meet him and said, "This way." They passed what had been a ballroom during the hotel's respectable past but which now served as a dance hall. A talented band played jazz on a large stage while girls with bobbed hair and beaded dresses shimmied across the floor with their dark-suited partners. A large bar sprawled across the side of the room and did a brisk business in mixed drinks while cheaply dressed girls tried to entice male patrons away from their friends.

Louie stopped to enjoy the view. "It's kind of quiet tonight. Usual for a Tuesday. You should see it on the weekend. The crowd is so big you can't move in there, let alone dance." He chuckled as he stepped away from the door.

Cabel shuddered. Tight or crowded spaces were something he avoided since his time in the trenches.

They walked past the ballroom and turned down a long hall that led farther back into the building. Men armed with machine guns and pistols stood along this hall at regular intervals, the menace and barely contained violence palpable, as was the message: we can kill you and no one will care.

The hall ended at a large, ornate door. After conferring with one of the guards, Louie opened the door and gestured for Cabel to walk in first. He hesitated and the men in the hall laughed. Clenching his hands to hide their shaking, Cabel stepped into a gaming room. Larger than it seemed possible from the hallway, the open room was filled with round tables and men who were serious about their cards. Chalkboards listed names and amounts but Cabel wasn't sure what they referred to. A small bar stood in the corner to serve the patrons and young women wearing tight dresses brought the drinks to the tables.

In the far corner Capone sat with his back to the wall, his eyes flickering between his cards and the people in the room. When he spotted Cabel, he jutted his chin and Louie took this as a sign to approach.

"Mr. Wrong-Place-Wrong-Time, I'm glad you could join us."

The men at the table laughed. They were all armed, Cabel realized, except for Capone. A gun in a shoulder holster and spats on shoes seemed to be the expected attire, and he was underdressed.

Capone threw his cards on the table. "Continue without me for a bit, boys. I need to have a chat with Mr. Evans."

Cabel followed Capone to a small booth tucked into the corner near the bar. Louie, wearing his own gun and spats, stood guard to assure privacy.

Drinks, unordered, were placed in front of them. Capone drank deeply and frowned until Cabel sipped his as well. He recognized Mack's whiskey the moment it touched his lips and he smiled.

"Good," Capone said. "I only trust men who have decent taste in liquor. Women, though, that's another story." He set his glass aside. "After our conversation the other day, I thought you should see the operations in person. Maybe you'll notice something we missed. Louie will show you around, what he found, how far he's gotten in his search."

Cabel listened to the gangster but was distracted by a young girl being led into the room through a small door near their booth. The second girl, probably in her late teens, wore a provocative, nearly transparent dress with clever beading that hid but also tantalized. Her makeup was applied with a heavy hand to accentuate her full lips and deep brown eyes and seemed more a mask than an enhancement. Perhaps that was the girl's intent.

The younger one was more child than woman, dressed in a simple frock that implied innocence and inexperience. Her long blond hair flowed long and loose giving her the appearance of a young girl who was ready for bed. Wide blue eyes filled with terror, swept the room looking for an escape. She looked at Cabel and said, "Please help me."

He stood but Louie blocked his way and Capone's hand grabbed his arm and jerked him back to his seat.

The gangster shook his head. "Don't worry about her. She's what you would call my product. In fact, I just purchased her this morning and Tanny is showing her the business. Usually takes the new ones a few weeks to settle in, but she'll be fine."

"You purchased her?" Cabel thought about the bars on the windows on the floors above and the the whiskey soured in his stomach.

"You really are a decent guy, aren't you?" Capone laughed and held up his glass for a refill.

The girl began to cry and Cabel turned in her direction. Strong fingers gripped his chin and forced his head back until he stared into Capone's dark cold eyes. "Don't be stupid, Mr. Evans. You can't save everyone. I would have thought you already learned that lesson during that war of yours." He released Cabel and reached into his vest pocket. "You should think about the lives you already have in your hands though, knowing you, I thought you might need a reminder." He opened his hand and showed Cabel the granite rock that had been on his desk in St. Joe.

Cabel's heart nearly stopped as he looked at it and understood all of its implications.

"I had a couple of my boys visit your house. They're young and still can look innocent when they want to. Your housekeeper let them right in when they said their car had broken down and asked to use your phone." Capone tossed the rock to Cabel, who caught it with numb fingers.

"Louie will take you into the tunnels and show you around. My men in the Levee District think that Alma and Fratti skimmed some money and that's why they're both dead. I want them to keep on believing that. Some of the men think that you came to me to collect the reward for killing her yourself, but others aren't so sure."

The young girl's crying grew louder. Cabel looked over and saw her huddled in a corner, hoping to escape the notice of the men while Tanny stood nearby, displaying what she had to offer. A few men looked their way but most were too absorbed in their cards to take real notice. Tanny leaned down and spoke to the girl, who shook her head and tried in vain to disappear into the woodwork. The terror in the child's eyes was too much to bear and Cabel started to rise from the booth. Louie pushed him back.

"You can't help yourself can you." Capone motioned for Tanny to approach then gave sharp orders to take the younger girl upstairs. Turning back to Cabel, he said, "You can't protect her. She'll be fine after a while and make good money too. Certainly more than she'd ever see living on a farm in Indiana. If you want to keep your family safe, forget about her. Figure out who stole my booze and where they hid it."

He accepted another drink and nearly emptied the glass before smiling at Cabel. "I bet right now you wish you hadn't saved me back at the Charades Club." He laughed when he saw the truth on Cabel's face. "Don't worry. Lots of people feel that way. Let's hope you're too smart to do anything about it. Go with Louie and let my men think you are being considered as Fratti's replacement." He finished his drink and stood.

"And Mr. Evans, be careful down there. It's easy to get lost in those tunnels if you don't mark your way." The gangster returned to his friends who dealt him into the game.

Cabel followed Louie out of the room, the terror in the girl's eyes seared into his mind. The sounds of merriment blended with the cries of the wounded as Cabel traversed his own no-man's-land of sanity. Fortunately nothing more was required of him than to trail behind his guide.

By the time they passed through the hotel's kitchen and into the cellar his mind had shoved the past back where it belonged. The world was still dangerous and uncertain, but at least it was real.

The cellar was large and well-lit. Shelves were built to create corridors filled with produce, flour, sugar, and other essentials.

Bins and barrels lined the walls closest to the stairs leading to the kitchen.

Louie walked past the barrels, snagging a ripe apple from one as he passed. At the end of the aisle, he turned left and led Cabel to the far end of the room and stopped in front of a large cabinet. Between the noticeable wheel marks and dirty footprints on the floor, it didn't take a detective to know that the cabinet concealed an entrance to the tunnels.

Louie sighed as he used a nearby broom to sweep the dirt away, removing all evidence of the hidden doorway. He looked at Cabel and said, "Capone would want someone's head if he saw this. If we're raided, it's like giving the cops an arrow pointing the way to our stash." He then gave the cabinet a tug and it rolled forward to reveal a doorway.

Cabel walked through it and onto a small landing at the top of a staircase that reminded him of the one in his home. Lightbulbs strung from wires near the ceiling provided ample illumination of the small room below. As with the cellar, wooden shelves lined the walls but these were built with a series of small openings that were filled with bottles. Three men played cards at a small table in the corner and one of them stood when he saw Cabel.

"It's all right, he's with me," Louie called out as he used a handle built into the back of the cabinet to pull it closed behind them. He stepped in front of Cabel and started down the steps.

The three men had abandoned their game and waited for Cabel and Louie at the bottom of the stairs. Louie made the introductions. "Boys, this is Mr. Evans and the boss is thinking about having him take over Fratti's job. I'm supposed to show him around and don't be surprised to see him down here on his own, checking our inventory and deliveries."

"Alone? I thought the boss said that no one could go into the tunnels by themselves except you," one man challenged.

"He did," Louie shot back, "but now he's changed his mind. You know Evans met with the boss on Sunday. He came out alive and Fratti didn't, so what does that tell you, Squib?"

"Louie's right. Floyd and I found this sap coming out of Alma's apartment building and took him over to chat with Capone."

Cabel recognized Ricky, the driver of the car that had taken him to the Metropole Hotel. The man named Floyd stood silently behind the others and stared at him with contempt. Cabel could understand the man's resentment. He'd been a complete outsider and two days later he was supposedly in a position of trust and responsibility far above Floyd and his companions who had been with Capone much longer. It didn't matter what this man thought. Cabel would maintain the ruse and do what was necessary to protect the Voss family and his cousin.

"Uncle Al wants me to show him the main tunnels, storage rooms, and key street accesses."

"Need a guide?" Floyd asked. "Capone won't be happy if we have to send a search party looking for the two of you and I know these tunnels."

Louie shook his head and smiled. In that moment, Cabel could see the family resemblance in the young man's eyes, now cold and flat with anger. "So do I, Floyd. Your place is here where you can't get into any trouble. It would be healthier for you if you remember that."

Hatred flashed in Floyd's eyes though his smile was as natural and sincere as Louie's. "Not everyone is lucky enough to be born into the right families. Some of us have to make our own way in the world."

Louie's bark of laughter was brief but genuine. "Being Capone's nephew might have started a few rungs higher up the ladder than you, but if I don't pull my weight or go against him being family won't protect me. If you think otherwise, you really don't know who you're working for." He shook his head in disbelief, never taking his eyes off the other man.

Floyd's scowl deepened but he didn't respond.

After a moment he turned to Cabel and said, "Come on, Evans. Let me show you the underworld."

CHAPTER 29

Louie led the way out of the room and into a large, wide tunnel that had probably been used to deliver coal in years past. The ceiling was at least eight feet overhead with the same electric lights leading into the tunnels in both directions. The air smelled fresher than Cabel expected, probably due to the large number of access points to the streets above.

Pressure built in his chest and his heart beat faster. Visions of the dirt-walled trenches shimmered and overlapped the rough cement sides of the tunnels. Sweat dripped into his eyes and his shaking legs would no longer support him. Leaning against a brick pillar, he closed his eyes and tried to will the trenches back to France.

Cabel opened his eyes to find Louie looking at him with concern. "You okay?"

"No, just give me another minute."

"Sure but you need to know that the boss won't care about your problems, only whether or not you do your job. He isn't a patient man so you need to find a way to be in these tunnels without going crazy or buy a black suit 'cause you'll be going to a lot of funerals."

The thought of his cousin lying in a coffin shoved all memories of the war aside. Jim had come so close to dying a few weeks ago that it was not difficult to imagine his funeral.

The tension in his chest eased but stayed nestled beneath his heart. It didn't matter. He was once again in control of his mind and body and could do what he needed to in order to protect those he loved. "I understand," Cabel said as he pushed himself off the pillar.

"Good." Louie studied him a moment. "Okay, let's keep moving"

They walked another thirty yards when they came to the crossroads of another tunnel. "We'll go down there later, but I want to show you some of the storage rooms."

Their tour of the underworld became a blur of twists and turns. Tunnels joined tunnels or stretched into unexplored darkness. Seemingly straight lines were proved to be curved when tunnels Cabel thought ran parallel to each other met at a junction. Someone had marked the primary routes with colored chalk symbols so that the men could get from a storage room to a delivery point without getting lost. This was important since most of the tunnels seemed indistinguishable from each other and Cabel could appreciate Floyd's warning about needing a search party.

Here and there, Louie would stop to point out where a delivery had been brought down from the street level and the hidden cubbyholes the thieves had used to stash a crate or two during the process. There was no doubt that they had prior knowledge of which street-access points would be used each time. The hiding places were invisible unless you knew what to look for, and they had to have been planned out well in advance. This was not the work of people who merely took advantage of a situation.

As soon as Cabel felt confident that he knew where he was, the maze of tunnels proved him wrong. There were rooms, and then rooms off of rooms. Storage rooms, delivery staging rooms, rooms holding nothing but crates of empty bottles, and something Louie called "party rooms" in a hushed, nearly reverent voice. Some of the places were clearly built as part of the coal delivery operations or for other maintenance purposes but others were kitchens, parlors, and bedrooms. Entire houses had sunk into the soft ground and forgotten, except for those who now used the tunnels.

Louie also showed him the doors that led to streets or bars, most of them were labeled as to where they led but others were blank. As they walked, Louie would point out doors that led to nowhere or tunnels that had not fully been explored. "We do most of our deliveries during the day so the bars are ready for the nighttime trade," he explained as they walked. "Even so, we have a lot of men down here at all times for emergency deliveries and general security. Since someone stole the cognac, the boss ordered that everyone must work in pairs and one of the managers makes the schedule so we don't have the same guys working together each night. The men don't know why everything's changed and some of them aren't very happy about it."

"And you're the only one he trusts to look for the missing cognac?"

Louie's smile held little warmth. "He doesn't want people to think he's weak, so yea, it's just me. Except now you get to help."

Although he had yet to get his bearings in this underworld of alcohol and violence, Cabel had seen enough to appreciate the task they faced. "It could take years to find the cognac in this maze, if it's even still here."

"You have days, not years. And if it's gone, well…" His eyes held sympathy but no mercy. Cabel's fate was his own.

When they arrived at a door marked "Lucky's," Louie opened it and invited Cabel to join him for a drink. Knowing his nerves would not survive another hour in the tunnels, Cabel agreed. The sturdy stairs ended at a door that opened into the backroom of the bar. Crates of bottles, either full or empty, were stacked in drunken disarray against the walls or left in small stacks. Cabel noticed that, despite the impression of disorder, care had been taken to keep the door clear. If the bar was raided, a hastily stacked tower of crates hiding the tunnel entrance would not look out of place.

Louie followed the sounds of laughter through the room's second door and down a dingy hallway into Lucky's. Cabel paused a moment to take in the brightly lit room. A bar ran about a third of the length of the longest wall and several patrons sat at the stools chatting, smoking, and drinking. Booths lined the remaining wall spaces and filled the center of the room. Cabel studied the bar a moment, remembering that this is where Fratti first encountered Alma. He now found it easier to think of her as two women, Amanda and Alma, but his heart felt the weight of the truth.

Several men greeted Louie, though a few also kept a speculative eye on Cabel. Louie was congenial but quickly separated himself from the men and motioned for Cabel to join him at a booth that gave a good view of the door.

"My uncle taught me to always know how to get out of a place in case of a raid. If the police come in, you run this way." He gestured to a short hallway behind him that led to the toilets. "If you take the door opposite the toilets, it leads to a hall behind the bar that connects with the hall we were in. From there you go down into the tunnels."

"Seems like a good way to get lost."

"Follow the blue or green marks and you'll find your way out eventually. Just listen before you open any of the access points to make sure there're no cops waiting for you on the other side."

Cabel nodded. "Is there a map or something to help me get a better sense of the tunnels? I felt like I was walking in circles down there."

Louie smiled but shook his head. "No maps allowed. The boss doesn't want the cops to get their hands on one and raid our stash. You have no idea how much money it cost to buy all that booze and how much more it will make us. I'm sorry, Evans, but the only way to learn the tunnels is to walk them."

"I was afraid of that."

"It isn't so bad after the first few times. You'll recognize landmarks like the water spot on a wall that looks like a duck or the places where the train tracks are still visible, stuff like that. I'll take you back down again to show you the rest of the storage rooms and the one that held the cognac." He shook his head. "Uncle Al was so angry I thought he was going to shoot Jake and Carlo just because he needed to kill someone." He swallowed the rest of his drink and set his empty glass aside. Gesturing to Cabel, he asked, "You going to drink that?"

Cabel looked down to find a full glass of something brown and fizzy in front of him. "No, help yourself."

"Thanks." Louie snagged the glass and downed a third of its contents. He looked at Cabel with eyes too old for his face. Cabel knew those eyes. They belonged to young men who had seen too much death and violence. They had peered at him from under the helmets worn by the men in his command and stared empty and uncaring from the dead strewn across the fields. He saw them in the mirror each time he had the courage to look himself in the eye. He felt pity for Louie, but he feared him too. Like a soldier, violence was a part of this man's world and he would not hesitate to kill on command.

"You know the men who work for Capone better than I ever will. Who do you think stole the cognac and the alcohol?" Cabel asked.

"Any one of them could, I suppose. That's the trouble when you work with gangsters. They don't care about the law or the rules. Capone took over the Outfit from Jonny Torrio and there're lots of guys who'd like to replace him or start their own gang somewhere else. Men talk about working their way up in the organization, but some Joes just decide to take over." He smiled. "I swear Prohibition was the best thing that ever happened to criminals."

"So no one in particular comes to mind."

Louie finished off his drink and shrugged. "Most men are too smart or too scared, or both, to even think about stealing from Capone. I guess that doesn't matter because there's always a few who might be brave or stupid enough to try it. There's a guy named Vic De Luca who might have done it but he's missing right now."

"Wouldn't that mean he could have taken the cognac and left?"

Louie finished his drink and set the empty glass on the table between them. "Maybe, but I don't think so. The day after the cognac was delivered, De Luca was part of the crew Uncle Al sent to Arkansas to pick up an order from Little Italy. I saw him leave and I know he came back a week later with the booze. A day or so later he didn't show up for work but we weren't too worried. Everyone knew he had a lot of gambling debts that he never could pay off so I figure someone got tired of waiting for something that was never going to happen and finished him off."

"But what about the truck he drove to Arkansas in?"

"No way he could have taken the bottles out like that. We searched those trucks top to bottom, and gave it an armed escort out of the Levee. It was empty when it left here and it didn't stop to pick anything up. Besides, I know a lot of the other guys on that crew. They're completely loyal."

"So why aren't they helping you search the tunnels?"

"Because my uncle's word is law," he said with both anger and resignation. "Something you need to keep in mind, Mr. Evans."

Cabel nodded, knowing he was trapped into working for Capone. The weight of the rock in his pocket proved to be a constant reminder. "Is there anyone else who comes to mind like Floyd or Ricky, or even Jake or Carlo?"

Louie shrugged. "Jake came up with Capone and wouldn't go against him. Carlo is another matter. The men don't trust him, he's too quick to kill, but he also would have warned any partners he had about the boss' change of plans that night, so I don't think so. Ricky is happy being a soldier as long as he's paid what he's worth, which he is. Floyd is different. Smart but sometimes too smart, you know? Still I don't see him doing something like this unless he tilted the odds in his favor. Even then, it would take more guts than I think he has. He likes to intimidate people but only those he thinks are weaker than he is."

"Like Fratti?"

"No. You didn't see Fratti the way that we're used to. He was confident and smart even if he looked like the wrong end of a pig. Then of course there's Alma. How does she fit into this?" He looked at his watch and stood. "I have a girl I'm seeing over at the Cullerton in a bit so I have to go. There're lots of cabs outside so you shouldn't have a hard time getting back to your hotel."

"Thanks." Cabel stepped into the bitterly cold night and watched Louie walk down the street before flagging a cab. The driver grumbled about driving to the Loop at that time of night but the promise of a large tip eased his concerns.

Cabel sat in the back of the cab and looked out over the dark waters of Lake Michigan, the young girl's terrified eyes still clear in his mind and Jim's granite rock a heavy weight in his pocket.

CHAPTER 30

Strong coffee allowed Cabel to put one foot in front of the next. Wednesday morning came too soon and followed a night spent dozing in a chair in his hotel room, an unsuccessful attempt to keep the nightmares at bay. Now he plodded down the street toward his office to prepare for the afternoon meeting with his father and uncle, a confrontation that would decide their fates.

As he reached the building, a gust of wind stole the hat off the head of the man in front of him. Both Cabel and the man scrambled to retrieve the fedora before it was crushed under the tires of a passing trolley. The rescue a success, the man hurried on his way but Cabel stood a moment. Something had caught his attention and he tried to push past his exhaustion to determine what it was. He scanned the streets until his eyes rested on a man slouched against a nearby building. Floyd lifted his hat in greeting, then turned away to be lost in the crowds of people on their way to work.

A coldness that had nothing to do with the brisk November day nearly froze him in place and the darkness within grumbled a warning. Cabel stood on the sidewalk, buffeted by the wind and the passing crowd, waiting until he regained control. He refused to allow Capone's threats to reduce him to what he had been five years ago. That thought steadied him as he walked toward the entrance to the office building.

Katherine met him at the door, no jacket to protect her from the cold. She grabbed his arm and pulled him to the side of the entrance, shivering yet determined.

"Whatever's wrong, we can talk about it inside. You'll freeze out here."

"No, this will be quick and I wanted to catch you before you came in to the office. Your mother wants to meet with you."

For a moment her words held no meaning. Of all the possible reasons for Katherine to meet him on the sidewalk, his mother's request seemed ludicrous. "Tell her I'll meet her tonight, tomorrow at the latest."

"No," Katherine said, hugging herself for warmth. "She said it was important that she see you before the meeting with your father and uncle this afternoon. Your father plans to be out of the house all morning so it needs to be now."

"But…"

"Mr. Cabel, whatever she needs to discuss with you it is urgent. I can handle the office until you get back. You're meeting with Christopher is at eleven thirty and I can push it to noon if necessary."

"Okay and thank you."

She nodded and rushed into the building.

IIIII

A cheerful fire warmed the parlor of his mother's home. Cabel poured himself a cup of coffee from the service set out on a low table in front of the sofa and idly studied the photographs and knickknacks on the mantle while he waited.

"Cabel, I'm so glad you came."

She looked lovely as always. Her pale mauve dress complemented her coloring without overpowering her delicate features and her hair was dressed in casual elegance. Her smile held genuine warmth. His heart stuttered a moment, unused to such a show of affection from this woman.

"Please sit with me, Cabe. We have much to discuss and not much time before you need to leave." She sat on the sofa and he joined her, pouring her a cup of coffee before refilling his own. Her hand shook as she accepted the cup and saucer. This was Cabel's only clue that his mother was nervous about meeting him and whatever she had to say.

"Mother, whatever is wrong, please tell me. Maybe I can help."

She gave him a sad smile. "My dear son, what troubles me is in the past and it's time you know of it. There are things that have happened that I believe may help you now." Setting aside her coffee she rose and stood before the fire, watching the flames dance in the hearth. "Your father was not my first love." She gave a harsh laugh. "I'm sorry to say but I don't think he ever was my love and I certainly wasn't his.

"As you know, I grew up in Boston and we had a large home on the Charles River in the Back Bay neighborhood. Our neighbors were famous politicians and writers, wealthy business owners, and those who inherited their fortunes." She gave a rueful smile. "And I fell in love with the Italian gardener who worked for us a few days a week. He was handsome and tall and seemed to care about me rather than who my father was and the size of my inheritance. And that was true, until I became pregnant."

Tears glistened in her eyes when she turned back to Cabel. "I hope that doesn't shock you, that your mother had a child by an immigrant gardener."

He struggled to keep his composure as he shook his head.

She laughed through her tears. "It's okay, Cabe. So many people see me as perfect, but truly I am just a woman in a cage of her own making." She selected a photograph from the mantle and returned to the sofa. "My father paid the gardener a large sum of money and the love of my life left me without saying goodbye. One of my cousins had been married for several years and was childless so she took in my daughter and named her Rose." She caressed the photo before handing it to Cabel. It was a formal portrait of a woman sitting in a chair holding a child with a man standing behind them, one hand resting possessively on his wife's shoulder.

"My cousin's name is Daphne and she raised Rose as her own. Too many people suspected what had happened and my father was desperate to see me married. A few months later, my brother was home from college for the winter break and brought your father with him to spend a few weeks with us. Edward fell in love with my money and status, and seemed to know that I was sullied." She gave a bitter laugh. "That was the word he used on our wedding night, 'sullied.' Edward made it clear that I was to make his father happy by producing a male heir. It didn't matter if it was the firstborn or the fifth, I was to lie with him until that blessed event and then he considered himself free to find his entertainment elsewhere. It never occurred to him that I was also free of his attentions, which were unwelcomed at best."

"Did he hurt you?"

His mother patted his arm. "No, dear, I was beyond hurt, beyond pain or love, even with my own son and for that I am truly sorry."

Cabel struggled to swallow the lump that had formed in his throat. "So I have a sister?"

His mother bit her lip and blinked away tears. "No, she died in the Spanish Influenza epidemic after the war. She had married, though, and had a son and daughter who both survived and live with their father in Boston."

Her pain was like a knife cutting through his soul. "You've never seen them."

She shook her head. "No, I don't think I could keep up the pretense if I did. Instead, I live here with a man who despises me and who can't see that I despise him as well. I have a son I couldn't love because I thought I was unworthy, and when you were young, I feared that you would have the same character as your father. I thank God every day for bringing Jon and his family into your life. Lily Warner was the mother I could never be and I am grateful that she accepted you as her own."

The mention of Lily Warner brought a different kind of pain. His heart ached to see her but he didn't have the courage to do so.

"Now that you understand a little more of your innocent mother's life," she said with a hint of irony in her voice, "let me tell you what happened with the business while you were away at war."

"I know some of it, at least," Cabel said. "I know that Father and Uncle Frank got into trouble by selling the government inferior products and they somehow managed to keep the company going despite having to pay heavy fines."

"That's true and I can tell you how they managed that feat."

IIIII

Boisterous laughter preceded Edward and Frank into the boardroom. Their attorney entered first, his stride confident and his conservative suit impeccable. The elder Evans men walked in next, their laughter cut off the moment they saw who was in the room.

Margaret Evans sat between her son and Christopher Stanton and smiled at the shock her presence created.

"There is no reason for her to be here," Edward said to Cabel. "Send her away so we can get our business handled. Frank and I are signing a lease on a building this afternoon and then we're going out to celebrate."

"Actually," Christopher said, "I think her contribution to our conversation is important. Shall we begin?"

Frank and their lawyer seemed bemused as they took their seats but Edward glared at his wife. "Remember, Margaret dear, you have secrets of your own that I don't think you'd want your precious son to know. Keep that in mind and tread carefully."

"Cabel knows all my secrets, Edward, and a few of yours as well."

Edward paled.

"Let's start this discussion by asking you, Frank and Edward, if you would reconsider your position on this new venture given the known repercussions from Sears and Roebuck if you continue," Christopher said.

"I'm Richard Davenport and I represent Edward and Frank in this matter. They understand the consequences their actions will have on Evans Manufacturing but feel that the success of their new venture will overcome any short-term losses that may be incurred." He and Frank smiled. Edward shifted in his chair and scowled at his wife.

"If that is the decision, we have no choice but to call in a loan taken out by Edward during the war." Christopher slid a stack of papers across the table. Richard thumbed through them reading as quickly as possible.

Frank turned to his brother. "What loan?"

"It isn't a loan. I married Margaret and the money is mine."

"How did you come to sign this loan?" Richard asked Edward.

"I told you it isn't a loan. The money is mine by right of marriage. I just signed those papers to make my wife happy."

"No," Margaret said. "My father put that money in trust for Cabel on the day he was born, to be paid to him when he turned twenty-five. He would have already received the funds if you hadn't borrowed them. You took out the loan because the trustees would not give you the money. It wasn't yours to take."

"So you signed the loan and used the money to pay the war office fines and keep the company going until Cabel came back from France. Once he did, he took over the leadership of Evans Manufacturing and returned it to financial stability, and later success," Christopher added.

"My failure of a son did not get this company back on track. We thrived under my leadership."

"Our leadership," Frank interjected.

Edward paused to glare at his brother. "*Our* leadership of this company kept it successful and allowed it to grow after our father's death."

Christopher raised an eyebrow. "Really?" Selecting a report from a stack of papers in front of him, he placed it on the table and tapped it with his finger. "According to this analysis of the company's ledgers, Evans Manufacturing would have gone bankrupt during the war if not for the loan from Cabel's trust. Although the company survived, it continued to flounder until he returned and worked like a fiend to bring it back to prosperity." He shook his head. "For a while, the partners at our law firm were concerned that this company would be the only one of our clients to lose money during the war rather than expand. If it wasn't for Cabel, we wouldn't be sitting here right now."

"If it wasn't for Cabel, I'd be standing here without a cane right now."

"You only use a cane when you want sympathy," Margaret said with disgust. "You did need it, for a while, but haven't for years. You carry it around in case someone asks about Cabel and you can blame all of your problems on him."

"How dare you," Edward shouted. "You are lucky I was willing to marry you and give you this wonderful life. Don't you side with your mad son over me."

"I'm not mad, just damaged," Cabel said, "by the war. It changed me, and not for the better. You used that to break me so that no one would notice that I was better than you at running the company." His father flinched at the words but Cabel continued. "You tried to destroy me and nearly succeeded. I won't let you destroy the company."

"You can't stop me, can't you see that? I win." He turned to his lawyer and said, "There is nothing here we need to address. Let's go close on that storefront."

"Actually, we aren't finished here. You need to repay the loan." Christopher held up the document. "According to this, you should have been making payments from your salary for several years now."

"Why should I? The money benefited the company, not me personally, so those funds should come from Evans Manufacturing."

"You could have structured the loan that way, but I think you didn't want people to know how you got out from under the pressure of repaying the government for the defective parts, and the fines as well. Instead, you took this as a personal loan, putting both your shares and Franks as collateral."

"You must be mistaken," Frank said, looking at Christopher and then Edward. "I never agreed to use my shares as collateral. I didn't even know about this loan. You said you'd take care of it and you did."

"Yes, and you didn't ask any questions," Edward shot back.

"But that means that my shares aren't at risk. I'm still fine."

"I'm sorry to inform you that you are the one who is mistaken." Christopher opened the loan document to a specific page and turned it for Frank to read. "You signed this paper giving Edward the right to include your shares as collateral. The trustees wouldn't have allowed the loan without this added surety."

Frank grabbed the paper and read the document. He turned to Edward and punched him in the stomach. "How dare you trick me like this."

Edward rubbed his stomach, his brother's lack of strength apparent in his reaction. "You mean like we did your son? You didn't seem to mind deceiving him."

Frank took another swing at his brother and soon both lawyers stood between them. Edward made no move to protect himself from the blows, merely laughing at Frank's ineffectual efforts, which increased his brother's anger. Cabel rose, intending to help separate the two men, but his mother placed a hand on his arm.

"Leave the children to their tantrums, Cabe. The lawyers can manage them and if you get involved I suspect Edward might hit himself with his cane then tell everyone that you gave him the black eye."

By the time she had finished speaking the brothers were separated and seated at the table, their lawyer between them. The man's expensive suit was torn at the breast pocket and missing several buttons. The look of exasperation on his face made it clear that only his professional reputation kept him from clouting his clients.

"For the sake of clarification, how much money does Mr. Edward Evans owe to Mr. Cabel Evans?"

"Nothing. I told you that money should have been mine through marriage and I have even a better claim now, given how Cabel attacked me."

Richard Davenport closed his eyes a moment then turned to Edward and said, "Since the loan occurred before your son attacked you," his glance to Cabel made it clear that he sympathized with the impulse if not the action, "that argument is not valid. However, if you would like to sue your son now, we will have to see if the statute of limitations has passed and if anyone will stand witness for you."

"Perfect. I want to sue Cabe and of course I'll have witnesses. There was a full board meeting that day."

"Really? I don't remember seeing anything," Christopher said.

"Me either," Frank added.

A brief scuffle ensued between the brothers but Richard forced them back in their seats with only a disarrayed tie as damage.

"Besides," Christopher added, "We will bring proof that you sought to harm your son, which I think will be fairly easy. And then there is what you did to Jim."

"What did they do to Jim?" Both Margaret and Richard asked.

Edward and Frank glared at each other but refused to answer.

"Edward, do you want to bring a suit for bodily harm against your son?"

"No."

"Then let's go back to our discussion of the loan," Richard said.

"Here you can see the loan amount and the annual interest on the monies lent. From my calculations, Edward and Frank owe Cabel close to eighteen thousand dollars." Christopher pushed a financial document across the table for the others to review.

Frank looked at the page and gasped.

"Can you repay the loan or will you give Cabel your stocks in lieu of money?"

"How long do my clients have to repay the loan?"

Christopher shook his head. "The terms of the loan state that if payments are not made as per the schedule, the loan is due upon call. We call it now."

The room went silent.

"That will ruin me," Frank whispered.

"There is another option that Cabel is willing to consider. Were the project to be abandoned, the company will continue much as it has, with a few minor adjustments. If not, either you must pay Cabel what is due today or you sign over your stocks to him. Once the stocks are his, he will cancel your project and demand repayment of all money you've spent on it."

"That includes the money you spent on your deception of Jim," Cabel added, thinking of the payments made to Amanda through the private investigator. "I suspect that came from corporate funds and I want them repaid."

Edward stood and slammed his cane on the table, shattering the heavy stick. "I will not allow you to push me out of this company. I helped build it and I will not give up my shares, especially not to you."

Cabel looked at his father with pity. "I understand your ties to this business, I share them, but I cannot allow you to continue taking actions you know will harm it and us. I would think your own finances would warrant a more prudent approach."

"My finances are none of your concern, Cabe. You will not force me out."

"Let me add one more incentive," Christopher said in a tone that had Frank and Edward glance at each other. "If you stop this project, in addition to keeping your shares and with a repayment plan in place, Cabel will not order a full audit of the books."

Frank paled but Edward waved his hand as if dismissing the lawyer's words. "Let him. What do we care? We own the business and we can take funds from it whenever we want."

Christopher asked Richard, "Are you familiar with the company's bylaws on compensation and dividends?"

"No, I haven't had a chance to review them."

"Here is a copy and I've marked the pertinent sections."

While Richard read the document, Cabel refreshed his mother's coffee cup and then his own, hoping the caffeine would continue to keep his exhaustion from gaining the upper hand.

Richard finished reading and said to Christopher, "Am I right in assuming that you claim my clients did not disperse funds as per these requirements?"

"Yes. Frank and Edward used certain accounts they created within the company as their own personal funds. Not only did this violate the bylaws but also these funds should have been credited against any dividends they received on their stocks."

"The amounts?"

"Considerable."

Richard sighed and turned to Edward. "You understand that this vastly increases the amount of money you owe, both to the company and Jim and Cabel as well?"

Edward refused to answer, which was answer enough.

"We will cancel the meeting with regard to the storefront," Richard said, raising a palm to halt Edward's protests. "We will discuss this matter, the three of us, and decide how best to proceed but I expect that your project is over, one way or another, and we need to assess how much money you may be liable for and how repayment will occur."

"I am liable for nothing," Edward shouted. "This is my company."

"No," Cabel said. "It's our company, something you have failed to appreciate."

"Call me when you have things sorted out on your end," Christopher said to his legal counterpart. "I want you to know that I have advised Cabel that he is being too generous with his offer. Fortunately for your clients, we'd like this matter closed quickly and quietly to avoid damage to the company's reputation."

"I understand." Richard left, his clients bickering as they followed him from the room.

CHAPTER 31

The shattered remnants of Edward's cane lay in the middle of the table. Cabel felt relief that at least one lie was now put to rest.

"Thank you for making this meeting possible," Christopher said to Margaret. "I fear the company would not have survived without your intervention."

She gave a small laugh. "I'm sure Jim and Cabel would have managed just fine without my interference, but I am sincerely glad that I could help." She sighed. "I should have spoken of this loan sooner and for that I am sorry."

Christopher enveloped her small hand between his. "I can imagine the competing tugs of family loyalties made your choice a difficult one. You were quite brave to be here today." He cleared his throat. "I must ask if we need to worry about your personal safety."

"I am also worried about you," Cabel added, relieved that his attorney had broached this sensitive topic.

Margaret shook her head. "Edward has never been violent toward me, preferring more passive ways to punish me for failing to meet his standards."

Cabel's jaw clenched as he imagined the mental warfare his father had probably employed against his mother. He had been subjected to it himself.

"I doubt he'd seek to physically harm me now," she added. "Though I have damaged his bank accounts, and therein lay all he truly values, so I don't know what to expect."

"I think you should pack a few bags and go to St. Joe for a couple days," Cabel offered. "I'm sure Jim would be glad of the company. He's healing but is getting quite restless with his confinement. Marta could probably use the help in keeping him occupied and she would take good care of you."

"I'm sure that isn't necessary."

"I disagree," Christopher said. "I think Cabel and I would both rest easier if we knew you were safe. Why don't you telephone your maid and have her pack your things. I'll have one of the office boys pick them up and meet us back at my office. We'll get you to the train as well."

Cabel sensed his mother's hesitation. "Please. Jim and I would both benefit from having you there."

With a sigh, she relented.

"I'll make the arrangements here and Cabel will call his cousin. In the meantime, please join me at my office. I think there are a few things we need to discuss."

"Of course," Margaret said. "Before we go, I'd like to have a private word with my son."

"Certainly." Christopher rose and gathered his papers before leaving the room.

After he shut the door, Margaret turned to her son. "Cabe, when we met at the house, I was so concerned about how you would feel when you learned the truth about me that I hadn't noticed how tired you are." She reached up to caress his cheek. "When I saw you at the hospital I was so happy that you looked well, better than you did after you came back from France, but something has changed."

Cabel tried to turn away, but she gently held his face and he would not resist her.

"Your eyes look haunted again and there is wariness in you that I didn't see a few weeks ago. What has happened?"

He closed his eyes. Reaching up, he removed his mother's hand from his face and drew it down to her lap but kept his fingers twined with hers. He shook his head, unsure of what to say. When he opened his eyes, he found her looking at him with concern but also genuine affection. He blinked hard to keep his tears from falling.

"All I can say is that Jim has asked me to find out who killed Amanda Channing. I've learned many things about her, some of them Jim knows and some he doesn't, at least not yet."

"And doing this for Jim has placed you in danger, hasn't it?" His silence was all the answer she needed. "Then stop, Cabe. Jim wouldn't want you to put your life at risk. You know that."

"I know," Cabel said. "The problem is that others are now involved and I have no choice but to continue. Please don't tell Jim. I don't want him to worry or blame himself."

He stood. Margaret joined him and together they walked to the conference room door and he placed his hand on the knob to open it.

"Please be careful, Son. You don't seem to know how many people love you and wish you well." She tugged on his jacket lapel and he leaned down, unsure what she wanted. Her arms went around his neck, tentative at first, then with more assurance. She held him close a moment, then released him and hurried out the door.

IIIII

Cabel placed a call to Marta, who seemed excited at the prospect of another guest but wanted to know when he would be home.

"Our Thanksgiving celebration is next week. I wanted to talk to you about inviting my daughter and her family, and the Arledge family, of course."

Of course, he thought. "I'll plan to be home Wednesday night, Thursday morning at the very latest. As for the meal, invite whomever you'd like and if you need more funds in the household accounts, let me know." For a moment, he thought there was a bad connection with the telephone line but realized that the sound he heard was his housekeeper's squeal of delight. Afraid of the leeway he had given her, he also worried that his forced servitude to Capone might require that he break this promise. Taking the coward's way, he asked to speak with Jim before he accidently gave Marta full run of his life.

When Jim came on the line he sounded stronger but still tired. They spoke for almost an hour as Cabel explained what had happened at the meeting. He didn't share his mother's secrets, those were hers to tell or not, but he did tell Jim what she had done for them and that she would be arriving at the train station later that day. He ended the call before Jim could think to ask about his amateur investigation into Amanda's life. He would need to tell his cousin about the woman's affair with another man, but didn't want to do so over the telephone.

Christopher called soon after to say that Margaret's bags had arrived at the office and they would be leaving for the train station in time for her to catch the four fifteen train to St. Joseph.

Cabel placed the earpiece on the telephone stand and rubbed his tired eyes. Something the lawyer had said triggered a memory. Despite his exhaustion, he forced his mind to consider the issue. His mother's bags had arrived at the office. And then he remembered.

Picking up the earpiece again, he asked the operator to connect him with the Metropole Hotel. Several minutes later Louie came on the line.

"Mr. Evans. I'm glad you called. I wondered when we could go back into the tunnels tonight. Uncle Al is anxious that you learn the ropes of Fratti's job."

From those words Cabel understood that Louie was not alone. "Not tonight, unless it's late," he said. "I've been working all day and need some sleep."

Louie laughed. "Okay. What time do you want to be here?"

"Actually, that isn't what I called about," Cabel said. "When Ricky and Floyd picked me up outside Alma's apartment I was carrying a package of clothes I had found hidden in a pie safe. I had wanted to look them over to see if there was anything there that would help me find out what she was up to." He didn't want to mention the odd drawing he'd found on the piece of paper tucked into her things. "Floyd took them from me and I don't remember seeing them since he placed the package on the floor of the car. Did he give it to you or Capone?"

"No." Louie's voice changed from relaxed to attentive. "No one mentioned a package and I'm sure the boss would have told me about it if he had seen it. Let me ask around. Oh, and meet me at the Cullerton at eleven o'clock. We've got work to do."

Cabel glanced at his watch. Just past three. He sighed and gave up the rest of the day as a lost cause. He grabbed his coat and hat from the coatrack, picked up his business case, and left to get a few hours' sleep before he returned to the underworld.

CHAPTER 32

Louie stood at the hotel entrance and nodded a greeting to Cabel. As they walked through the lobby, Cabel paused a moment. Several women lounged on couches or chatted with men who blushed and tugged at their ties, but the young girl he'd seen yesterday was not among them.

Louie shook his head and nudged Cabel to keep him moving. "Uncle Al told me to let him know if you asked about the new girl. You haven't, but I know what you're thinking. Forget about her. If you don't get the job done, you'll have bigger problems to worry about."

Cabel nodded but knew that as soon as he'd finished with Capone, he'd find a way to help the girl and keep his family safe. He wouldn't leave her here. Angry at being forced to do the gangster's bidding, exhausted from his fight to save his company and his family, he needed to tread carefully to protect all that he held dear.

"Did you learn anything about the clothes?" he asked, more to change the subject than any real curiosity.

"No. Ricky and Floyd both said it was in the car like you told me, but they don't know what happened to it," Louie said. "I told the boss about it and he's not happy. I'll have to talk to the boys again and see if I can help them remember."

They trudged through the kitchen, down the cellar stairs, and to the hidden door at the back of the room. Cabel braced himself to return to the tunnels but found that the experience wasn't as difficult as it had been the night before. He wasn't sure if exhaustion or familiarity helped to take the edge off of his anxiety, not that it mattered. Phantoms of the trenches lurked at the edge of his vision but kept their distance, which was all that mattered.

Louie led him down a tunnel, pointing out bar entrances and other landmarks that he used to navigate the maze. He reached a crossroad and stopped. "Last night we followed the tunnels under the businesses on Cullerton Street and Wabash Avenue up to roughly Michigan Avenue." He pointed to the right. "Not only do most of the bars and speakeasies have tunnel access for deliveries down here but we also store most of the beer and the booze distilled in Cicero in rooms off of those tunnels. If the police ever raided us, they'll mostly get the local stuff that the boss can easily replace." Louie looked at Cabel. "He wouldn't be happy about it but at least the cops wouldn't find the Canadian beer and booze. It's stored this way." He turned left and Cabel followed.

The string of electric lights buzzed overhead. The concrete walls had bits of brick showing through here and there, proof that something lay beyond the utilitarian service tunnel. People had marked on these walls with paint or chalk. Some were faded with time while others were sharper in color and shape. The floor had been paved in concrete that was lighter than the color of the walls and Cabel wondered if this was how Capone found the tunnels or if this was an addition to make the movement of crates and barrels easier. As he pondered the question, he was surprised to realize that he was able to take note of these details. Last night, memories of the trenches had overcome his ability to take in his surroundings.

Louie stopped at a rusted service door but, even in the yellow glow of the lightbulbs, Cabel noticed that the hinges were new. With a sharp tug, the door opened. Louie stepped aside for Cabel to see within. Crates were stacked in neat rows and nearly filled a room he estimated to be roughly forty square feet.

"The whiskey is on this side of the room, the gin at the back, and the vodka is over there," he said, pointing as he spoke. "Most of the time we have just one room like this. We don't want to keep too much on hand, just in case. But with our supply cut off for a few months, we have four rooms about this size to keep everyone happy through the winter."

He pulled the door shut and continued walking. "We have some wine down here too. Uncle Al likes to have some with Sunday dinner, especially when there's a big crowd. And there's the Irish whiskey a local makes for us. Don't know how it's different, but it is."

They came to a smaller, unlit tunnel that connected with the main one. Louie stopped and opened a wooden cabinet standing near its entrance. Three flashlights sat on shelves. Louie grabbed one, turned it on, and shone the beam into the tunnel.

"One of the other storage rooms is down here and the rest are off of side tunnels like this one. When the booze in the room I showed you gets low, we restock from these."

Cabel felt relieved when Louie turned the flashlight off and replaced it in the cabinet. Although he could manage the main tunnel, the smaller, narrower ones presented challenges he didn't know if he could overcome.

"Where are we now?"

"We're under Cullerton Street, going west toward Clark, though we'll be turning off of the main tunnel soon."

"How far are we from Alma's apartment building?"

Louie turned and studied Cabel. "Not far, I think. Is it important?"

"I don't know. It's just that she's tied to the thefts and it made me wonder."

"If there's tunnel access from her apartment, we haven't found it."

"Has anyone looked?"

"No, but why would they?" Louie continued on, following the main tunnel for another quarter mile or so and then turned left at the crossroads with a secondary passageway. They continued in silence, passing more tunnels and the occasional storage room, Cabel's nerves stretching tighter with each step. A few of the side tunnels were strung with electric lights, but most were unlit paths that led into blackness. Cabel noticed that flashlights were stored near some of these tunnels but not others. If the police ever did raid this part of the maze, these small lights would become beacons, pointing the way to hidden storage rooms.

At the next unlit tunnel, Louie picked up two flashlights from the concrete floor and handed one to Cabel. "The boss wants you to see the room where the cognac was stored." He flicked on his light and started down the tunnel. Cabel hesitated a moment before he did the same.

A few yards into the narrow space Cabel's hands started to sweat. His body shook and the flashlight beam wavered. The cement walls seemed to drip with mud and the air grew foul with the smell of desperation as men awaited the call to battle.

Louie stopped and shone his light on a pristine metal door that boasted a shiny new lock. Swallowing his terror, Cabel forced himself to notice these details in an effort to keep his mind from betraying him.

"Uncle Al has the only key. He wanted you to see this door so you understood where this tunnel is in relation to the others. Now we're supposed to go in the back like the crooks did." He turned to retrace his steps, passing Cabel as he led the way into the light.

When they reached the larger passageway again, Louie glanced at Cabel then looked again. Pulling a flask from his coat pocket, he offered it to Cabel, who shook his head.

Louie's jaw tightened and his eyes grew cold. "We have to go down some more tunnels. I won't ask if you can manage it, because you need to if you want to protect your family." He held out the flask again. "This will help."

Although Cabel's stomach protested, he sipped the whiskey, waited, and sipped again. The harsh liquid flowed through him bringing warmth and a measure of calm. He returned the flask to its owner and they began to walk again.

Several yards later, another side tunnel created a crossroads. The left side had electric lighting but did not lead where they needed to go. Turning on their flashlights, Cabel and Louie took the path to the right. The passageway was narrow but straight. Other small tunnels crossed it and Louie took one, then another. Cabel knew he wouldn't be able find his way back on his own and felt his panic grow despite the alcohol-induced calm. At the next turn, the tunnel changed as the concrete floors gave way to dirt and cinder. Old bricks lined the walls and the ceiling height dropped at least a foot. Rocks and old railroad tracks made walking difficult and Cabel kept his flashlight and eyes pointed down to keep from tripping. The effort needed to keep his footing, combined with the whiskey, helped to keep the war at arm's length.

Louie stopped and shone his light on a pile of rubble. "I think this is where the thieves first tried to dig through to the locked room but they were stopped by the rocks behind it." He walked a little further. "They tried again here and got lucky."

A large section of bricks had been removed from the tunnel, as well as slats and lathe that had once been part of the wall of a house. The broken bricks and other debris had been shoveled to the side of the passage. Louie stepped through a gap that was wide enough to accommodate a man and a cart loaded with crates of cognac.

Cabel followed him into a surreal world. From the style of the bits of furniture, he guessed that the sunken sitting room had last been above ground sometime in the eighteen forties. Molding curtains still hung over empty window frames. Chairs stood in front of a collapsed fireplace, their cushions now home to a family of rodents that scurried away from the beam of his flashlight.

A path had been cleared to the far side of the room where Louie waited near a wood-framed opening that might have once led into the family's dining room. A large hole had been made in the concrete wall behind it, so the doorway now opened into the room where Capone's prized cognac had briefly resided.

"Strange place," Louie said, "There are more like this, one here and there. We find these sunken rooms in the oddest places." He walked through the doorway.

Cabel followed.

The smell reached him in the same moment Louie shouted.

The ground shook from the mortar blasts and his men screamed in fear.

"Cabel, go to the main tunnel and find the entrance to the hotel. Get a message to Capone."

He heard the words, an anchor to the present if only he could grasp their meaning.

Stepping over the body of a good man who would be grieved, he reached the ladder that would take him to the top of the trench and into the battle. He tried to climb the rungs but they were slick with mud and he could not keep his footing. Above him, someone cried out in pain.

"Damn it, Cabel."

The ground shook again, or did it? Strong hands gripped his arms and shook. A sharp slap to the face pulled Cabel from his hell.

"Can you walk?"

It seemed an odd question until Cabel realized he was lying on the floor of the lost room.

"Come on. We need to get you out of here so I can go for help."

Cabel let the man, Louie he remembered with relief, pull him to his feet. His first steps were tentative but grew stronger as he crossed the room. His flashlight lost and his footing unsteady, Louie grabbed the front of his shirt and forced him through the maze of tunnels and, finally, into the light.

Once there, Cabel staggered to the far wall and sank to the floor. He expected Louie to leave to report the dead body in the cognac room. Instead, the young man slid down next to him and offered his flask with a shaking hand.

The flask passed between them for several minutes.

When they had drained it, Louie turned to Cabel and asked, "Did the war smell like that?"

"Sometimes it did. Sometimes it still does." Cabel closed his eyes ashamed that this secret had escaped.

"I've seen dead men before, even killed a few, but I've never smelled anything like that and never want to again."

"Do you know who it was?" Cabel didn't care, not really. He just wanted Louie to talk about something besides the smell of death.

"Vic De Luca. I told you about him last night. The gang called him Badger because he was so mean and ornery no one wanted to work with him." He shook his head. "Someone shot him in the head and left his body there to rot." Louie looked at his empty flask in sadness and sighed. "He was alive the night the cognac was stolen and we knew he went missing a few weeks later. If I hadn't shown you the room, I don't know if we'd ever have known what happened to him." He shook his head. "I didn't think he was stupid enough to have been part of this mess."

"Maybe he wasn't. Maybe he had the bad luck to come across the guy who did steal the cognac," Cabel offered.

"No. He was killed in that room. The only way into it without a key is through that little sitting room. The only men who knew about that were the ones who stole the booze." He leaned his head against the wall and closed his eyes.

Cabel began to wonder if the younger man had fallen asleep when Louie opened his eyes and said, "Now we have to tell the boss what we found."

The dread in his voice matched Cabel's own.

IIIII

Capone held court at the Metropole Hotel but quickly cleared the room after Louie had whispered into his ear. The three of them sat around a small table and Capone listened intently while his nephew recounted what they had found.

When Louie finished, Capone asked, "Did you tell any of the men in the tunnels what you found?"

"No. I was going tell the boys guarding the stairs to the Cullerton access, but Evans told me to wait."

"And why did you tell him that, Mr. Evans?" his icy anger finding a new victim.

Cabel failed to suppress the chill that slid down his spine. "The body is in a room that is supposed to contain crates of French cognac. Your men couldn't help us with the body without also learning about the theft."

Capone's eyes widened a moment and Cabel thought he saw respect hidden in their dark depths. This thought chilled him more.

"De Luca's father and I worked together in New York before I came out here. That's why I took Vic on." Capone seemed to be speaking more to himself than to his audience. He scowled. "We don't tell anyone that the sap is dead until we know who killed him. I don't want problems with his father or his gang."

"So what do we do with the body?" Louie asked.

"Leave it where it is. No one will see it and he can't get any deader." Capone cut the tip from a cigar, lit it, and puffed until the flame took hold. "The way I see it, this job took at least two men. De Luca was one but who is the other? What do you think?"

Louie shrugged.

"And you, Mr. Evans?"

"For my thinking, this all started with Amanda, the woman the people in the Levee knew as Alma." He had grown to hate this woman he'd never met. But for her, Jim would be well and he wouldn't be forced to do a mobster's bidding. "Could De Luca have known her somehow? She mostly worked in the East. Maybe he was the one who hired her."

Capone blew smoke rings from his cigar as he considered the situation then shook his head. "Vic wasn't smart enough to come up with this plan on his own. He was impatient and angry at being sent here from New York. If he knew the girl, he would have brought her in long ago, stolen what he could, and have left. No, the doll was hired by someone who heard about the cognac and wanted to steal it. Whoever that is has more patience than any De Luca I ever met."

"So why would that person bring De Luca in as a partner?"

"Maybe he knew the job was too big to do on his own or maybe he wanted another sap to pin this on," Capone said, shrugging away the question. He tapped the ash from his cigar and studied the glowing embers. "Have you learned anything more about this Alma, or Amanda, or whoever she is?"

Cabel shook his head. Suddenly weary from the long day and still shaken from the discovery of the body, he wanted to return to the relative safety of his hotel. "What about the package? Has it been located?"

"What package?" Capone asked.

Louie glared at Cabel before responding to his uncle. "When Evans searched Alma's apartment, he found a package she'd hidden. Says he gave it to Floyd. I've asked and he says he doesn't have it. I haven't had a chance to tell you about it and honestly I don't' think it's important."

Capone turned to Cabel. "What was in it?"

"A dress and pair of shoes like the ones she wore when she was Amanda Channing. She kept the same thing at her other apartment, except they were clothes she wore as Alma. I searched through the ones I found in the Northside apartment but hadn't really looked through this new package yet, though I wanted to."

"Why?"

"I found a key to the Levee District apartment in the toe of a shoe I found in her Northside apartment. There might have been something else hidden in the other bundle that I missed when I looked through it the first time."

"So you searched her other apartment too?" Louie asked.

"The police had searched it after she was killed, trying to find information about her next of kin. Someone else had been there too. I found the place was torn apart just like her apartment here."

Capone studied him a moment. "So you just happened to find these hidden things in both places after others had searched there first?"

Cabel hadn't thought of the situation that way and now realized how suspicious it looked. "I don't know what to say except that I spent a lot of time at a friend's home. His mother took me in as one of her own and his five younger sisters thought of me as a big brother." He smiled as memories drifted past. "I quickly learned that women think differently than men. I found the first bundle of clothes in an unused oven. At the Levee apartment it was more luck than thought. I knelt down to pick up a piece of paper and was at the best advantage to see the pie safe tucked under the lowest shelf in the pantry."

Capone leaned forward. "And you saw nothing in the package that seemed out of place?"

"Yes." And this was true. The small piece of paper with the odd symbol was on top of the bundle, not in it. Until he knew what it meant, the symbol would be his secret.

"And you're sure Floyd took the clothes from you."

"Yes. Ricky was driving and Floyd took the package."

He turned to Louie. "Find Floyd. I want to speak with him personally. Tonight."

The clock on the mantle chimed once.

Capone chucked. "For an honest man like yourself, your workday is long over. For me and my boys, it's barely begun. Louie, get this sap a cab before you find Floyd. Tell the boys in the hall I have a few calls to make and I'll let them know when I need anything."

Cabel and Louie stood and walked to the door.

"Oh, and Mr. Wrong-Place-Wrong-Time, you have until Saturday night to find my booze. Understood?"

Cabel nodded, exhaustion the only thing keeping his panic at bay. They were in the early hours of Thursday morning. He had three days until his family members started to die.

CHAPTER 33

The November sun was too bright, the morning too warm. Cabel used the brim of his fedora to shade his eyes. People who passed him on the sidewalk either eyed him with suspicion or smiled and nodded. Both groups seemed to believe he had drunk too much the night before. But it was the war, not drink, which had him squinting in the light.

Sleep had been filled with nightmares, some of the worst he experienced in years. His night became one where the line between sleep and wakefulness was blurred by dreams, memories, and shell shock that turned the past into present. Threaded through them were visions of a young girl with frightened eyes who begged him to save her. There were moments when he felt as if his fingers scrabbled to find purchase on the rim of sanity as a hungry darkness yawned below.

Unrested and unsettled, it was a relief to step out of the sun and into the cool gloom of the Monadnock Building. He stepped off the elevator on the executive floor of the Evans Manufacturing offices to find the executives and staff in inordinately good moods. People cheerfully greeted him and joked among themselves. There was a general sense of joy and while Cabel didn't begrudge them their happiness, he didn't want to join in either.

He continued down the hall toward his office. Katherine's empty desk surprised him. She seemed to make an effort to be there to greet him each morning and then follow him into his office to review the day's schedule. Feeling slightly ill-used, he opened his office door.

Katherine stood near his desk with her arms flung around the shoulders of a tall man as she sobbed against his shoulder.

Nonplussed, Cabel stared a moment and then began to back out of the room. Katherine saw him and gave him a watery smile as she gently removed herself from the arms of the man who held her.

"Look who came to visit us today," she said in a happy tone that was at odds with her tears.

The man turned to face him.

Cabel's smile rivaled that of everyone else in the building. He rushed forward and hugged his cousin tight. "Jim. I suspect you shouldn't be here, but I'm so glad that you are."

Katherine closed the door quietly as she left the room, leaving the cousins to themselves. Their first awkward moment occurred when they both moved to sit behind the desk. The second followed quickly as they realized the implications of Jim's return to the office.

They spoke at the same time. "I should have told you I was coming." "I'm so glad you're here." Together they laughed.

"Let's move into the board room," Cabel suggested, gathering papers he wanted to review with Jim.

Soon they were seated side by side, coffee cups in hand and papers stacked nearby.

"You're looking well," Cabel said.

"You're not." Jim studied him with concern. "I overheard Aunt Margaret telling Marta that she was worried about you, and now I see why."

Cabel gave a silent curse at his thoughtlessness. Although he knew he needed to get his mother out of Chicago, he should have realized what would happen when she arrived at his home in St. Joe. He shuddered at the thought of what awaited him when he returned. Knowing that there was a sixty-two mile stretch of Lake Michigan between here and there gave him some comfort.

"I hope you didn't rush here on my account. I'm tired, that's all."

"No it isn't." Jim turned his face away but not before Cabel saw the disappointment in his eyes.

"You're right. I'm sorry I lied to you." He sighed. "When we spoke yesterday I told you where things stood between us and our fathers, but nothing has been truly decided yet."

Jim faced him again. "I know, and I know that standing up to your father to save the company was difficult, but I believe there is more. Please tell me."

Cabel bit his lip to keep from sighing again. How much to tell? "Dealing with my father has been trying. Realizing that he has no place in my life has been harder," Cabel began. "But yes, there is more. I've learned new information about A-A-Amanda," he stumbled over the name as there were so many to choose from, "which has placed me in an awkward situation."

"Awkward or dangerous?"

"Some of both." Cabel gave a rueful smile. "There are things I can't tell you, for my safety as well as yours." He knew his cousin would join him in the tunnels without hesitation but he would not put Jim's life in any more risk than it already was.

"I heard Aunt Margaret say that she thought you were in danger. Are you?"

Cabel nodded. "As I looked into who killed Amanda, I have crossed paths with Al Capone."

Jim's face darkened. "I never should have asked for your help. This happened because of me. Stop, just stop and walk away. You've done enough."

"I can't." Cabel held up a hand to stop Jim's protests. "Truly, I would but I can't. Capone's threatened you, Marta, and Jorge. I need to help him with something or you will all die."

"No," Jim said, shaking his head with disbelief until he saw the truth in Cabel's eyes. His shoulders sagged. "I'm so sorry, Cabe. I never suspected anything like this."

"Why would you? She played her part well."

Tears glistened in Jim's eyes and he quickly blinked them away. "I loved her so much that I could never imagine hating her, but now I think I might. Who was she, really?"

"I promise I will tell you all that I know when this is finished, but not yet."

"But…"

"No, Jim, this isn't the time. Let's talk about the company. Are you ready to come back to work?"

Jim nodded and seemed relieved at the change in subject. "I am so bored and restless that I'm surprised Marta didn't send me here in a box days ago." Jim smiled. "I had forgotten how wonderful she is. You should know that as much as I'd like to be back, I know I'm not able to be at work full-time. I tire too easily. I came because I was worried about you, but if I'm honest, I'm worried about my place here. You saved the company when I couldn't."

Cabel shook his head, touched by his cousin's honesty and the fear behind it. "The company isn't saved yet and if it is, it's because of my mother rather than anything I did. I almost feel sorry for my father. After this he will be quite alone."

"My family as well. I've decided to get an apartment or house of my own. I can't live with my parents after what my father did and knowing that my mother was part of it."

"Perhaps it was past time for both of us to reach this place."

Jim smiled. "I think you're right." His smile dimmed. "What about you and the company. Will you stay on?"

"I will be here for as long as you need me, but after that no. I've watched our fathers bicker and compete with each other, with us, over the prestige of this company, and the credit for its success. I don't want to repeat their mistakes with you."

"It doesn't have to be that way. We aren't our fathers."

"True," Cabel said, "but we both have the desire to be the best and to be in charge. I've come to realize how important family is and you're part of mine. I will not risk that for a place in the company and, once you've recovered, you won't need me here. I think it's time I start something of my own."

"That sounds wonderful, as long as you don't compete with Evans Manufacturing."

"I promise."

Cabel drew a report from the stack he had brought and together he and Jim reviewed the information it contained. As they did, Cabel smiled to himself. He enjoyed being here with Jim, working at the company they both loved, but he also felt at peace. This interlude, however long it would last, allowed him to appreciate his cousin as a true business leader, which gave him the freedom to seek a new path. Only Capone stood between him and this unknown future.

After a brief knock on the door, Katherine stepped into the room. "Mr. Cabel, you have a telephone call but the man wouldn't give his name."

"Thank you." Cabel left the room, looking back only long enough to see Jim and Katherine with their heads together over a report.

In his office, he picked up the earpiece. "Hello?"

"It's me, Louie. The boss wants you to know that Floyd is missing. I've talked with some of the men and a few of them say that they've seen Floyd and Vic drinking together a few times, which surprised them because De Luca never drank with anyone."

"What else do you know about Floyd?"

"I've been asking around since he went missing last night. Seems he heard Capone wanted to talk with him and suddenly was nowhere to be found. Anyway, I asked around about him. From what they tell me, he grew up over in Michigan somewhere. Benton Harbor, I think, and worked on a farm."

With those words, Cabel understood. He reached for the file with the investigator's notes and pulled out three photographs. Two showed Amanda in front of the House of David Amusement

Park gates. In one she was with her sister. In the other she stood next to… "Floyd."

"What?"

"Did Floyd work on an apple farm?"

"How the hell would I know?"

"It doesn't matter. I think I know how Floyd knew Amanda, or Alma, or whatever you want to call her. He's the one who hired the girl and is behind all of this."

"Are you sure?"

"Yes." Cabel studied the photograph again and felt like an imbecile for not recognizing Floyd sooner. The day he had followed Cabel to the office, he had the same tilt of his head and angle of his hat as he leaned against the building across the street. So many things now made sense. They just needed to find him.

"I'll tell the boss what you said. This helps, of course, but you still need to find that stolen booze. You have less than three days." The earpiece buzzed, indicating that Louie had ended the call.

CHAPTER 34

Cabel returned to the conference room to find Christopher Stanton sitting next to Jim, deep in discussion. A stack of legal documents sat on the table between them.

"Hello, Christopher. I'm glad you could join us," Cabel said as he sat next to his cousin. "Did someone call to tell you that Jim was here or was his presence a pleasant surprise?"

"A very pleasant surprise indeed and a fortuitous circumstance as well. Your fathers' lawyer came by my office yesterday morning with demands from his clients." Christopher shook his head, a small smile played at his lips. "I always respect my legal colleagues even when their clients' interests run counter to mine. Until yesterday, I never pitied one.

"Edward and Frank made several demands that his own attorney knew would never be met but was legally required to present to me. He knew he was fighting a losing battle and together we worked out a compromise that I believe is in the best interests of the company but perhaps not your own, Cabel."

"You know how I feel. What is best for the company is what we will do."

"Wait. What is the issue here?" Jim asked.

"It has to do with the repayment of the loan. Edward and Frank have agreed to repay the loan to the company, not Cabel. This will also allow them to return the funds they used without authorization over the years without feeling that they were in the wrong. You will both receive additional dividends from these funds, as the amounts should have been included in the income of the company from the start." He sighed. "I am appalled at their treatment of their sons and this company their father worked so hard to build and you both run so well. Anyway, in addition to the return of the loan, they will no longer be involved in the day-to-day running of the company. As shareholders, they will continue to share in its profits and sit on the board, but that will be the extent of their involvement."

"But what about Cabe? The money should be his."

Cabel shook his head. "I didn't know about the trust and the income from my shares is enough for me to live on. It doesn't matter to me."

"It should," Jim said.

"You don't understand. My father needs to repay the loan to the company rather than to me to protect his reputation, at least that is how he sees it. He needs that more than I need the money. This is also one small way I can atone for what I did to him five years ago."

"No. You don't owe that man anything," Jim said.

"I have to agree," Christopher added. "That said, by allowing Edward to repay the loan through the company, we can resolve this matter today and that is worth considering."

"Jim, I appreciate how you feel, but the executives of Sears and Roebuck are watching us closely. The sooner we stop any discussion of opening retail stores, the stronger you look as a business leader. The fact that this is happening on a day that you are in the office increases your credibility in the business community."

"I agree with Cabel. As I said from the beginning, this is best for the company and that is who I represent."

Jim frowned at his cousin and then smiled. "All right, I will agree to this, on one condition." He turned to Christopher. "This morning Cabe and I discussed our roles in the company. He feels it is best to have one strong leader, me, rather than confuse the staff and the business community by both of us having an active role."

The look Christopher gave Cabel held respect and a hint of sadness. "I have to say that again, I agree."

"I will only remain as president of Evans Manufacturing and allow this travesty of an agreement with our fathers to go forward if Cabe agrees to attend the monthly board meetings and to be available for consultation as needed."

Cabel felt his heart swell with pride for his cousin and joy that he might still have a small role in the success of this business. Perhaps he did not need to fully shed his past to find his future.

"I can accept those terms, though as I said, I am thinking of starting a small company of my own."

"Excellent idea," Christopher said. "It is time you reentered the business world and that is a perfect way to do so."

"There is one demand I will make in this as well," Cabel said. "You know I have the same number of shares in this company as Jim but when I turn thirty next year, the company trust will end I will acquire both my grandmother's and grandfather's shares as well." He turned to Jim. "As head of this business, you need to be the majority shareholder. These shares have to come to you. Neither of our grandparents anticipated that we would find ourselves in this place, but here we are. We need to correct this and now is the best time."

"No, Cabe, Grandfather wanted you to have them."

"You're wrong, Jim. He wanted the president of the company to have them and that person is you." Cabel turned to Christopher. "How do we make that happen?"

The lawyer stared at the cousins a moment. "My father knew your grandfather better than I did, but I know that he would be very impressed with both of you at this moment." He turned to Jim. "Cabel's correct. As president, you must be the majority shareholder. There can be no doubt that, while everyone in the family can participate in the company and voice their opinions, the final decision must rest with you. Cabel trusts you with this authority, as do I. Are you ready to accept it?"

Jim stood and walked to the windows. The traffic on Jackson Street seemed to hold great fascination. In this moment, Cabel realized just how young his cousin was, how young he himself had been when he was forced to take over the management of the company. Jim had already proven himself to everyone else, but would he trust himself enough to continue to serve as head of the company? Cabel remembered a question he had asked Katherine his first day in the office and realized he needed to address it to his cousin.

"Jim, do you want to be president of Evans Manufacturing?"

Still looking out the window, Jim seemed to grow taller. He turned. "Yes. I love running this company and I do want to continue as president. With our fathers out of the way, just think of what could be accomplished."

IIII

The rest of the day was a blur of paperwork and telephone calls. Katherine kept them supplied with strong coffee and fortifying sandwiches. Each time she left she room, her gaze would linger on Jim, as if assuring herself that he was here and well.

Throughout the day, Jim spoke with confidence and made each decision with decisive authority. He worked with Christopher and the various department managers to apprise himself of what had happened during his absence and to begin to correct the damage caused by Edward and Frank. Throughout the various meetings, Cabel noticed that Jim's concentration wavered whenever Katherine was in the room. He was pleased to see that his cousin was healing emotionally as well as physically.

Around two o'clock, exhaustion caused Cabel's vision to blur, making it difficult to see the words on the pages in front of him. By three, he realized that Jim had pushed himself too far. What had been intended as a short visit had become a full working day, and his cousin was not yet up to the demands of the job. It was telling that Jim made no complaint when Cabel called the meetings to an end.

When the cousins were alone once again, Jim said, "You have done all that I asked and more with regard to the company and Amanda. I had hoped I was strong enough to return to work but I'm afraid that Marta and Dr. Lewis are right. I need more time to heal."

"Marta is rarely wrong in these matters."

Jim laughed.

"You can stay in the hotel with me tonight," Cabel offered.

"Tempting, but I promised Marta and Aunt Margaret that I would take the train back this evening. I know that if I stay in Chicago I'll want to come into the office tomorrow and it wouldn't be good for company morale if I collapsed during a meeting."

"True, though people will be disappointed. You have no appreciation of the positive effect your presence has had today."

Jim smiled. "Thanks, Cousin. And thank you for running the company when I couldn't and for dealing with our fathers' messes." He sighed. "I'll work with Christopher to assure that you are fairly compensated for your trust shares. I know what a generous sacrifice it was for you to make that offer."

"Honestly, it wasn't as much of a sacrifice as I expected. You deserve them."

"If you hadn't gone to war, you would be sitting here now."

Cabel nodded. "True. And where would you be?" The question had no answer. "In the end, it doesn't matter. Here is where we are and I am so proud of you."

"And I you, Cabe. You'll stay until I am ready to come back full time?"

"Of course. Until then, I'll take you to the train station and return you to Marta before I find myself in trouble."

"Maybe you should come with me," Jim said. "You look as if you could use some of her care as well."

Cabel shook his head. As tempting as the offer was, he had less than three days to meet Capone's demand. Since he had no idea how to accomplish this task, he needed to get back to the tunnels and hope he would see something he missed before.

"At least get some food and sleep."

"That I can manage."

They reached the conference room door when they heard Eunice's sharp voice. "Where is my son? I want to see him now."

Cabel and Jim looked at each other a moment. "If we take the back hallway, we'll be at the elevators before anyone knows we're gone," Cabel suggested.

"Lead the way."

CHAPTER 35

The countdown to Capone's deadline ticked relentlessly toward zero. Cabel awoke Friday morning with the weight of the passing seconds sitting uneasily on his shoulders.

After dropping Jim at the train station the night before, he had returned to his hotel and showered. A quick meal, a brief nap, and he would return to the tunnels. He would not leave until he found Capone's treasure, save his family, and maybe rescue a young girl from a horrible fate. The situation would be laughable if it wasn't so deadly.

The last thing he remembered was sitting on the edge of the bed.

He awoke to find shafts of morning sunshine shining in his eyes. Turning to the bedside table he saw that he should have been in the office an hour ago. Although the battle against his father and uncle appeared to be over, Cabel knew he should go to work and address the needs of the business. Instead, he calculated how much time he had until Capone would make good on his threat. Thirty-six to forty hours at most. The company would survive his absence for the day but unless he met Capone's demands his family would not.

Using a payphone in the hotel lobby, he called Katherine, and then Christopher, to make excuses for his absence. They both quickly accepted his claim of feeling unwell, which had him realize how exhausted he had looked the last few days. Their concern sounded genuine and Cabel was surprised that he found this to be a comfort rather than a burden.

Shoving more nickels into the slot, he placed calls to the Metropole Hotel and then the Cullerton. Louie was nowhere to be found.

If he couldn't find Capone's nephew, he would need a new guide to the tunnels.

Adjacent to the telephone boxes, a shoeshine boy polished the leather oxfords of a clean-shaven man who never looked up from his newspaper. Cabel studied the scene a moment and knew who might help.

IIIII

The bell tinkled above the barbershop door as Cabel entered. Mack glanced over and smiled at his visitor before wiping the last bit of shaving cream off of the face of the young man seated in the red chair. Money exchanged hands, along with a bottle of hair tonic, and the pink-cheeked customer stepped into the cold November day.

Mack studied Cabel a moment. "You look like a man in the soup." He smiled at Cabel's blank expression. "It means that you look like a man in trouble." The barber walked to a small sink and rinsed the shaving brush. He looked back at Cabel. "The question is, did you bring the trouble with you or are you looking for it?"

Cabel considered the question. "Some of both, I suppose."

"Ah, you must have a bit of Irish in you then, to be giving an answer like that." Mack finished at the sink and looked at Cabel. "You're needing my help then?"

"I need to get into the tunnels, and I need a guide."

Mack stilled. "I can let you into the tunnels, you know that, but taking you where you aren't supposed to be? I'm sorry, no. The Italian gang tolerates me because I'm married to a good Sicilian girl." A quick, bright smile lit his face. "My fine whiskey helps too, especially since Mr. Capone has a taste for it." Mack's eyes lost their humor. "Neither will protect me if I'm found to be helping someone I shouldn't."

"I understand." Cabel struggled to find the words to convey the essence of the situation, if not the details. "Capone has, um, encouraged me to help him locate something that has gone missing in the tunnels. I've been down there with his nephew, Louie, twice but I can't find him today and I'm running out of time."

"Louie's taken you, then? And you're sure Capone told him to do this? Sometimes that young man likes to go his own way and that could get you killed."

"I'm sure. I was with Capone when he ordered Louie to take me into the tunnels the first time and I've seen him since then, to report on my progress. Or rather, lack of it." Cabel didn't understand the barber's concern. "I have less than two days to find the missing items before my family is harmed."

Mack studied him a moment. "Is this problem you're dealing with the same one that got my neighbor killed?"

"Probably," Cabel admitted. "Please. I just need you to get me to the main tunnels. I'm sure I can manage from there."

"I'm thinking you'll be needing a bit more help than that." He shook his head. "I'll close the shop and take you into the underworld. I'm just hoping we can find your missing treasure without having to pay the devil for the privilege."

Cabel waited while Mack finished cleaning the brush then locked the front door, flipping the sign from Open to Closed. The back office looked the same as before, neglected and slightly disorganized, with a stack of boxes against one wall. Mack shoved them aside and opened the concealed doorway.

At the bottom of the stairs, Mack checked the flame under the still. He selected two small logs from the wood stacked against the far wall and added it to the fire. Cabel watched the smoke rise up and disappear into the vents near the ceiling.

"My wife worries about me having a fire down here, but I tell her that God designed these tunnels for those of us wanting a safe place to brew a fine whiskey. There's always a breeze and the smoke is pulled above ground with nary a hint of a scent left behind. She says God had nothing to do with it. It's just my family's luck for finding a good spot for illegal trade. Same thing, to my way of thinking." Mack smiled but it didn't reach his eyes.

"Thank you for helping me," Cabel said to acknowledge the man's concerns. "I promise you I am telling the truth. Capone wants me in the tunnels to find what he's lost."

"I believe you, Mr. Cabel. The problem is, there's also someone down here that doesn't want it found, isn't there?" Mack didn't wait for an answer as he turned from the still and took two flashlights from a shelf near the tunnel door. He handed one to Cabel along with a piece of chalk.

Cabel stared at it, then at Mack.

"Put that in your pocket."

Confused, Cabel did as he was told. Mack unlocked the door. Both men turned on their flashlights and stepped into the darkness.

As promised, the air moved well and held only a hint of smoke. Cabel knew that they were several blocks from the Cullerton Hotel but fairly close to several of the bars that Capone's men kept supplied with alcohol and beer. Their underground route would take him through parts of the tunnel system he hadn't seen yet, which might help him with his search.

The small tunnel led to a slightly larger one. Mack took one turn after another. Soon Cabel couldn't tell whether they were headed east or north.

"How do you keep track of where you are?" he asked.

"By my marks, of course."

"Your what?"

Mack turned and shone his flashlight near Cabel's face, but not in his eyes. "Are you saying you've been wandering these tunnels, guide or no, without chalk or marks?" He shook his head and continued walking as he spoke. "When you're in the main tunnels there's always landmarks, doors to the speakeasies, storage rooms, and such. In other places you'll be wanting to make sure you can find your way, so you mark the walls."

Cabel remembered the first time he went into the tunnels. Capone said something about marking his way and he knew about the marks in the main tunnels, but no one had told him to make his own.

"When I started delivering my whiskey to the storage rooms near the Cullerton, I didn't want to lose my way, so I drew my mark on the wall each time I made a turn. Like this one."

His flashlight beam stopped at a low spot of the wall about a foot from the juncture of the next tunnel. A pair of squiggled lines was drawn a few inches above the floor.

"Like most of the men, I mark my path near the ground. I need to see where I'm walking, don't I? Because my flashlight is already pointed down, it's easier to see my marks if they're low as well. Now, Capone's gang draws their marks at the edge of the crossroads, sometimes with arrows so they know to turn or keep straight. I'm putting mine farther back where no one is looking for them. I don't want unexpected company knocking on my stillroom door."

Cabel nodded, though Mack couldn't see him. This explained how Louie was able to find the way to the thieves' tunnel so easily. The path had been marked.

"You learn who travels where in the tunnels by their marks. You'll be wanting to make up one of your own, just to be safe."

"Like what?"

"Could be anything, couldn't it? A cross or a circle, though you want to make it a bit different, so you know which one is yours."

Cabel stumbled.

"Are you all right back there, Mr. Cabel?"

"Have you ever seen a circle with a dot in it or a crescent moon with a line above and below?"

"No, but I don't take the tunnels anywhere except from my still to the storage rooms. Are they marks you're wanting to claim or ones you've seen?"

"Neither, but I think one of them will lead me to the, um, thing I'm searching for."

Mack paused and waited for Cabel to stand beside him. "So you think you know what to look for now?"

Cabel nodded.

"That will only help you if you know where to find the first mark so you can follow the trail. Any thoughts on that, Mr. Cabel?"

"Yes," Cabel said. "If you get me to the main tunnels by the Cullerton, I think I can manage from there."

"Now then, I'll be helping you look a bit more than that. Don't you worry. I'm Irish. I know to leave before trouble starts. Of course, being Irish, that doesn't mean I won't stay for the fun, does it?" He laughed and continued on a path that now Cabel could follow as well.

CHAPTER 36

Cabel and Mack searched offshoot passageways of the main tunnel near the cognac room for almost an hour before Mack found a crude circle with a dot in its center drawn on a dirty wall.

"Here it is, then," Mack said as Cabel joined him. The chalked symbol seemed to glow in the beam of the flashlight. "The newer tunnel stops here and there's nothing but brick and dirt beyond. I haven't looked for the next mark, but the fact that this one is drawn on the left wall, I'm guessing it's telling you which way to go."

Cabel nodded. The cement-walled tunnel ended at a T with a narrower passageway leading in both directions. His flashlight revealed rubble and broken bricks on the floor of the right side of the decrepit corridor. Shining the light above, he could see that a ceiling had once arched above but most of it now lay scattered on the ground. Bits and pieces still clung to the dirt overhead. Cabel shuddered at the thought of being buried alive in this place that seemed both past and present to his war-ravaged mind.

Lowering his flashlight, he shone the beam down the left side of the tunnel. Here the rubble had been swept aside but the packed dirt shared no secrets.

"I'm thinking someone was needing this tunnel clear for a reason. Maybe carting off something that wasn't theirs."

Cabel nodded. Realizing Mack couldn't see him, he said, "You're right." Probably Floyd and maybe his partner, De Luca, had used this passage. He shone the flashlight down the corridor that led to the answers he sought. "Mack, please go back to the main tunnel and see if you can locate Louie. Ask the men if you have to, and if Louie isn't around, find Capone."

"Are you sure this is what you want to do?"

"No, but it is necessary. Don't come down this tunnel yourself. Just lead them to the first symbol and they'll know what to do from there."

Mack left and the light Cabel held seemed to dim.

He turned left and swept the flashlight's beam back and forth across the floor, wary of tripping over broken bricks or missing another symbol. The passageway split again and Cabel found the symbol directing him to go right. Despite the obvious signpost, he paused. The floor had been cleaned of debris in both directions.

Curious, he took a few cautious steps into the other side of the tunnel. A bit farther down it joined another, wider one, that seemed to link back to the main tunnel system. A few yards later it met with the junction of another passageway. Here he found the chalked symbol of a crescent moon with a line above and below. This was the mark he found hidden at Amanda's Levee apartment and he wondered what it meant.

He retraced his steps until he returned to the dot within the circle mark and continued to follow where that trail led. A door, like many others he had passed, stood ajar a few feet from where he stood, the circle and dot symbol drawn above it. The answers within were Capone's, not his, so he would wait where he was until Louie or his uncle arrived.

The door swung open on well-oiled hinges. Floyd appeared in the entryway, a heavy gun in one hand and a flashlight in the other. "I suppose a swank like you is waiting for an invitation. Come inside and let's finish this."

Floyd stepped back and motioned for Cabel to enter before him. The modest room held a small camp stove, bedroll, tins of food and a small water barrel. Floyd kept his gun pointed at

Cabel as he lit an oil lamp on the floor near the entrance. He lit another near the bedroll before turning off his flashlight. Cabel did the same.

"Cozy, isn't it?" Floyd's mirthless laugh echoed off the cement walls. "You asked too many questions, put too many things together, and now I'm stuck down here until we finish the job." He stalked closer to Cabel. "Do you know what she did with it?"

"What?"

He leaned close to Cabel and said softly, "Ada. Do you know what she did with the cognac?"

Floyd's question made no sense. "I thought I'd find the cognac here."

"I'm not surprised. This is where De Luca and I left it but it isn't here anymore, is it?" He turned, kicking an empty can out of his path. "I brought Ada in on this and then she fell for your cousin and betrayed me." He turned to face Cabel. "We had this all worked out, I just needed a girl and I knew Ada would be perfect. I visited her sister over at the House of David and found out how to contact her. Ada and I didn't part ways on the best of terms so I had to encourage her to come back."

"You threatened her sister."

"And her mother. Ada comes back and before I know it the mother and the girl have gone back to whatever hill country they came from."

"She sent them away," Cabel said, trying to understand. "Then why did she stay and help you?"

Floyd kicked another can, hard enough for it to bounce off the wall. "I thought it was because she was loyal to me. I taught her how to play men, be what they wanted and make money at it. So maybe I got a little jealous. She was too good at her job, so I smacked her around a bit and she left. Doesn't matter. I taught her everything she knew. She owed me but then she fell for her mark."

"Jim?"

"Yes, Mr. Swanky with his money and clothes. She actually carried a torch for the big shot," he shouted, looking around for something else to kick. Finding nothing nearby, he leveled the gun at Cabel. "She was smart and I guess she figured out that we weren't just setting up Fratti as the fall guy. She had to die too, right after she was supposed to move out of her apartment."

With those words, Cabel understood a little bit more. "These tunnels connect to her apartment building, don't they? It has to be nearby. She was going to pack up her things and leave, using a truck that was going to hold cognac and alcohol instead of furniture."

"You're almost as smart of Capone thinks. Yea, we were going to move it that way, but somehow the tunnel entrance was sealed over at her end. Real professional job but I can't figure out how she did it."

Cabel thought of the young man he had met at Ada's apartment. Billy was good with his hands and liked doing favors for his friends. Maybe he had helped Amanda hide the cognac before he sealed the wall in their apartment building.

"We met here." He waved his empty hand to encompass the room. "We traded information and planned everything out. No one could find this room and everything was Jake."

"But Capone found out about the theft too soon."

"Yeah, he did. I wanted to wait a few more days to steal the cognac, but no, he said it was best to move it right away, so we did."

"Who told you to move it?"

"I did."

CHAPTER 37

Louie stepped into the room, swinging the door shut behind him and continued the story as if he had been listening at the door. "I knew my uncle's plan and also that I needed an alibi." He glanced around the room, disgust apparent on his face. He looked at Cabel. "I wanted more power, to be given real responsibility and all he said was for me to earn it like everyone else. But he didn't earn it, did he? No. He just took it, so I decided to do the same." He smiled and turned to Floyd. "Maybe I moved too soon in stealing the cognac, but so did you, when you killed the girl."

"How was I supposed to know she stole it?"

"If you had followed the plan, it wouldn't have mattered. We could have threatened Jim Evans' life to get it back from her, or let her go like she wanted."

"Well, I didn't know that before I killed her, did I?" Floyd shouted.

"You look confused, Cabel. Let me explain." Louie lowered his gun and Floyd did the same. "I wanted to steal my uncle's cognac. He needed to see me as a leader, not a follower but he never gave me the chance. To Uncle Al, I'm just an errand boy, and so I decided to show him different. I knew I couldn't pull this heist on my own and that De Luca was unhappy at being handed off to Capone, so I brought him into the deal. He told me that Floyd might be useful as well, so two became three."

"Useful? I was more than that. I brought in Ada, made the plan. Without me, you two would still be standing around trying to figure out what to do."

Louie shrugged. "You did help, Floyd, more than I expected. Not that it matters now. You mucked everything up and I still don't have the cognac." He turned back to Cabel. "I knew where Uncle Al planned to store his prize so De Luca and I found a parallel tunnel. We all took turns digging through the walls until we found the room that backed up against the wall we wanted. Then we waited."

"We dug? I don't remember you down there with a pick and shovel," Floyd said. "You're just like your uncle, taking credit for everyone else's work."

Louie was distracted by the bickering with Floyd, but he stood in front of the only door in the room and he had a gun. Cabel didn't like his odds but he knew something these men didn't. Amanda just might save his life tonight.

"Shut up. You don't know what you're talking about," Louie shouted, then turned his attention to Cabel. In a calmer voice, he said, "The night the cognac was delivered, the men were ordered to clear out, except for the guards near the Cullerton and above ground where the crates were brought down. No one knew about the other access points, like a nearby apartment building. Floyd and De Luca waited until four in the morning before they broke through the wall and moved the cognac here. My uncle should have come and gone by then. Instead, he arrived much later than planned and discovered the theft. He was furious. Then he treated me like a servant, sending me into the tunnels over and over to find the cognac. Of course, I didn't have to actually look for it because I knew where it was all along."

"You act like you have it so hard, but you're sitting pretty, aren't you?" Floyd snarled. "Capone doesn't know you're involved, so you can walk out of here any time you want with no one the wiser."

Louie glared at Floyd. "I'm nothing to my uncle but a patsy to use as he wants. I get no respect and that's the thing I want. It's what the cognac will get me."

"Except Amanda stole it?" Cabel asked.

"Yes," Louie snapped. "She moved it somewhere. She had to have help, but we don't know who. Then she leaves a note for Floyd telling him she'll give him the cognac if he lets her out of their deal. She wanted to be Amanda and marry the man she loves. But before he gets the note, he shoots her. The only smart thing he did was kill her as Amanda rather than Alma," Louie said.

"I did a lot more smart stuff than that. I'm the one who figured out how to work this scam."

"And I'm the one who can make the most money from it once we find it."

"But how are we going to do that? We don't know where it is."

"What about De Luca and the private investigator?" Cabel asked, hoping to keep them fighting and distracted.

Floyd picked up the story. "I convinced De Luca that Louie was double-crossing us. I took him to the private dick's office to find out what he knew and to cover my own tracks. He knew about my connection with Ada, and I had to make sure he couldn't tell anyone else. The next day I told De Luca that I had the goods on Louie and arranged to meet him in the original storage room. I knew he wasn't happy, and if we didn't find the booze soon, he'd start mouthing off to the wrong person. We didn't need the stooge anymore, so I shot him."

"And maybe you helped Ada move the cognac and then killed her so you wouldn't have to share the profits," Cabel said.

"If I had helped her, I'd be long gone. Besides, we'd always planned to kill her. I tell you, it wasn't me."

Louie nodded. "That's what I thought." He raised his gun and fired.

Cabel fell to his knees, hands over his ears, as the sound of the blast reverberated through the small room. Head pounding from the noise he looked up and saw Floyd on the ground, blood pooling beneath his body. Louie stood looking at the body, one hand over an ear, the other holding the gun at his side. He walked to Cabel and knelt, offering a flask. He accepted it with a shaking hand.

They both sat with their backs against the wall sharing the flask, though their earlier camaraderie was absent. Louie took a last swig, capped the flask, and returned it to his coat pocket.

"Can you hear now?" Louie asked.

Cabel nodded.

"Good." He stood. "I ran into Mack and he sent me here. There were too many other people around to kill him but I'll catch up to him later."

Cabel rose to his feet. "You don't have to hurt him. He didn't come down the corridor and doesn't know anything."

"He knows enough, and I'm sure he will start asking questions when you disappear. Tell me you know where the cognac is."

Cabel gave a harsh laugh. "Why would I tell you if you're going to kill me anyway?"

"To save your cousin and mother, and anyone else you care about. If you help me, I'll convince Uncle Al that Floyd killed you, so he won't have a reason to go after your family." Louie's smile was bright and cold. "As my uncle told you, you can't save everyone." He laughed. "Seems like you can't even save yourself. Now take me to the cognac." He pointed his gun at Cabel.

Cabel's legs shook as he walked to the door and remembered feeling the same way the first time he'd marched into the trenches. He'd thought death a certainty then. He did now as well.

CHAPTER 38

He opened the door and fumbled for his flashlight. The tunnels in this part of the system were pitch black. He had a flashlight, but so did Louie. Despite his fears, if he saw an opportunity, he'd turn off his light and dart down a side tunnel. Maybe he could lose Louie in the dark.

"Stop stalling," Louie said as he shoved the barrel of the gun between Cabel's shoulder blades.

Cabel nodded, the beam of the flashlight wavering from his shaking hand as he led them to the junction where Floyd's mark led in one direction and Amanda's in another. It was the best place he could think of to make his move and reach the main tunnel. He swept the light across the passageway to find the mark and assure himself that he was in the right place.

He turned and used the flashlight as a club, smashing it into Louie's nose. The snap of the bone gave Cabel hope that he might make it out alive. Louie yelled in pain and dropped his flashlight but not the gun. Cabel kicked the flashlight away then took the turn at the junction and ran.

"I will kill you," Louie called out, his voice echoing through the tunnel.

Cabel followed Floyd's marks and ran, though his speed was hindered by the rubble strewn across the floor. He looked back and saw the beam of a flashlight. Either Louie had found his own or had gone back to retrieve Floyd's.

At the next crossroad, he realized that Louie was getting closer. The young man knew the tunnels and was tracking Cabel's every sound. Despite his growing terror, Cabel understood that the darkness might be his only chance to survive. At the next juncture, he wiped away Floyd's mark and used the chalk Mack had given him to draw a new one that would lead Louie in the wrong direction. After he finished, he took the correct passage and turned off his flashlight.

Impenetrable darkness enveloped him. He could see nothing, yet his mind filled the void with terrible images of the trenches and bloody battlefields. Fighting against his fear and the past, he took quiet, tentative steps away from his hunter.

"The darkness can't hide you for long, Cabel. But we'll see who finds you first, me or your ghosts."

Keeping his hand against the wall, Cabel continued to creep forward. His heartbeat sounded so loud he was surprised that Louie couldn't hear it. He thought he heard a rustle in the dark ahead of him and wondered if Louie's prediction would prove true.

"I don't want to play hide and seek with you, Cabel. Lead me to the cognac and maybe I'll let you live. Of course my uncle will kill your family, but at least you'll survive. That's the best deal you'll get. Come out and let's get this done." Louie's voice faded as he took Cabel's bait and walked past the entrance to the tunnel.

Underneath the sound of Louie's voice, Cabel could hear a murmur. Perhaps the dead had come to escort him home. "No," he whispered under his breath. He did not die in the trenches of someone else's war and he would not do so in these tunnels today. The anger he worked so hard to control struggled against its tether.

"You tricked me!" Louie shouted in the distance. "When I find you, I will shoot your kneecaps until you talk and then I'll kill your cousin." His voice grew louder as he retraced his steps.

Cabel continued his slow progress to safety and considered his options. If Louie found him before he reached the main tunnels, he would fight to stay alive. Once again he gripped his flashlight as if it were a weapon, knowing it wouldn't stop a bullet, but it was all he had. Distracted by these thoughts, he tripped on some debris and fell hard.

"I hear you," Louie called with glee.

Cabel looked over his shoulder and could see the beam of the young gangster's light. Knowing he would become a target if he turned on his own, he stayed in the dark as he struggled to his feet. He flattened himself into a wide niche in the wall behind him, hoping it would hide him until Louie was close enough to hit with the flashlight.

Louie's beam grew brighter. "Come out, Cabel. There's no one here to save you. Let me have my cognac and I'll kill you fast, I promise. Turn on your light so I can see you."

Several flashlights turned on at once. Cabel blinked against the sudden brightness and saw Louie standing in the middle of the tunnel with his arm thrown up to shield his eyes from the light.

Two men rushed forward and grabbed Louie's arm, taking his gun and flashlight away. Then they dragged him to Capone. The gangster stood in front of his nephew a moment. "You disappoint me." He then spoke to the men who held Louie. "There's a truck waiting outside. Take him up to the Wisconsin compound so I can deal with him in private."

The men nodded and began to drag Louie away.

"No, Uncle Al, please. I was just trying to help find the cognac. It was Floyd and Cabel who were in on this, not me." His shouts faded as he was taken to his fate.

Capone turned to Cabel. "We heard Louie yelling so I had my men turn off their lights and wait in the tunnel to see what would happen. I heard everything." He shook his head. "I knew he had a wild streak, but I had no idea he was stupid." Capone's shoulders sagged as he looked down the tunnel where his men had taken Louie. He turned back to Cabel. "My nephew told me how you hated being in these tunnels, that they reminded you of the war. Knowing that, I have to say that I am impressed by your courage." He slapped Cabel's cheek gently, then leaned forward and stared at him with cold and determined eyes. "Did you find the cognac?"

It took a moment for Cabel to find his voice. "No, but I know where it is."

"Is it down here?"

Cabel nodded.

"Good." He stepped back. "Your friend Mack found me after he'd seen Louie. Lucky for you, he doesn't much trust my nephew. Lucky for him, you didn't tell him more than was necessary to help you. I'd hate to have to kill a man who has such talent with a still." He turned to his men. "Ricky and Squib, you two come with me. The rest of you get back to what you were doing. And, if any of you talk about what you've seen down here, you'll be joining Louie in the back of that truck."

The men shuffled out of the tunnel.

Capone returned his attention to Cabel. "My nephew was working with Floyd and De Luca, right?"

"Yes. Floyd knew Amanda and brought her in to help them. She wanted out so she stole the cognac from them, hoping to trade it for her freedom. They killed her before they realized she'd taken it."

Capone laughed softly. "I'm really sorry I didn't get a chance to meet that doll." His smile faded. "Take me to my cognac and you might live through this yet."

Cabel walked to the end of the corridor and remarked the passageway. He then led Capone and the two men through the warren of the tunnels. He followed Amanda's chalked symbol, wondering if she was deceiving him as she had all the other men she had known.

The last turn ended at a collapsed tunnel. There was nothing there.

"I guess the doll took her secret to the grave."

Cabel could hear the fury in the gangster's voice. "Maybe not," he said more as a prayer than a hope and walked down the short pathway, shining his light over the brick wall.

Ricky searched the other side of the tunnel. "Here."

Cabel turned to find the young man shoving aside a fallen beam to reveal an opening in the wall.

"Give me that," Capone snapped as he grabbed Ricky's flashlight and climbed through the hole.

A tense moment later the gangster called, "It's all here." Cabel sagged against the wall, shaking with relief.

Ricky walked over to Cabel. "What's in there?"

"Don't be too curious, Ricky, or too greedy. You don't want to end up like my nephew," Capone said as he emerged from Amanda's hiding place clutching a bottle of his precious cognac.

"Sure, Boss," Ricky said with a squeak.

"Actually, I have a couple of jobs for you and Squib."

Capone gave orders to move the cognac and stolen alcohol to a secure room closer to the Cullerton Hotel entrance and to clean the room where Floyd had camped. Finally, he told them where to find De Luca's body and ordered them to take it to an undertaker.

Cabel focused on the harsh voice and sharp orders. He kept has hands pressed into the rough bricks at his back. Still the past intruded. Doughboys wandered by, smoking or talking as they waited for their orders. Others read letters from home or heated rations over a small fire. No one, living or dead, took notice of him leaning against the tunnel wall.

"Hey, I'm talking to you."

A kick to the shin forced Cabel's attention to Capone, who studied him with undisguised curiosity.

"Come on, sap. Let's get you above ground."

CHAPTER 39

Cabel sat at a table in the card room of the Cullerton with only a vague memory of his walk through the tunnels that brought him to this place. Capone took a bottle and a couple of glasses from behind the bar and joined Cabel at the table. Two armed men stood guard by the door. There would be no other witnesses to the coming conversation.

Capone poured whiskey into the glasses and slid one across the table. "It's Mack's. He told me you were partial to it."

Cabel opened his mouth to speak but found he had no voice. Instead, he sipped the whiskey and let its smooth heat warm his soul. His hands shook as he set the glass down but he was calm enough to face the man across from him.

"Tell me everything."

Cabel did, with the exception of Billy, who had probably helped Amanda move the whiskey and seal the entrance to her apartment building. When he mentioned the private investigator Jacob Martin, Capone called one of the men over and sent him to search the dead man's office. Cabel continued his story, stopping to answer the gangster's questions until he reached the part when Capone's men had joined him.

"I know you sent for Louie but I'm glad the Irishman decided to find me as well. He saved your life and my cognac," Capone said.

"Mack did as I asked, but doesn't know anything except that I needed help. Please tell me he is safe."

Capone's harsh laugh made Cabel's skin crawl. "He's fine. You're lucky he trusted you enough to help find that mark on the wall without asking too many questions."

"And Louie?"

The gangster refilled their glasses with slow, controlled motions. "Do you remember what I said I would do to the person who stole my cognac?" His words were clipped.

Cabel looked at Capone and saw rage.

"I asked you a question."

"I think you said something about killing him slowly."

Capone smiled as he reached over and patted Cabel's cheek. "That's right and that is what I intend to do." He held up a hand to cut off Cabel's protests. "I know what you're going to say, that he's young and my nephew, and I should give him a second chance. But if I did that, my men would think that I'm weak. They would know they could use my family to get to me, see? No. Louie will die. Yes his mother and my wife will be upset for a while, but Louie has two brothers and a sister, so they'll be okay. Besides, Louie's mother was born into this life. She might not like it, but she knows the rules.

"And that brings me to you. Do you remember the rules, Mr. Wrong-Place-Wrong-Time? Unlike me, your family *is* your weakness. You tell anyone what you've learned about my business and they die. I have a sudden raid or too many police nosing in my business, they die. Understood?"

Cabel nodded but thought of the young girl he had seen in this room.

Capone shook his head. "The first time I met you was at the Charades Club. I thought you were a sap who made the best of a bad situation. I gave you a ring as a reward, one I still expect returned if you ever need a favor." He sighed. "I had some of my people look into your life and found that you are, unfortunately, an honest sap, which means I can count on you to do what you think is right. And I think you're still worried about the little blond, aren't you? You're trying to figure out how to rescue her and keep your family safe."

"It's just…"

"Shut it. Listen, Mr. Evans, you can't save everyone but the problem here is that, no matter what I say, you're going to try anyway. Louie is a lost cause. He will get what he deserves and my men will know that if I'm willing to kill my nephew, I won't think twice about killing one of them. But the girl… You really are a sap."

The guard who had been sent away returned with a bundle in his hands. Capone motioned him to the table and accepted a small stack of mail.

"It was on the floor. I guess the post office don't know he's dead yet," the guard said, then returned to his position by the door.

Capone thumbed through the letters, setting one aside before shoving the rest to the floor. He picked up the envelope, studied it a moment, and then handed it to Cabel. "It's addressed to Ada Cummings. Looks like her family wrote to her."

Accepting the letter, Cabel nodded. Jim could now contact Amanda's family.

"I don't want to have to kill you or your family, so I have something waiting for you in the lobby. But I need you to listen to me very carefully, Mr. Evans. You have now wandered into my business twice. I am not a fool and yet I believe that both times were because you were trying to help a friend and a cousin. Twice are all the chances you get. I find you in my business again, I will kill you. I'll keep the promise I made to you with the ring, but otherwise stay out of my world, Mr. Evans, and I'll let you live in yours."

Capone rose. Cabel did as well and was surprised when the gangster held out his hand. Cabel returned the gesture.

"I could use a man like you, if only you weren't so honest."

One of the guards opened the door. Cabel nodded his goodbyes to Capone, hoping never to see that scarred face again. He followed the guard to the lobby and found the young blond girl huddled in a dress and shawl too flimsy for the weather.

A beautiful woman with too much makeup and knowing eyes stood next to the girl. "Mr. Capone told me to give you a message. He said that you can't save them all, but he'll let you save this one. He must like you because he said he'd rather lose this product than have to kill your family." She shrugged and walked away.

The blond girl looked at him with big, sad eyes and started crying. Cabel took off his coat and placed it around her shoulders. Guiding her outside, he hailed a cab and together they left the Levee.

CHAPTER 40

A sergeant ordered her troops to lift and carry the supplies. Cabel groaned. Another trench to build, another field to soak in blood.

A telephone jangled, pulling him from the dream. Yet the orders continued to be issued, pausing only to answer the ring.

"Cabel, you have a telephone call. Are you coming down soon? There is much to be done," Marta called.

Cabel groaned again. Dragging himself from the bed, he found some trousers draped over the back of a chair and pulled a shirt from a drawer. Stumbling downstairs, he glanced at the chaos of the dining room and parlor, and escaped to his office, shutting the door firmly as he entered.

He sat at his desk and picked up the handset of the newly installed phone. "Hello?"

"Hello, Cabel, this is Greg Finch."

"Hello, Greg. Do you have any news?"

Cabel heard the young detective sigh. "I have, but I'm not sure if it's what you want to hear."

"Did you locate Myrtle's family?"

"Yes. They live on a small farm in Southern Indiana. It took the local police a while to locate them as the farm is very remote."

Less than a week ago, Cabel had brought Myrtle to Michigan then returned to Chicago and contacted Greg Finch to help locate her family. The girl had been largely unharmed and the Arledge's had taken her in until she could be returned to her family.

"They must be anxious to get their daughter back."

The line was silent.

"Don't they want her back?"

"It isn't that simple, I'm afraid. The family is having a rough time of it and the policeman I spoke to suspects that they had sold the girl for money to keep the farm going." He paused. "They actually are quite anxious to get her back."

"They want to sell her again." Cabel felt the darkness stir. "She's a sweet, smart girl, and they want to sell her?"

"Some farmers are having difficulty bringing in their crops. I'm afraid this situation isn't as unusual as you might think."

"I'm not sending her back."

Greg chuckled. "I knew you would say that. You'll take responsibility for her then?"

Cabel thought of the Arledges who had recently lost a daughter. Myrtle couldn't replace Kittie, but she would certainly be welcomed into the family and he could provide any financial assistance necessary. "Yes. I'll make sure she is cared for."

"Thank you. I guess that's one more thing to celebrate today."

Something large and heavy crashed to the floor. Cabel felt it reverberate through the boards beneath his feet. Shouting and recriminations could be heard.

The sound was loud enough that Greg had heard it over the telephone line. "It sounds as if your celebration is off to an exciting start. Happy Thanksgiving, Cabel."

"To you and your family as well, Greg."

IIIII

A long table nearly filled the dining room. A slightly smaller one stood in the parlor. Cabel had been assigned the role of host, answering the door, greeting the guests, and inviting them into his home. Beyond this meager contribution, his housekeeper Marta was the star of the event and she seemed to be enjoying every minute. Anne Arledge and Myrtle collected coats and placed them on the couch in the study. Jim was responsible for drinks and Kaye Arledge accepted covered dishes that guests brought for the meal.

Jorge Voss and Walter Arledge found a safe corner to stand in to observe the comings and goings. They were joined by Dr. Lewis, and a young man that Cabel guessed was Jorge's son-in-law. As they talked, they kept a close eye on Nate and another boy about his age.

"That's John, the little paper boy," Marta said when she saw who Cabel was studying. "I invited the boy's family to join us as well, but I don't think they were comfortable coming to a home they'd never been to before, especially one on the bluff. I'm so pleased they let John come and I sent a basket for the family with the Arledges that they dropped off when they collected the boy." She paused, letting her eyes roam over the collected guests. "Thank you so much for this, Cabe. I've always wanted to have a large Thanksgiving dinner and never had the chance. You've made me very happy."

He put his arm around the woman who had started him on the path into the light. "I wouldn't be here without you, Marta. If this small thing makes you happy, we'll have to do it again soon."

She looked up at him, her eyes bright with excitement. "Christmas is only a month away. We've never decorated this house up proper, because your family was usually in Chicago for the holidays. Oh, thank you, Cabe. It will be wonderful." She hugged him tight then rushed off to the kitchen.

"What did you just agree to?" Jim asked, grinning.

"Christmas."

Jim laughed. "You've been in the city all week so you missed all the cleaning and cooking that went into this, but you'll get to be in the middle of it next month."

"Was it that bad?"

Jim laughed again and went to join Jorge and the other men.

He looked well, his cousin, Cabel decided. Although Amanda's betrayal had hurt him deeply, knowing that she had truly loved him seemed to lessen the blow. Jim was ready to return to work on Monday, and Cabel was surprised to realize he was ready to be home. Even though his father and uncle had surrendered their shares of the business and the situation was settled, Cabel couldn't be in the office and not think of their betrayals. St. Joseph was also a safe distance from Capone and the tunnels beneath the Levee.

The doorbell rang again. Cabel opened it to find Katherine Anderson standing on the doorstep, her cheeks rosy from the cold. He ushered her inside and Jim came over to continue making the young woman feel welcome.

Soon they were all seated at the various tables. Marta sat nearest the kitchen so she could refill dishes and check on the pies. Cabel sat at the head of the table, which afforded him a view of the parlor across the hall where Nate sat looking clean and well behaved. Cabel wasn't taken in.

Platters were passed, plates filled, and complements were given through full mouths. Marta waved away the praise, but she flushed with pride.

Cabel mostly concentrated on eating, but bits of conversation floated past.

"How long will you be visiting your son, Mrs. Evans?"

"Please, call me Margaret. To answer your question, I'll be staying with Cabel another week or so now that he is back home and won't be working in Chicago. We haven't had much time to talk and we have much to catch up on. After that, I'm planning a trip out east to visit my family."

"There is a new jazz band coming to the Chicago Theatre next week, Katherine. Would you like to go with me?"

"Oh, Mr. James… I mean, Jim, yes. I would enjoy that very much."

Throughout the meal, Cabel noticed that Kaye's attention would drift to the parlor. At first he guessed that she was keeping an eye on Nate and her youngest daughter, Belinda, but, although she smiled at the sight of them, her eyes kept searching.

Cabel's mother leaned over and touched his arm to get his attention. "Don't worry about Kaye. She is a mother who lost a child. All mothers cherish the ones that surround her, but they can't help but search for the ones who are lost, even if they know they can never come home."

Cabel looked at his mother. "Like Kittie, and your daughter, and Jon."

She nodded. "For Lily Warner, that list also includes you."

He felt as if he'd been punched in the stomach.

"Cabe, I'm sorry."

He gave her a tight smile and excused himself from the table.

Stepping onto the front porch, he took deep breaths and kept his face turned into the strong winds blowing in from the lake. Anyone who cared to notice would assume that was the cause of his tears. All these years he had been ashamed to face Lily, guilty at being the one to survive. Now he had a new shame to bear. He had witnessed so many family betrayals in the last weeks, but it never occurred to him that his unwillingness to face Lily dishonored the love and acceptance she had so freely given to him.

The door opened behind him.

He turned to find Nate studying him.

"Oh good, you're awake."

Cabel shook his head. "How could anyone sleep out here in this cold?"

Nate's inelegant shrug effectively conveyed his lack of understanding of the oddities of adults. "You need to come in now. The tables are cleared, but we can't have pie until you come in." He leaned forward and motioned Cabel to do the same. "Miz Marta promised me I could have a piece of pumpkin *and* apple pie if I behaved myself all through dinner. We need to eat it soon because I don't think I can last much longer."

Cabel laughed and let Nate lead him back to the Thanksgiving feast.

CHAPTER 41

The snow-covered walkway muffled the sound of his steps. Light spilled from the parlor windows and glinted on the heavy flakes as they fell silently from the sky. Cabel lifted his face and felt the snow melt on his skin before falling like tears down his cheeks. He wiped the moisture away with a gloved hand and walked up the porch steps.

The soft notes of a Mozart sonata awarded his efforts. Someone in the house was playing the piano and he wondered which of Jon's sisters sat at the keyboard. All five of them had taken lessons, he remembered, but only two showed true talent. That thought, like a cork loosened from a bottle, let other memories spill forth. Unlike those from his own home, these held nothing but love and laughter that were so pure that even the war couldn't taint them.

He stood on the porch in the gathering darkness and knew how fortunate he was to have been Jon's friend and, through him, a part of the family who dwelled in this house. How could he face Jon's mother or father, or his sisters, all grown up now he was sure? His courage wavered and he fought the urge to run down the steps and disappear into the gloom.

Instead he lifted the brass knocker and let it fall against the plate. The clang reverberated through the house, followed by the sound of quick steps. Before he was ready, the door opened wide.

A young woman of twenty or so stood before him. Her dark hair and sparkling brown eyes were so like Jon's he knew this was a sister, though which one he couldn't say. They stared at each other a moment, he and the girl, before she turned and shouted, "He's here. Oh mother, he's here."

Lily Warner stepped into the hallway, brushing her skirt as she came. "Charlotte Florence Warner, you know better than to yowl like an alley cat when announcing a visitor." Her eyes widened when she saw Cabel standing in the doorway. Face lit with joy, her arms opened wide as she rushed forward.

He met her part way, bending down to cling to her as tightly as she did him.

"Oh, Cabe, my dear, dear boy. You've finally come home."

AUTHOR'S NOTES

While I created this world of fiction, it is as historically accurate as my imperfect attempts allow. St. Joseph, Michigan, stands on the Michigan shores of the lake; and while the Silver Beach Amusement Park of 1927 is gone, bits and pieces have been brought back to life.

The House of David in Benton Harbor, Michigan, thrived for many years before and after the fateful loss of its leader. In November of 1927, Benjamin Purnell was tried on charges of molesting several girls who lived in the compound. He died before a verdict was delivered. To this day, he has staunch supporters who claim his innocence and others who believe in his guilt. I don't know what the truth is and did not present an opinion in this book.

The Levee District of Chicago is now the Near South Side. Located south of the Loop and Printer's Row, it served as the city's red-light district from the 1880s through 1912. The famous Everleigh Club, owned and operated by sisters Minna and Ada, was considered the most famous and luxurious house of prostitution in the country. The Mann Act, also known as the White Slavery Traffic Act, was enacted in 1910 in response to the activities of the Everleigh sisters and other brothels in the red-light district.

After less than a decade of respectability, the Levee District became Al Capone's south side base of operations. He owned many businesses there including the Cullerton Hotel, which he ran as a brothel. White slavery was still rampant, though many victims now came from Europe. The Cullerton Hotel had over twenty-five miles of tunnels beneath it, and there were party rooms where drugs, alcohol, gambling, sex, and other vices were fair game. The tunnels were also used by patrons in the Levee District to avoid being caught during police raids. Remnants of old homes and other buildings could be found beneath the Levee District. Many sank into the soft soil and were either built on top of or forgotten.

Capone brought in booze from the Canadian distilleries across the river from Detroit and also flew Canadian beer into the country on seaplanes that landed on a lake on his Wisconsin property. Neither of these activities could have occurred during the winter months.

This is the point where my imagination took over. I used this information to create the plausible decision to hide extra beer and liquor in the tunnels in preparation for the winter. The confusion of the tunnels and the proliferation of the sunken rooms were also of my own creation. I developed the system for marking the tunnel walls and how that would have been used.

The Cullerton Hotel later become the Blue Star Auto Stores and is currently in the process of being redeveloped into condominiums. If you look online at pictures of the Blue Star, you will notice the small window on the side of the building. During its use as Capone's brothel, the sides and back of the building sported these small barred windows to keep the women trapped inside.

Thus, I blended fact and fiction to create key elements of *Cold Betrayals*. I hope you enjoy the journey and forgive any mistakes.

Please visit www.erinfarwell.com or https://erinfarwell.wordpress.com to learn more about myself, Cabel's world, and his next mystery.

CPSIA information can be obtained
at www.ICGtesting.com
Printed in the USA
LVOW04s0526040916
502952LV00004B/5/P